19433

£ 5·00

THE SOUND OF
THE SEA

THE SOUND OF THE SEA

Colin Mackay

CANONGATE

First published in 1989
by Canongate Publishing Limited,
17 Jeffrey Street, Edinburgh

The publishers acknowledge subsidy of
the Scottish Arts Council towards the
publication of this volume.

British Library Cataloguing in Publication Data
Mackay, Colin, *1951*–
The sound of the sea.
I. Title
923'.914[F]

ISBN 0-86241-173-4

Typeset by Rowland Phototypesetting Limited
Bury St Edmunds, Suffolk
Printed and bound in Great Britain by
Billing and Sons Limited, Worcester

Contents

For my parents Hugh and Margaret,
and for Robert Ogilvy who loved the stars
too fondly to be fearful of the night.

The Waves

Mine is a city by the northern sea. It sits on the coast of Lothian at the point where the river Forth suddenly broadens into a wide estuary dotted with small islands, and, if you stand on the embankment above the water and look to the north, you can see the green fields of Fife on the other side veering away sharply to a blue horizon of hills, sky, and a sea that stretches to Norway. And at night the lights of the coastal towns—Burntisland, Aberdour, Kinghorn, Dysart and the others—shine over there in little clusters between black hills and black water as far as Largo Bay, and sometimes there is a glimmer of light on one of the islands or on a ship out in the firth. Edinburgh.

When I was a child I first heard of the sea in which my Highland grandfather had died serving the Royal Navy, and though the village where I was born was some miles inland in green Lothian surrounded by farms, a presentiment of the sea floated over it; sometimes the wind bringing its scent, sometimes flocks of white gulls that would descend on the ploughed fields crying horribly. And still of an age to be put to bed while it was yet daylight, and not knowing what death was, I would lie in the little room at the back of the house wallpapered with patterns of ships, boy sailors, and red-coated kilties, and dream of glory and the sea where my grandfather lay. There, I was sure, all bad things would be put right.

Then, when I was four, we came to Edinburgh to live here by the coast in the docklands of Leith. Twenty-seven years later I live alone in this same house my parents bought, sleep much of the day, and patrol a large empty building all night. And still, very occasionally, I dream of glory and the righting of ancient wrongs.

I

My work is the 'graveyard shift'. From eleven at night until eight in the morning I look after the security of a large council-owned leisure centre, sweep the floors, make sure the tea urn is ready for the morning cleaners when they arrive, and listen to their talk. The building is made of concrete breeze blocks and is very ugly. Inside, it is air-conditioned, stale-smelling, dusty, and lit by fluorescent tubes. The litter bins are always choked with juice cans and chocolate wrappers; crisp packets and cigarette butts lie on the floor. Nightwatchmen, like burglars, policemen, and some lunatics, inhabit the unsociable hours. In winter I clock in when it is black outside, and it is still dark when I clock out; in winter the sun and I are strangers, and criminals come out like vampires from the crypt; but in summer the midnight sky is still streaked with faint lemon light, and by three the dawn is already breaking. Sometimes, when the night is at its darkest, I will stand before a window and switch the lights off behind me, and out there the city with its half-million souls will gleam like a magic lantern, while on the railway line on the other side of the road the sleeping trains rush past. And then in the morning when I walk home, I pass the docks, pass the warehouses, and walk along beside the embankment which separates Edinburgh from the sea, and the smell of salt is on the air, and of fish crates and oil, and there is the sound of the waves and the herring gulls, the churning machinery of the docks, and the horns of ships that come to anchor. This morning, walking home, I saw the arrival of a rusty merchantman, and from the kitchen window as I waited for the kettle to boil, I trained my binoculars on it, read its name, *Ivan Susanin*, and saw the Soviet flag. Then I went to bed.

And time, tick tock, the hourglass and the cowled reaper with the scythe passed over this fourth of May, 1982, and over turbulent Edinburgh—the regional and district councils, the offices, the factories, the shops; over all its domains, bleak Niddrie and bleaker Wester Hailes, Corstorphine over whose hill the sun nightly goes to set, neat Craigentinny, neater Braid, unlovely Leith—tick tock, it went, the trickle of the hourglass, the padding steps of the reaper with the scythe. Morning turned to midday, turned into afternoon over streets of cars, houses where televisions played, and already busy pubs. And when an Argentinian missile struck the destroyer *Sheffield* in the South

Atlantic, I slept, slept so peacefully I cannot remember my dreams, and as I dreamed them twenty of its crew died in the flames.

Tick tock, time, the hourglass and the cowled reaper.

I woke up at last, lay for a while fretting aimlessly, then got up yawning and scratching myself, and shambled through to have a wash. En route, by reflex action, I switched on the radio.

I ran water into the sink and shaved carefully . . .

Tick tock, said the clock on the wall.

Tick tock, as I shaved, came the reaper with the scythe.

And somehow, hearing that news, I could not face coming to work, clocking in, putting on my blue boiler suit, and spending the night sweeping floors in a leisure centre of all ridiculous places. So I phoned the supervisor and told him I was sick. Perhaps it wasn't such a great lie at that. I switched on the television news, but there was a quiz game or some damn thing, and *click*, I switched it off fast. Tick tock. Do you know what it is like when the bleak room you are sitting in becomes a black pool that threatens to brim up and swallow you, oh do you know? I saw myself drowning in it and scrambled out. I virtually ran down the tenement stairs and out into the street where the traffic rumbled past Leith docks. Ironically this unlovely road is called after the mythical lizard that can live in flames Salamander Street, and on the other side of it is the sea: and standing there on the pavement that summer evening, thousands of water miles from where men were burning in the South Atlantic, I could hear the sound of the waves hitting the shore beyond the line of warehouses, and smell its bitter salt above the exhaust fumes of the lorries.

Tick—

tock . . .

It was a calm April morning when we suddenly found ourselves at war. When the day shift came in to work they were talking about it. I picked up a paper on the way home and read the screaming headlines. Attack on the Falkland Islands, of which so few people had even heard. Over the next days the homely, familiar, frightened faces of the islanders stared out from newspapers and TV screens, folk like us living under foreign invasion.

3

And I thought—War? My grandfather knew 1914, my father —'Pa' as I always called him—knew '39. This was surely the war I had missed. I wondered what I should do.

It was a sunny April day, a watercolour afternoon. Dove grey ships of the Task Force like beautiful toys sailed from Southampton and military bands serenaded them. On the TV news I saw the docks there packed with relatives and well-wishers—the bands were playing 'Sailing', a pleasant melody—and amongst the weeping women and Union Jacks a man held up a placard saying 'Give Them Hell'.

It was a watercolour day, an Indian summer adventure fit to be painted, framed, and hung up on a wall beside the red uniforms and crossed swords of our glory days. We forgot all about NATO and the Warsaw Pact, the nuclear winter, the four-minute warning, the batteries of Soviet missiles aimed at us with their thousands of miles range, their megaton and multi-megaton warheads, their appalling apocalyptic power.

And it was a watercolour evening, that evening of the day the ships sailed, *Sheffield* among the others so rich in living men. I stood at the window beside the television set and stared out at the sea. And then, with some notion of talking to God, and because mine is the top flat of our stair, I opened the skylight above the stairwell and climbed out onto the roof. The sky was clear and snell, and standing there on the weatherbeaten slates beside the chimney-pots and television aerials with Edinburgh behind me and the docks far below, I looked north and west over the waters of the Firth of Forth and saw the islands of Inchkeith and Inchcolm lying between us and Fife; then eastwards to the sea where the Bass, Craigleith, Fidra and Lamb rocks lie off the Lothian coast; and I saw the white haze of gannets and kittiwakes, cormorants and guillemots on the tossing waters where the fishing-boats go. That night when darkness came down on Edinburgh, and on the ships on another sea sailing to the war, I saw a light from the direction of the Isle of May's lighthouse where the Forth estuary meets the North Sea, and heard the wild geese pass over with their lonely cry.

What should I do, I asked myself again and again—go to work, watch television, eat, sleep? I needed something more dramatic and violent. Should I join up? Write war poetry?

Oddly, the atmosphere was indeed for 1914's bunting and patriotic ballads round the piano. A ballad came into my mind then, one that was in all the school poetry books many moons ago, about Sir Patrick Spens who was sent by his king to Norway (*Noroway*, it was quaintly spelled, *Noroway o'er the faem*) to bring a princess home to Scotland; but the treacherous waters drowned him before he had quit the Forth. And sitting there on the roof in the night the old words ran through my head:

> *Half-owre, half-owre to Aberdour,*
> *Tis fifty fathoms deep;*
> *And there lies gude Sir Patrick Spens,*
> *Wi the Scots lords at his feet!*

That was but a few miles from where I sat that night, and the little port of Aberdour, where I had gone for my holidays a quarter of a century ago and played with a dog called Bobby on the beach, was one of the specks of light now showing on the distant shore.

The next night my shift recommenced. The back-shift men I relieved were still talking about the war. The daily tabloid had war headlines covering the whole front page. Thereafter, as the days crept by with no real news and it seemed that it would all pass away in a flurry of UN resolutions, they talked about it less and less, and though it clung barnacle-like to the front page of the *Daily Record*, the nudes and bingo and gossip steadily reasserted their importance. While I swept floors.

Yes, tick tick tick tock. Time what had you done to me? At thirty-one I felt myself already edging towards middle-age. Living alone, I was becoming set and funny in my ways. My day had the surreal logic of the nightworker who reads the morning paper before he goes to sleep and is up to breakfast in time for the evening news. We are candidates for insanity, all of us. So at thirty-one my patience with the world was growing crusty. I had a routine which seldom varied in a life that was at complete variance with all else. I worked ultimately for a district council I despised. My shaving mirror heard my querulous complaints regarding those lethargic bureaucrats, the intimidated managers they employed, and the incompetent supervisors who were employed by them. Oh how I longed for adventure, as all men do who have a house and a modest salary! By day when I slept my

5

bed flew the jolly roger and sailed the Seven Seas. So now my heart went south with the Task Force as from my armchair in my woolly pullover and slippers I wished 'the boys' good luck, then went out to sweep floors again in a time of threatening disaster.

Then of a sudden came the cowled reaper.

April passed into May, and on the second of the month we sank the Argentine cruiser *Belgrano*. And I, sitting in my blood-thirsty armchair, applauded. GOTCHA, said the headlines. 'That's shown them!' men said in the pub. 'That's shown they fucking Argies!' And I agreed, may God forgive me. On the third, I walked with a swagger, I think we all did, the men I saw on day-shift, the men I met in the pub. We had rediscovered the sense of belonging to an important country, one which had the power to chastise the wicked, and the wisdom to do so with justice. The second and third days of May were a watercolour time, red white blue and bells across the meadow Maydays, and the sneer machine of 'them' which had ground down on us so hard for the past twenty years was silent.

Mayday, Mayday, Mayday. And on the fourth Mayday came the scythe.

The news was simple, matter-of-fact. As I stood in the kitchen making my meal the radio told me that earlier in the afternoon our destroyer *Sheffield* had been attacked by three Super Etendard fighter-bombers of the Argentine Navy, two Exocet air-to-surface missiles had been launched, one had hit slender grey *Sheffield* and set her on fire. She was burning, said the radio, and there were casualties among her crew; the aluminium alloy in the superstructure was melting, the plastic-covered cabling was on fire and filling the ship with poisonous black smoke. So stark, so simple was this damage report of burning flesh and melting alloys that I stood there at the sink staring out of the kitchen window at the sea, the six thousand miles of water that lay between Edinburgh and the Falkland Islands flew away, and I saw those burning sailors—I whose grandfather had died in a burning ship at Jutland—there before me on the ballad water where Sir Patrick Spens and his men had drowned half-owre to Aberdour. Dear God, I thought, is life so vulnerable?

And so I went out and walked in the early evening of this May day that is still so beautiful but no longer seems to be washed in

6

watercolour. I walked along Salamander Street and past Leith docks at the time when the lights were coming on in the streets of Edinburgh and across the water on the Fife shore. There were the sounds of the city sliding towards night, the harsh noises of the docks where cranes old as dinosaurs hung over high ships, the clip-clop of pedestrians on the pavements, the growl of evening cars on Baltic Street and Commercial Street driving past Leith's Western harbour and Newhaven harbour with their silver and red lights exploding for split seconds like starshells on the windows of darkened shops, the rumble of a tired bus heaving its way along Starbank to Lower Granton Road. And I walked to a place I knew of where I could reach the water's edge.

Here. Look.

The lights are coming on now over there in Aberdour, Kinghorn, Dysart, and all up the Fife shore to sweet Largo Bay.

Listen. Do you hear the sound of the sea?

A misty wet tunnel runs underneath the railway embankment that hugs this bit of the shore, and the bairns of Granton use it when they run to play on the shingly beach beyond. It is nearly suppertime. As I walk towards the tunnel two wee boys come running out, shouting to each other. Kicking a football. Playing soldiers. Doing things I used to do.

'Bang! You're deid!'

'No I'm no!'

'Aye you are, I killed ye!'

'D'ye think we'll get a half day if we beat the Argies?'

'What d'ye mean *if* we beat the Argies? 'Course we'll beat the Argies! They's only fucking Argies!'

'Think we'll get a half day. . . .'

And they pass, neither giving me a glance. They dodge the traffic with the practised grace of dancers and disappear into a tenement stair. And I walk alone into the tunnel, the cold darkness swallows me like a whale, and the sound of the sea greets me on the oily sands. The dark embankment hides Edinburgh now, and there is not another soul in sight but the lights on the water. There to the left is Granton harbour, over to the right Newhaven, and beyond is Leith with its cranes; and the breakwater there along which a wee laddie used to go to see if he could hear seals singing out in the Forth, and where now a ship with a

Soviet flag called *Ivan Susanin* rides near motionless at anchor in the oncoming night.

Suddenly, on the switchboard of my memory, two half days cross wires. And suddenly out of the past there comes—

A classroom. Grey light on white walls. Cold radiators. Rows of dirty, carved-upon desks.

Years: tick tock . . .

Yes, it was twenty years ago, on one Monday awful morning in 1962, and we were all there in school assembly as usual, and the bell was ringing in the tower above; ding dong said the school bell to the grey morning sky. And there were hundreds of boys and girls in that assembly room lolling around chattering, swapping homework, bubble-gum, comics, while teachers sat at the rows' ends chatting to each other, ignoring it all, ignoring us, ignoring me, ten-year-old me, whom I can see in there with the others. Ding dong, said the bell. Suddenly hundreds of boys and girls were standing at sloppy attention like a parade of midget soldiers, and the teachers all alert and respectful, when entered headmaster Foulis in a temper, black gown winglike fluttering behind him in the cold stale air.

'Right! Good morning, school.'

'Good morning s—'

'Right! Silence! SILENCE! Open your hymn books and turn to number—'

Brrrr, I remember it, even now; and yet there was nothing odd about that morning, all was as usual. We opened our grubby little hymn books (the cheap cover dye came off on your fingers) and turned to number whatever-it-was, some Victorian dirge, and dirged it out. The heady stood behind the lectern. He was supposed to have been a Spitfire pilot, half his face was certainly burnt purple with fire or rage, and he glared angrily at us through the Love and Blood of the Lamb who had taken away the Sins of the World as though he suspected us of stealing them. Strange how after all these years I should mind the teacher at the end of our row jangling the change in his pocket, or how, when the hymn ended and there was a noisy shutting of books, we all sat in the seats' clatter and the spinsterly music teacher at the piano clipped her handbag mouth shut, folded thin hands primly on her lap, looked just once at her ringless fingers and sighed. High on the wall a pastel-coloured Jesus was walking across the water and smiling softly to a flock of all-coloured bairns that was waiting for him on the bank. Jesus was fair and blond and had glazed eyes and a dopey expression. The headmaster had a sheaf of papers, the papers were rustling with announcements—And somewhere in among the next sportsday, the football match with another school, and the black burning shame of McCulloch or Macconnachie or Macgregor or whoever it was caught smoking in the bog, I slid off into whatever adventuresome world wee boys slide off into when adults are talking nonsense. But I jerked awake to hear this said from the lectern as the head folded his notes away:

'. . . And in the event of nuclear war, school will close at twelve-thirty until further notice.'

He said.

A time of gloom: the reaper and the scythe.

1962, the best of years, the worst of years. Unemployment was scarce heard of. Our parents all worked, older brothers and sisters worked, no one knew anyone who did not have a job. Working boys were going to universities for the first time, or so it seemed; accents other than those of Oxbridge were being heard on the BBC; television showed cowboy series, and radio played *The Archers*. Times were still austere enough to keep boredom at bay. Bairns played with sticks, with marbles and with catapults; holidays were taken in Burntisland, or, more exotically, in the nearest Butlin's camp; no school had a drugs problem, all schools had violence problems; gangs fought with bicycle chains, flick-knives and cut-throat razors; in some of our wynds and back streets policemen on foot patrolled in twos, or not at all. And the razor gangs who ruled the outside world did so without hindrance. A slow incessant drizzle of humiliation came upon our heads: the colonies of the empire fell away into corruption, a procession of coal-black dictators in western suits made bombastic speeches in the halls of the United Nations, and we, who had not profited from the colonies presence one bit, resented their departure as a personal slight.

All this was 1962. The docks were full in those days, through the gates at Leith passed thousands of men, the harbours were crowded with ships, and the railway line that curved around our house between Salamander Street and the sea was a continuous roar of coal trains passing dockwards from Monktonhall, Woolmet, and all the rich pits of Lothian. The coal that fuelled the steel works that made the missiles that I knew about but did not understand about, being only ten years old, even when the word 'Cuba' was on everybody's lips.

When did it begin? I remember a reference in some teatime news bulletin to the Bay of Pigs, and the jokes we made about yon funny foreign name in the playground, me and my mates. *Bay of Pigs*! we said, the name of some funny Walt Disney cartoon, wasn't it just? And Fidel, that big guy with the beard growing out of his eyes—! We had a teacher with a beard and we called him Fidel. The Yanks would soon take care of Fidel, we said. In the school swimming baths we played the Sands of Iwo Jima. The Japs lined the deep end and the Marines and USN Seabees paddled down the baths and stormed the diving board. We took it in turn to die spectacularly off the diving board. The instructress sat glumly in her cubicle listening to the radio and sucking pandrops.

A time of gloom. American spyplanes detected Soviet missiles in Cuba with nuclear warheads. There in the jungle paradise they sat raising their snouts skyward in the gleaming tropical sun. None of us understood why our parents were so doleful. Kennedy was just going to send in the Marines, we said, it would be as simple as that. Bang bang finito! All the glory-soaked Saturday evening Sunday afternoon war films would spill from the television screen, and we would slaughter Fidel's Japs and Nazis, or whatever they were, on the carpet and the fireside rug. We speculated on the size of an atom bomb. We thought it was probably the size of a football, black, with the word 'Bomb' painted on it in white letters. We tried hard to talk American, refought the battles of Iwo Jima and Guadalcanal, chewed gum in wedges, and walked like John Wayne in 1962.

On the switchboard of my memory boys are playing football. . . .

Morning break. Me and Andy and Dougie and Eck kicking a battered ball to each other. In the playground boys' voices are cold sharp splinters of glass.

'Think it will?'—'Whit?'—'Blaw up.'

'Whit?'—'The world?'—'Aye.'

'Naw.'—'How?'

'It might but,' said Eck with a half-hearted kick at the ball.

'Dinny see it,' said Dougie.

''Spose no.'

'I mean, where would all the folks go with no world to stand on?'

'Aye, there's that.'

'And all they animals and fish and whales in the sea and that.'

'See them swimming aroond in the sky?'

And I laughed, parting the air with my hands.

'Splash splash, here's me a dolphin.'—'A taddy, ye mean.'

'Aw, just a wee puddock,' said Andy. And I jumped on Andy and began battering him. The ball rolled off. A while later we chased it.

'And it's five minutes into extra time—'

'The score is still nil nil—'

'Whit's nil?'—'Nothin!'

'And Hibs have got two minutes left to equalize—'

'They's equal already.'—'All right, it's wan nil.'—'And it's McGilpin!'

'McGilpin passes to Moran!'—'Moran passes to Lauder!'

'And—'

Hughie!

Pa's voice.

Pa. My father Donald. A tall, grey, sober-looking kirk-elder of a man, studious and self-possessed. As a child in another age he had spoken Gaelic, and though he had forgotten all he ever knew of it by now, his carefully acquired English still wavered uncertainly between the schoolroom-proper and the Edinburgh street. He was in his schoolteacher's voice now, the voice he kept for seriousness. Lauder passed back to Moran and scored in silence.

'Carry on with your game, boys. Hughie, I want to speak to you.'

Next door to us was the big secondary school where Pa taught

11

English. The two schools were twins, primary and secondary (frying-pan and fire, said Pa), huge red sandstone buildings that outdid each other as some Victorian architect's idea of Dracula's castle. They stood within spitting range of the little river called the Water of Leith. On one side was a refuse works, a dreich public park with its grass all trodden to the bare earth, a dogtrack, and a graveyard. On the other side was a neat row of bungalows and an office block. A few old Anderson shelters still stood around, doubling as bicycle sheds. The Water was full of rubbish, and a laddie of my age had once drowned in it, his feet tangled in the rubbish. The big chimney of the works smoked day and night, day and night, and inside the cold school windows we children of the New Elizabethan Age chanted tables, dates, and formulae by rote. There are 4 gills to a pint, 2 pints to a quart, 4 quarts to a gallon. . . . The teachers either seemed to be men who had survived Hitler's war with their nerves in shreds, or women whose men hadn't survived it at all. And one of these men was my Pa.

He sat himself down on the school steps. 'Hughie,' he said.

'Aye?'

Our heads were level since I was on the step above. Yes, he was a gaunt man, my Pa, and his hair was white. We had called each other by our names ever since Ma died.

'Aye, Donald?' I said.

'Hughie, would you like to come away with me? A sort of holiday, just the two of us, down the coast somewhere maybe. What do you say?'

'You mean now—the day?'

'Aye.'

'Will we see the sea?'

'Aye,' said Pa, 'we'll see the sea.'

He ruffled my hair.

'Great!'

'Tell no one,' he said.

'How, Donald?'

'Just tell no one,' he said. 'It's our secret. Just you and me, son.' Just you and me.

'That's magic!' I said.

The Train

We took the afternoon train eastwards.

Waverley Station was an adventure then: great long platforms and more noise than I had ever met. I had only been in it a couple of times, the first time when the railway police ('polis' we called them) still wore helmets like PC Murdoch. But me and my pal Dougie often hung around on the iron footbridge that crossed over the lines from Princes Street Gardens and waited for the old puffers to come shunting under us *chuga chuga chuga chug—whee whee*! because neither of us liked the new diesels.

The place was spattered with strange signs, crudely drawn circles with upsidedown catapults in them, and the letters CND. I had seen them about a lot, but paid them no heed, less than I did the Bovril hoardings which had Highland cattle round a dazzling blue loch with a red-cheeked woman like my mother smiling in the radiant sunlight.

I was smiling too. I was going to see the sea.

Pa bought the tickets. He had a duffle bag under one arm, and on his back was a rucksack older than I was. There was a silence between us. I wondered at it. He looked sidelong at the polisman, sidelong at the ticket inspector. I kept on asking where we were off to, but he didn't say, and eventually he lost his temper and told me to wheesht or he'd belt me one. He never did, but I closed my mouth round a gobstopper and thought, it's worth it to see the sea.

In the train I grabbed the window seat and sat, legs dangling. Pa had made me change out of my school uniform, the daft blue blazer and the shorts that I hated, into a pair of jeans and a nondescript jacket that I liked better and kept for playing football. The jeans had a tear in the arse of them that I had sewn up as well as I could, which was not well. My Ma would have sewn them up better, but my Ma was dead.

'I've got bad news for you, laddie. Your Ma's deid.' Pa was crying.

The year before. I'd got the tear skimming a wall, the polis in pursuit. Why? I can't mind. A ball had broken a window, something like that, and then Andy with his red-skiffed knees was waving his arms from the street corner, and the big polisman was bearing down on us, and there was me running, running.

'I'll get you, ye wee bugger!' the polisman shouted.

He knew me fine. He was round our house that same night, saw the wreath on the door. 'It's the wife,' said Pa, 'the wife, she's. . . .' And the polisman said nothing about that window then or ever. 'Your laddie's, er, lost his ball—I think,' said the polisman uncomfortably. Pa nodded and said he would buy me another one. But he wasn't looking at either of us, he was just looking somewhere into the air, and the polisman sat there on the edge of the best chair, so big and blue, dangling his cap in his hands and rubbing the band. And on the wind, it being that flat of ours high above Salamander Street with all its windows open in the mild evening, between the occasional sound of a lorry and a car, I heard faintly—so faintly it seemed—the sound of the waves on the shore.

'I've got bad news for you, laddie. . . .'

And when I go back in memory and grope around in the dark cupboard of those years, there is no Bomb, no Kennedy, no Cuba, none of these things precious there. What my hands uncover first is the sight of my father crying, and that big polisman, and the distant sound of the sea.

Your Ma's deid, he said. Your Ma's deid. Your Ma's—

And the sound of the sea—

Deid.

'Hughie, don't do that,' said my father.

The train was rattling along through vast green fields. I stopped picking my nose. 'What's wrong, Donald?'

'Just don't do it. It's no polite.'

An ancient lady with a polite mouth was sitting beside me in the carriage. She smiled. 'Oh he's a fine looking wee man,' she said, creasing her old face.

'Aye,' said my father.

'Is it a school holiday?' she asked.

'Aye,' said my father.

'Oh you'll be glad to be away for the day,' she said to me, and her eyes were all shiny like two wet pebbles.

'My Ma's deid,' I said to the window, 'and we're all away to see her.'

'Hughie!' said my father.

'He means,' he said to the old lady, 'that we've the week off for the funeral.'

The old lady was so sorry, she said. She asked where we were going. Berwick, said Pa, the funeral's in Berwick. We looked out the window and there was North Berwick station passing us.

'Berwick-on-Tweed,' said Pa.

When the old lady got out and we had the carriage to ourselves, he gave me a whack on the knee.

'What did you say that for, you tattie? You wanting everybody to know who we are?'

'Should they no then, Donald?'

'No! Leastways no yet. Give me time to think,' he said, and put his head in his hands.

'But what's wrong, Pa?'

'Look,' he said, 'it's like this. You don't have the day off, do you? The head didn't give you it, did he; we just took it, all right? You should be learning at school, and I should be teaching at school, and instead here we are, sciving, the two of us. That's a fine thing now, isn't it? And do you know why? Because in the event of a nuclear war you're going to get a wee half day; so we're just taking it the now, and if Khrushchev sends one of his big bombs over to blow up Rosyth navy base on the other side of the Forth there, then—Chrissakes, I don't know—maybe we'll survive it. Now d'ye understand?'

A while later he said:

'It's the other people, Hughie, they won't understand it at all. They'll just see a father taking his laddie away from school

15

without permission. *Without permission,*' he said, 'and the rest they won't understand at all.'

I tried to understand, but failed. It worried him—therefore, because he was my father and I loved him, it worried me. But as to the thing itself, no, I didn't understand it either.

The Bomb was so big and I was so small: and I mean, where would all the folk go with no world to stand on? . . .

We got out at last at a wee station in the midst of strange hills that Pa called the Lammermoors. There were a couple of friendly voices on the platform talking strange fluting words. The street where we were standing was one line of stone houses and a pillar box and a couple of shops, and no cars at all. Then *Wheeeee* the train was away, and the city with it, a whistle among green fields. Oh lonesome train. There was a man sitting on the kerb eating an icecream cone who smelled of cow dung. And we set off hiking up the slope of a hill with the sun over our shoulders, and walked, walked, and walked with strange things growing about us that I didn't know, for I was no country boy. There was a warm smell of animals and greenness on the hillside; strange birds were crying overhead, and I asked and asked about them, but Pa would tell me nothing except that soon we would be there. And where, I asked, where? But no, he wouldn't say.

We hiked on and on that evening, until my feet hurt and the shadows were awful long on the grass before us. Over braes we went, down into shallow glens where the sun was hidden and our feet splashed the darkness, and more than once heather roots and bracken tangled round my ankles and sent me headlong. But, 'On, Hughie, on and you'll see the sea!' said my Pa, striding onwards like a hero, so I scrambled to my feet and on we went, Pa stepping it out, me trotting at his heels.

Then at length, when the sun was near its setting, and I was so scratched and sore and stung with nettles that I was fain to lie down and die just where I was in a heap, at length we came to a final moorish hilltop where three bent, twisted trees were standing against the sky. And then of a sudden I felt a new wind blowing in my face, and taking a step or two further—and ignoring the bevy of timid sheep that galloped away from us, and the rabbit that vanished down his burrow—I could smell the familiar salt on it, and hear the sound of gulls screaming in the distance. Then, as we climbed a rickle stone dyke, Pa suddenly pointed and gave a shout. And there, twenty years ago, knee-deep in bracken, I saw the sea.

A Story About Noroway

It was dark and strange that night. We slept in an old schoolhouse building, Pa and I. Its walls were strong, its roof intact, and inside it was cold and smelled all stale and full of dust. I winced at the word 'school' engraved in the weatherbeaten stone lintel above the main door. Pa saw me and laughed. 'No teachers and blackboards for you here, laddie!' he said. But I was feared of the beasties in the darkness. I saw a spider that was about as big as my fist scuttling into a great crack between the wall and its wooden doorpost. The light worked to the switch. We saw the greyness all around; the desolate look of a house that was unlived in. Pa pulled out one of the sofas, turned the cushions upside down, and we slept on it in our clothes, exhausted with walking so long in the strong fresh air.

That night I heard the waves on the shore far far louder than they had ever been at Leith. I woke twice during the dark hours, and still they roared. Before night drew its curtains on us, we had sat by the water's edge where the waves came running in. The sun was away over the hills, and there were no lights on the sea. I asked Pa, where was Burntisland, where was Kinghorn, where was Aberdour, whose lights had all shone out in such a friendly fashion over the Forth? And he told me then that this wasn't the river Forth any longer. This was the sea, he said, the *real* sea. It was a great darkness, and on the other side of it was Norway, where a princess had waited for Sir Patrick Spens, and Jutland, where the battle with the Germans had been. Oh, I said, and stared.

'Pa,' I said, 'I can't see anything. Will we see them in the light of day?'

No, said Pa, some things could not be seen even in the light of day. After a while I asked, how did he know they were there, then? And he said that some things just had to be taken on trust, as an act of faith, like. And I looked at Pa as he stared out into the darkness, and was surprised, because Pa was a Freethinker and a Socialist, and had no time for the ministers and what he called their lies and fairy-tales.

So there we sat together on the rocks looking at the sea, and the moon came out and made a path of silver to us across the angry waters.

'I often think of the Old Man on nights like this,' said Pa, 'him that's dead over there.' And I knew that he was talking about his own father who had died in the great battle when his ship was sunk by the Germans and the waters had come in over his head. My father had been no older then than I was now. So we sat there looking along that white path, cooling our sore feet in a pool of water, and I was fair expecting to see the Old Man come walking to us across the top of the waves like Jesus in the picture, only more real, when Pa gave himself a shake and said, 'Ech, the damn crabs!' And he pulled my feet out of the water, and his own, and he laughed.

'The perils of dreaming, Hughie, are that you're likely to get your toes bitten off.'

We let our feet dry on the sea air, then clambered back up the beach and the slope beyond in the moonlight, and so returned to the door of the cold-smelling house.

'It's peaceful here,' said Pa as we lay together in the darkness on the sofa in that strange room.

'Aye, Donald.'

'I think we'll stay,' he said.

A while later he asked me if I was cold; and, no, I said, I wasn't cold, only a bit feared; and he told me that in the daylight everything would be fine—even if we couldn't see Norway. Then he wrapped me tighter in his coat, and I asked him to tell me a story, the way Ma had done when I was a bairn, and he began telling me about the King of the Golden River. And I could hear the waves hammering the rocks on the shore where we had been, and in the midst of it I fell asleep, and when I woke it was broad daylight, and the sun was blazing like a great fire through the nearest window.

19

Well!

There was a road, and a fence, and a yellow field, and the sea; and I ran the road, and jumped the fence, and swam the field, and came to the sea at the top of a red sea-cliff, and stood there, staring. How am I to describe the sea now except to say that it was huge? Huge it really was. It was the hugest thing I had ever seen in my life. Nothing like it was at Granton or at Leith; not even from the top of Arthur's Seat: no, not even from the top of Scald Law out in the Pentland Hills, though I had been up there once on a clear day when it wasn't raining and you could see for miles.

I saw a boy in a cartoon once. He stood on a planet, and stared at another planet, and knew that he could never touch it. So I stared at the sea.

Pa was calling me back to the road. He was wearing a shapeless sack of a red pullover Ma had knitted for him once. There was a van of some sort standing beside him. I saw his white head and red pullover there above the yellow cornfield, and I waved, and turned back to the sea.

The cliff was high, but the rocks had plenty of footholds, all worn jagged and dusty, and when your hands brushed them they came off all red-brown splotches because the salt was eating into them and they were crumbling. And I ran along the surf singing to myself about those who go down to the sea in ships, and all the other Bible stuff my Ma had told me evenings when Pa was out, and I saw the wonders of a great work in the moon rocks and the sand and the driftwood and seaweed on the wetness of the shore.

When I was a child I saw as a child. I wheecht off my rubber shoes and clarted barefoot in the waters till the jeans hung heavy on my knees. A crab came and waved his pincers at me, and I waved my toes at him, and he made off into a rock, and I pursued him and keeked in at him in the crack where he was, but kept my fingers to myself. Then I clambered the rock with a driftwood gun and fought redskins, Apaches and Creeks—I, Hawkeye—in among the tumble stones of the pounding shore where the waters rushed at me laden with war canoes. Were there still bears in Scotland then? There were as many as there were screaming Hurons, for Chingachgook and I had our work cut out fighting them off, so fierce and many were they with their arrows and musket shots thudding into the redwood logs around us all the time, until their whoops died away and they floated with their brown shoulders on the foam and their heads crowned with feathers, that were gulls' feathers on a piece of shattered planking the waves played with while my pebbles raised bullet splashes all around. This was the finest beach there was in all the world. All the world I knew was a bit of Edinburgh and the Pentland Hills and the shore of Fife, but this beach was finer than any in Edinburgh, which was so cluttered and noisy, and finer still than the shingle shores of Fife where King James had burnt witches, and I had once played with a dog called Bobby and yelped loud as he did when the same wave had come and whacked both our rumps.

Round a corner of the red cliff there was a river that ran over the sands, and I followed it upward ankle-deep in its yellow bed, and it was a shell made of fern and hill walls for it held the sound of the sea all in one place. And I turned to the sea and saw white foam horses riding for the beach, and turned to the valley and heard their hooves among the bracken and the falling waters.

Once upon a time, said Pa (and a very good time it was, said every dark corner of that strange and lovely night-time house), there was in a place called Styria, where the folk are all German, a beautiful rich valley. And it was surrounded on all sides by great big mountains towering way way up into peaks—

'High as Arthur's Seat?'

Higher, much higher; high as ten Arthur's Seats standing on each others' shoulders; and so cold at the top, these peaks, that they always have snow lying there, even in midsummer—

'Higher than Scald Law?'

Aye, higher than Scald Law, for it's no often that you can walk through the clouds on Scald Law, but in Styria the clouds are always below the mountain peaks; and out of these peaks, away above the clouds, where the sun is cold and the air is ice and the snow is always lying, come burns splashing down over the rocks so cold they'd burn your mouth if you drank of them, and set your hands on fire. And as they go plunging down the mountain-side, said Pa, these burns become—

'Torrents!'

Torrents, and these torrents become—

21

'Glaciers!'

Rivers, puddinheid! And one of these rivers fell westwards over the face of a crag so high that when the sun had set on everything else, and all below was darkness—like the room here—his beams still shone full on this waterfall so that it looked like a shower of gold. And so the German folk in the valley all cried it the Golden River: and one of them was a wee laddie like yourself called young Gluck. Now Gluck lived in that valley with his two bad brothers called Hans and Schwartz, and one day—

One day: one day I will find words to describe all this, I thought. ('Words,' said my socialist Pa, 'are the stamp of property.') And I turned to the sea every time I was on a height, every time I was on a shelf of rock all shiny with the splashing water, or found an overhanging ledge with bracken spilling from its shoulders so tough you could swing on it. And every time I was high up like that, I could see it behind me, that northern sea, with its waves sweeping inward like great wings.

I knew the red cliffs were crumbling, so slowly no one could see them crumbling, but it was happening; and the great stone breakwaters they had built round Leith all shored up with iron and concrete were crumbling too, though no one could see it; and one day in maybe a million years they would all have crumbled away, and the sea would be everywhere, like Ma said it was in the beginning, a waste of waters—

And careful, said the girl, you'll be falling in.

I looked to see who it was, shy-like, me being a laddie and her no being. She clambered down the bank where the trees were and looked at me, brown-haired and freckled and stoury, head on one side, and she said again,

'Mind ye dinny fall in. Are you dreaming or whit?'

'I'm okay,' I said.

'You dinny look it'—the impertinent bisom.

'I'm okay, I said.'

'Well whit are ye doing—clarting?'

'Aye,' I said, my face turning red at her spoiling the sea's crashing for me.

'Och,' she said, 'whit are ye doing that for?'

''Cos I want to.'

'Och,' she said, 'you're a right half-wit.'

'Away ye go!' I said.

'A right half-wit,' she repeated.

'I dinny want you here,' I said.

'Dinny worry. I wouldny be seen dead with you.' She sat down.

Silence.

'D'ye have your shoes off?' she said.

'Aye.' They were around my neck.

'Can I take mine off?' she said, taking them off.

''Spose so.'

'It's cold,' she said, landing both feet splat in the water beside me, soaking the few bits of me that were still dry.

'Aw fucking Jesus!' I said.

'You shouldny use words like that,' she said.

'Och, fuck off,' I said.

She sat herself down then on the rock beside me. Her legs were real brown, like a tink's. Mine were thin and white and pimply.

'Where are you from?' she said, putting a straw in her mouth.

'Edinburgh,' I said.

'Whit are ye doing here?' she said.

'Clarting,' I said.

''Sides clarting?'

'On holiday. Come with my Pa.'

'Oh,' she said. 'We've no got a holiday.'

'We have,' I said, ''cos of the atomic war.'

'Has there been wan?'

'No yet, but we're having a holiday if there is.'

'Oh, that'll be great!' she said.

'Aye, magic!' I said.

When I got back, Pa was in a temper. He was kneeling beside the grate in the schoolroom cleaning out old ashes. He wasn't happy. Ever since Ma died we had split the housework between us, each doing what he could and what was necessary. Once a week a charlady came in to do all the things we hadn't bothered with.

'And where the hell did you get to?' he said.

'I'm no going to be your bloody skivvy!' he said.

23

He pointed to a rickety-looking Hoover.

'The carpet's filthy,' he said. 'Get started!'

'I was down at the sea,' I said, over the racket of the Hoover.

I was running the surfline and raking the pools and listening to the crashing of the waves, I said.

I didn't say anything about meeting the girl.

Pa didn't approve of me talking to people. He thought people, collectively, were stupid. 'You talk to stupid people, you become stupid yourself,' he said in his English-serious voice. He was that proud of his learning and his books.

In our flat at Leith he had thousands of books.

So had his friend Joe. Thousands and thousands of books.

'Books will never betray you,' he said. . . .

I was sitting in Joe's bookshop where nobody ever bought anything, at the top of a wooden stair in a close long since demolished, marching my toy soldiers over a plateau of books, and Joe and Pa were deep in learned talk in a valley of paper, with the books, not shelved as ours were at home, but stacked three, four deep against each wall, and the one wee window near the ceiling top was ashen grey with dust on the inside and streaked by dirty rain without. Joe was my Pa's age, and bald, and bent, and yellow-fingered, and wore a black tammy on his head, and smelled of Woodbines.

And Pa was complaining about the boys at his school. Do you mind how it was, he said, when we were out there at Alamein and bloody Salerno fighting Hitler, the things we hoped for? Oh, I ken they were naive. The great red dawn!—he said, and smiled sadly. Maybe it was all just fading away into darkness and midnight stars, but it was something for all that, it was a vision! Look at these laddies now. They've got the privileges we could hardly dream of, they've got the opportunities we never had, and what are they? I was talking to them the other day, one of these class debates I organized. The Head doesn't like the idea, afraid I might teach the lads democracy! He needn't worry. We were reading *Saint Joan*, so I asked them about the death penalty. What should happen to murderers? I asked.—Hang them! they said, all of them. How about rebels, revolutionaries?—Hang them! shoot them! they said.

—How about rapists? said Joe, sucking on his fag.

24

—Oh, castrate them! Dangle their balls over a tank of piranha fish!—It isny funny, said my Pa. I've got to teach a bunch of Hitler Youths. I've got Nazis in my class.

—You should have left, like me, said Joe.

Pa snorted and was silent.—Aye: maybe I should have, he said at length.

And all the time I was happily murdering my toy soldiers.

Joe was my godfather, yellow fingers and all. He and Pa went back a long way, to the tenement where they were laddies, playing on the same twisting stair. They had been apprentices together, they had been communists together, together they had followed John Maclean. Joe had gone to Russia and seen Stalin; Pa had sheltered him from the polis; outside the City Chambers Pa had had his head cracked open hunger-marching by Joe's side; they had been in the war together; become disillusioned together; drifted apart. Joe had wanted to call me Vladimir Ilych, after Lenin. Pa, thank Christ, had refused.

Joe owned the old schoolhouse as an occasional but-and-ben. His socialism was canny, based on good capitalist property investment. It was how he lived, for his bookshop was a hobby, and Pa and a few other fanatic fellow bookhunters were for cracking with, not taking from. To Joe's shop we went often. To Joe's we went that day after school (after *we* had left the school; all the other pupils and teachers were still in it, not yet three as it was), and I didn't have my soldiers with me, so I dawdled round the piles of books, tracing their meaningless titles with my finger, and wondering what was going on, while the two men talked together in low and anxious voices. . . .

'They call it Redheugh,' said Pa, breaking the evening's silence.

'How?' I said.

'How do ye think, tattie?' he said, and grinned.

He was sitting in the armchair. I rolled over on the carpet and leaned myself against his legs.

'Don't go off like that again,' he said. 'I was that worried.'

'Is it called Redheugh 'cos of the cliffs?' I said.

'Aye,' he said.

'But you should have seen the sea!' I said.

'I've seen it all afore,' he said.

25

'It was huge,' I said. 'It really was.'

'Folk die in it,' he said. 'Be careful, son.'

'Tell's about the Old Man,' I said, for there was no television set at Redheugh.

—Ah. I've told you it all before.

'Tell's again!'

He died when I was your age. That was a long time ago, sunshine, a long time ago. 1916—can you imagine being as far back as that? Old King George and Queen Mary still there, folk talking about Victoria and driving in horse-drawn cabs! And radio was still called the wireless in those days, and gey new it was too, and television had not yet been thought of, far less invented. And Germany had a Kaiser who had a grand brass eagle on his hat, and our King had a lot of feathers on his. And it was in the days of High Society when ladies wore balldresses and waltzed with hussar officers on polished floors, for every posh house was like a palace with a ballroom and palm trees and a fountain, and that; while the people who paid for it all worked in docks and coal mines and went hungry.

Then one day, for some reason, God knows why, the Kaiser with the big brass eagle on his hat and the King with all the feathers on his went to war, despite the fact that they were cousins and friends and had danced with each other's wives and drunk champagne together.

And when I was eight, we had a half day—just like they're going to give you, Hughie—because the soldiers were going off to the war, and we stood there on Princes Street to watch them pass. The Old Man was wearing a bowler hat, and the Old Lady had a wee union jack in her hand, and everybody was cheering. Then along the road the soldiers came marching, Highlanders they were in their kilts going to the trains at Waverley; and there were young officers with swagger sticks, and pipers playing *Hey Johnnie Cope Are Ye Waukin Yet?*, and the old colonel riding a white cuddy, his whiskers white too, his face beery red, and his back straight as a bloody poker. We bairns all ran alongside the soldiers and carried their packs, and me and your godfather Joe, we carried a soldier's rifle in between us like a pole, and the man hugged us both and said we were that like his own bairns. And they all got killed, those soldiers—every one of them.

26

Well, they gave the Old Man a white feather because he wouldn't join up, cried him a coward because he wouldn't fight in their bloody imperialist war, and a year later they took him anyway for the Navy; and still he wouldn't have it, so they beat him and made him a stoker on a battleship—the *Queen Mary*, launched by the old bag herself. And at the battle of Jutland the German shells got her—Admiral Hipper, the bastard, bullseye every time. And the officers all buggered off, and the marines and ratings on the decks, they had a chance; but not the poor bloody stokers down in the holds, nobody told them what was going on, so when the ship capsized they were caught there and they couldn't get out. And the water poured in on top of them and drowned them all.

Well, to be fair, I suppose the officers died too.

Everybody dies in the end. The wealthy Society dames in their fur coats and jewels who had been that patriotic and handed out their white feathers, they stayed at home and died of old age, and that can be a painful and cruel thing too. And the men who owned the coal mines and the docks, all of them. But their riches are still there, *and* the bastard warmongering system they operate.

And until the day I die, I will never forgive them for it!—Said my Pa.

Wanted

And night is down now; the sea takes the city; the embankment behind me is black as the sky above. Only the harbour lights flicker along the shingle between Granton and Leith, and the shore lights of Fife over there under swart hills.

Look. . . . Listen. . . .

My father's voice.

These were the days of twenty years ago before the final supremacy of television. Fathers still found time to tell stories to their children then, and I heard many stories while walking in my father's shadow. Sometimes even now, sitting alone in my room above Salamander Street staring at the fire, hearing the monotonous rumble of television sets from the neighbouring flats, I remember those eerie tales.

The Old Man, my father's father, came from mountainous Sutherland in the distant north; and now, wandering back and forth here on the dark shore, I blink my eyes and see that Sutherland of the mountains where I have never been. And, *Come*, I hear Pa's voice saying—

Come, he says. To the north-west. This is our place, here where the floods meet. See? There's the Atlantic and the North Sea fighting each other for control of the skerries, the splintered scatter of the Orkney Islands, and Scapa Flow, dark with rain. Here the coast sweeps west of John O'Groats, the earth suddenly heaves up mountains, and rocks and grass soar into the clouds. Sutherland. The coast sweeps on past Strathy Point, Strathnaver, the Kyles of Tongue and Durness to Cape Wrath, makes a sharp southern turn into the Atlantic, and her cliffs face the waters of the Minch under the shadow of Ben Dearg Mhor, down to

28

Kinlochbervie, Scourie, Handa, Badcall, Eddrachillis, and the slopes of Ben Stack.

All this desolation was our Eden, said Pa, this Sutherland that the Gaels called *Duthaich MacAoidh*, 'the land of the Mackays'. They had come from God knows where, half Gael and seemingly half Norwegian, and they called themselves *Morgainn*, 'the Sons of the Sea'. They took the lands of Strath Halladale and Strathnaver, even as far as Reay Forest and the shores of Loch Assynt, and they held them by plough and by sword fighting all comers, hunger and winter, Norwegian jarls and Scottish lords alike. Aye! said Pa, his eyes shining, they were grand fighters our forebears! He told me all about battles, some pronounceable —Lochbroom—some with outlandish teuchter names like Drumnacoub and Aldicharrish. He told me about the crofters and their hard life in a land that yet sounded so beautiful. It was a place of high mountains, he said, with fertile glens, and forests that went stepping down to the sea. And it was so remote up there in the cold north that the folk had had to warm themselves with legends, he said; and he told me some of those foolish legends. They had believed (in their ignorance, said Pa) that seals were womenfolk wrapped in animal skin, and sometimes one of the seal women would come on shore and leave her skin under a rock by the water's edge and walk all naked and lovely along the sands when the evening sun was shining over the waves of the Minch. Pa's eyes became soft and dreamy. If a man captured her sealskin, he continued, she was his for life because she could not return to the sea without it: she would stay with him and mother his children in the hope of getting her sealskin back. And sometimes these children could see into the future, he said. If you were the seventh son of a seventh son you could look into the peat fire flame and see the future there before you. I sometimes think there is something in it, said Pa wistfully. He mentioned names —the Brahan Seer, of whom I hadn't heard, and likened him to Nostradamus, of whom I hadn't heard either.

He said all this sucking on his pipe. Then he blinked and shook himself. 'Ach, nonsense!' he said. He leaned forward, and stared at me intently. 'Do you know what happened next?' he said.

He told me. Sometimes I think my father *bled* history.

'The lairds!' he cried. 'The damned lairds!'

It was the time of the Clearances. The Duke of Sutherland had taken to his heart the cause of economic progress and wished to develop the potential of the country in such a way that the mists of medieval poverty and superstition would be parted and a new age of civilization dawn for Sutherland. He meant so well. The people would stop scratching a living on their wretched crofts, concentrate instead in the new fishing villages—all neatly planned and hygienic with schools and kirks—that he would have built along the coast, and devote themselves to the lucrative herring industry. Meanwhile the hinterland would be turned into one great sheep pasture, and so Sutherland would flourish, said the Duke, and he set his factors to the great work.

Pa never made the connection between this engineering with human clay and the vastly greater exercises in social engineering made during this century in his beloved Soviet Union. No: he told me in horror and in rage how one old woman had died when the laird's men fired the roof over her head; that was what the Tories did, he said; God curse the black Tories! The millions who were killed by socialists in Russia and the Ukraine belonged to another galaxy; they did things differently there.

'They burned Sutherland!' Pa shouted, his face turning red. 'They drove the folk out and gave their land to the sheep! And no story prepared them for what was going to happen! None of these bloody legends was any use! *Look!*' his voice insists.

I look and I see flames.

We had an ancestor called Andrew, a crofter who had gone for a soldier in a red coat with a sprig of wild broom in his bonnet and a swing to his kilt in the war against the French Revolution and the armies of Napoleon. And the guns fired in Flanders and Egypt, they fired over the bloody fields of Spain and at Waterloo, and when he came home from that last battle a one-armed invalid he found that the Duke's factors had burnt Sutherland from the mountains to the sea, and the croft he had left twenty years before was a mere scattering of broken stones on a hillside where the sheep wandered.

Then Andrew sat and wept, having found that the gentry were altogether without honour, and he turned to the sea as he had been told to do; and perhaps some sealwoman did come to him, for he married and settled on the coast to try being a one-armed

30

fisherman, and found he could not succeed. Nor did the others. *Duthaich MacAoidh* emptied itself towards the coast as the Duke had wanted, but there the crofters heard foreign voices calling them, and they crowded into immigrant ships to try for a new life in Nova Scotia or Manitoba, by the Great Lakes or the Rocky Mountains. So one day Andrew stood on the deck of a ship in Tongue harbour that was waiting to raise its anchor and set its sails for Halifax in distant Canada, and with him stood his young wife and a hundred other migrants with their belongings. But even as the anchor was rising, Andrew turned (so the story goes), and looked back at the shore, and he could smell the land, and in his mind he could see the heather bloom on Ben Laoghal and hear the sound of the salmon jumping the falls of the Naver; and Canada was so far away. So he turned and left his uncle and his cousins, his second cousins and his third cousins, his sister and her man, and all his folks, his neighbours and his friends bound for distant English-speaking places, and he stepped back into Sutherland with his wife, and the ship sailed without them. Then Andrew wandered year upon year like a tink, knew hunger, fathered a son and knew the joy, saw his wife die and knew the sorrow. At last, in the little village of Scourie, hugging Eddrachillis Bay, he settled in old age, employed variously as one-handed bellringer, occasional carpenter, and, when all else failed, story-teller for the price of a dram, clinging to his Sutherland even as Scourie clung to the cliffs of it. And his son was a carpenter after him.

This story my father told me, who had it from his father who was a carpenter too, the drowned Jutland sailor.

In the pub at the foot of the stair, sometimes in the saloon bar when the TV is quiet and the jukebox is stilled, I hear men of my age and older talking about the way things were when they were children. In those days, they say, there were no drug addicts, no football hooligans, no mass unemployment. And they will turn to me and ask me what my good memories are. And I say, when I was a boy folks told me stories.

'So listen,' Pa would say grimly, telling me about the terrible years of the Clearances, and how the landlords had burned fair Sutherland from end to end.

'Listen,' he would say, telling me about the Old Man, his Highland father.

'Listen,' he would say, telling me about the war, the horror of war, and the wickedness of Hitler.

'Listen!' he said.

Listen.

And I listened. But I preferred it when he told me the legends of Sutherland, or about the King of the Golden River.

Of course only a townsman would have seen such story-telling mystery in the green land, but Pa was a townsman for all his Highland ancestry, and I was very much a townsboy in those days, and the country was a strange world of which I knew nothing, so I peopled it with all sorts of fantasies.

'I sometimes used to come here by myself, me and Joe maybe,' said Pa, as we stood together on the lip of the valley I had gone clambering up the day before. A narrow bridge stretched over it, and on the other side were the remains of a fortress tower, inglorious enough it seemed now, a mere rickle of fallen stones jungle-deep in nettles where men had fought each other long ago.

'In the days of the Covenanters,' said Pa, 'Cromwell—you know about Cromwell?—he marched his army up along the coast to the valley just about here.'

'And did he cross it?'

'Oh aye, he crossed it,' said Pa sourly, 'and it's a good thing for us that he did, because he was a democrat, and we were being oppressed by the Kirk and the bastard ministers. The same ministers,' said Pa, 'who have sucked up to the landowners and betrayed the working people throughout history!'

We walked back from the bridge, Pa telling me all about the wickedness of the ministers, and the landowners, and of the people's struggle against them. It was a fine story, full of blood and bravery, but I thought of the Old Man, and how Pa must have missed him when he was my age; and I wondered if in the end all the killing was worth it.

'Is there anywhere in the world that men haven't been fighting over?' I asked.

And Pa said, no, for this was the time of tyrants and the rule of the beast. And we walked on without saying a word. After a while I noticed that Pa rubbernecked whenever he heard a car on the road behind us.

'Keeping shote for the polis,' he said. 'We shouldn't be here, son.'

There were police stations in Cockburnspath to the north and Coldingham to the south, but Redheugh wasn't big enough to have one. This dot on the map had been the parish schoolhouse to which bairns who were now pensioners had tramped from the hill farms before the country buses came. There was a smithy too, though that was finished with, and the old smith lived there in retirement. Otherwise there was only a green wooden shed owned by the Women's Rural Institute, though I don't think they used it once all the months we were there. Further away, what was left of a mill was owned by a troglodyte, rumoured to be an Edinburgh doctor, whom nobody had ever seen. All else that was left of the village that once was were a few stumps of crumbling foundation sticking out of the nettles on the roadside like broken teeth.

And down the coast road to Coldingham went little old ladies in Morrises at thirty miles a fortnight, commercial travellers in Rovers at a hundred on the wrong side, phlegmatic farmers in tractors built like battle tanks, and shopkeepers in vans of all descriptions with battered mudguards, clarty radiators, and strange signs hand-painted on the sides:

DUNGLASS LICENSED GROCER
VEGETABLES, FRUIT, NEWSPAPERS, SWEETS,
TOOLS, IRONMONGERY
AND ANYTHING ELSE YOU WANT

And on the Lammermoors the sheep grazed.

And that, said Pa, pointing with the stick he carried for walking, was what was left of the old kirk of St Helen's. It had been Catholic, he said, from before the reformation, when Coldingham had a priory that owned all the land hereabouts. But Johnny Knox and his lads got at it with firebrands, and now it was just a desolate stone arch standing against the sea, halfway between the road and the cliffs. And yonder, he said, pointing to a distant promontory round which the waves were white and angry, would be the ruins of Fast Castle where the local laird had once lived in Stuart times, but his line was dead and the place all fallen into ruins. It was a terrible place for wrecks, said Pa. And he chuckled fiercely over the killings, ruins and burnings of the past.

'Still,' he said, pointing back to St Helen's, 'to be fair to them, those monks worked. Monastery land is always good rich soil. They had their uses, the buggers.'

When we got back to the schoolhouse there was an old man leaning against the roadside fence with a stumpy pipe in his mouth. Pa greeted him and lit up his own briar, and the two began cracking. Pa always ignored me when there was someone else for him to talk to, but the old man introduced himself and solemnly shook my hand. Bob Purves was the smith, though he had shoed his last horse perhaps about the time I was born, and—barring the troglodyte and the invisible ladies of the green shed—he was to be our only neighbour.

'But wheesht, don't tell anybody,' I said to Bob Purves, ''cos we shouldny be here.'

The two men took the pipes out of their mouths and laughed.

'Bob isn't a secret agent, ye daftie,' said Pa.

'But how are we hiding from the polis?' I asked, thinking of the blue man at home when Ma died. 'Are they after us, then?'

I went down to the sea and told the Old Man that we were wanted by the polis on account of our being revolutionaries and fell dangerous; and he sat beside me there on the rock with his feet in the sand and looked at me sadly out of his unblinking dead man's eyes, and the water streamed off him onto the gleaming shore.

The Old Man's face kept changing, for I had never seen it. Pa kept not a single photograph of his own father in our house—or if he ever had he had long since destroyed it. For Pa had no time for such sentimental rubbish. He said that gravestones should be bulldozed, and dead bodies turned to lime and used as fertilizer, like they did in the Soviet Union, that wonderful place (or so he said they did). And so the Old Man's face kept changing. He was a rugged sailor with blue tattooes; he was a stolid Highlander

34

with sandy hair; he was an Edwardian gent with a droopy moustache and wide, believing eyes. And he was dead and drowned, and so the water streamed off him onto the golden sand. But his face kept changing; and I told each face in turn that we were dangerous, we descendants of his, he could be proud of us, brave rebels and revolutionaries that we were, *wanted by the polismen* who spoke German—of course—and had squat steel helmets, and carried machine-guns, and got killed in great numbers. And the dead man just looked at me and looked at me, and at last I was silent and listened to the sea.

When I was a wean and newly arrived in this world, my folks put a lead on me and took me from the nearby village of Broxburn, where we lived then, into Edinburgh, the big city, to see my Pa's mother who was awful old and living in a stair in Marchmont.

She looked like Old Mother Hubbard, and she dwelt in an old house, on a ground floor, with a great black range that had a great black dog lying in front of it, and a wicked black cat that eyed me evilly, and huge black iron saucepans boiling up great steaming bowls of stuff that she had helped her mother make, who had helped *her* mother make them, who had helped *her* mother before her. And on the dark and never-washed walls were many other strange black-looking things, and I did not know what they were.

There I sat in a high hard chair in a sombre corner and listened with the innocence of a flower in the garden outside to my Pa and Ma, and to my Pa's brother, my uncle Jimmy, and my Pa's own mother, whom he called the Old Lady, all talking dark, mysterious words to each other about the bad days back long ago before the war when there were the hunger marches, and mounted constables had ridden up and down the High Street with their long wooden batons; and of how there had been a younger brother, Willie, who had got pneumonia tramping the streets in search of work, and had died of it because there had not been enough money to pay for a doctor.

And I listened to all these terrible things about the dark times, and understood none of it, except that they were bad. Then the cat with the evil look came stalking me where I sat alone in my corner. *Help!* I cried, *help!* because I was afraid of the cat; but I was only three, no more than that, and my words did not come out properly. Then the cat came with its sharp sharp claws, came and vanished and left me wailing, more in fear than pain, and everybody, turning round and seeing no cat, wheesht at me, and frowned, and Pa called me a damn nuisance. But the Old Lady, who was awful old, I remember how she came over to me then all wrapped up in her oldness, with her black gown and brown knitted shawl and strange dry lumpy hands; and in a voice that whispered like starched sheets,

'Shush, my wee mannie,' she said. 'Shush, and I will tell you a story about the land beneath the sea.'

The land *beneath*—?

She drew her chair in and sat down slowly and heavily, and the chair creaked.

Aye, Hughie, that's right, she said. Listen. Once—upon a time, yes—there was a man called Conn who was a great king and a grand warrior, so folk called him Conn of the Hundred Battles. Now Conn had a son, and his son was called Conla, and Conla was a prince—just like you, Hughie—and a fine bonny man he was too, with hair golden as the wheat and blue eyes like the very sky. But it was a bad time, and there was war, and the young men had marched off to the war, and there had been battles on land and on sea, and so many had died and not come back that the land was hurt without them, and weeds grew, and no one milked the cows, and the crofts were desolate.

Now Conla the prince was kind, and he was that sickened with men's cruelty that he went down to the sea and stood at the edge of it and listened to the white waves coming in; and he asked the waves if there was a land anywhere that was not full of suffering —and the waves spoke to him. Aye, they did. At first he thought he had gone daft, a voice coming like that from nowhere; but then as he looked closer he saw a mist forming on the sea, and out of this mist came a shiny seal creature, all wet and glowing. And then the seal shed her black seal skin, and out of it stepped the bonniest lassie he had ever seen in his life, all tall and fair was she, and her skin was smooth as the water. And she said to Conla, 'Come away with me, laddie, and be my man, and we will live together for ever in land-under-the-sea where there is no death or sickness, and all the folk are kind.' And Conla stretched out his arms to her.

But Conn, his father, had heard all this, and he couldn't see the lassie, he heard only a voice enchanting his son that came out of the thin air; and he was feared that it was a demon come to put a spell on his son and drag him down to hell. So Conn of the Hundred Battles called on Kernann, who was a wizard, and Kernann took an alder twig and stuck it into the earth, and drew the power of the earth, and then he held up the twig and it burst into a sheet of red flames that came in between Conla and the elfin girl; and so Conla was held to the earth. And Conn did this out of love, because he knew he would lose his laddie to the little people and never see him again.

—And what happened next? I asked, and my eyes were wide as fists. The stillness broke in the room.

'Ach!' said my Pa. 'Filling the bairn's head with nonsense!'

The great black dog opened his eyes and blinked.

One cold day in the newness of the twentieth century the Old Man and the Old Lady had come south from Sutherland, last refugees from the land of sheep; and the Old Man was a young cabinet-maker of Scourie with a dozen or two English words seeking the work that the empty glens no longer had, and the Old Lady was a lass from a moorland croft with nothing but the Gaelic and warm round cheeks and the bairn in her who would be born to grow and become my own Pa. And with them they had the cabinet-maker's tools, and a table and a mattress, a press full of linens and rugs wrapped round the china that tinkled within; and black iron saucepans, some bowls, a kettle, and a great black Bible, all in an unsprung trap. And they drove *clip-clop* out of the wasted land of peat fires and memory and ruined steadings and ghosts of those who had gone to die in Canada, and they drove south over stony Highland roads till they came to Stirling where the road forked, and the western road went to Glasgow, and the eastern road went to Edinburgh.

Then my Pa's father, whom I was never to know, sat there on his wooden box with all his tools in it and looked to one and looked to the other, and both were English places where the Gaelic wasn't spoken. So he asked the first man he met on Stirling bridge, 'Will it be Glasgow or Edinburgh that will have the best employment for a willing and hard-working cabinet-maker, do you think?' And the man (whoever he was, God knows, for his name is not recorded) said, Oh fine it would be Edinburgh, for the new town was filling up with folks all wanting the finely crafted furniture for their living-rooms. And so the Old Man who was to be drowned in the waters thanked him, and turned his cuddy's head to the east, and came to Edinburgh, to this same ground-floor flat in Marchmont by the Meadows, and began making tables and desks and fine dressers with drawers in them out of hard black wood with brass knobs and handles on.

And did he, I wonder, ever walk in the Meadows or picnic in the Braids, or look up at the Calton Hill or at Arthur's Seat from the window of his wee shop on London Road and think of the quieter, greener, harder land he had left, where his folks had lived since records were first kept; or mind the Sound of Handa, and Scourie, Badcall and Eddrachillis bays as he walked the promenade of Portobello; or see his own bloated body floating up to him out of the bloody waters of Jutland, and a child he would never know searching for him in his own dead eyes?

The Old Lady outlived him by forty years, and I never saw her but that once, when she told me the story of prince Conla and the elfin girl of the sea, for she was dead by the year's end, and my Pa said some words in Gaelic over her cremation. And that was the last of the old language my family ever spoke.

('The last they ever spoke,' I say to the girl whose mouth is all red with berries.)

But to return to that story. . . .
The feasts of Beltane came and went and the year moved swiftly, but there was no rejoicing in it for Conn of the Hundred Battles, for he could see his son fading before his eyes. Conla had eaten a golden apple the elfin girl had given him so that he might escape from the place of sorrow and come to her in the land of the ever-young that is beneath the sea. Every night he ate the apple and placed the core by his pillow. Every morning he found the apple whole. So it was with Conla. He took no mortal food or

drink, and with a diet of longing he paled away from the lands of death and of his father's hundred fights. And from the white-capped waves he heard his lover's voice calling him—Conla. . . . Conla. . . .

'And was she really bonny, Grandma?'

—Oh she was tall and lithe and her skin was smooth as the water, and when men looked on her needles of fire prickled in their throats. . . .

Then she must have been like my mother, I thought, for Ma was that bonny old men would lift their hats to her in the street, and young men would turn and stare when she walked by, blushing happily, with bright eyes dancing as she held my hand.

I can remember our returning home that evening to Broxburn where we lived, which was then a village, a crossroads with eight short rows of houses, no more. The mist came rolling off the sea and over the flat fields of West Lothian until the green country bus was like a great galleon voyaging through a sea of strange vapour. Ma was sitting by the window of the bus, while I was between her and Pa, and looking at her she seemed so bonny I thought she was indeed just like that girl of the sea, and that my own father was the man of the Hundred Battles whose memories of old wrongs were weighing me to a world that was immense and frightening. I believe I hated him then.

That night I saw my first darkness. I suppose it must have been closing towards winter and the nights lengthening. I had never seen darkness before. It was daylight when I went to sleep and daylight when I woke; daylight when I played in the yard and stole raspberries; daylight when I chased the fly-away birds that circled and scolded me in a flutter of feathers; daylight when I used to make arrows and a Red Indian's headdress in that backyard with the goat and the hens and the hedge at the end beyond which the green land stretched.

Darkness was new and I was afraid. I lay awake in it listening to the stillness into which the world I knew had disappeared, listening to the night sounds of a village, and the odd car passing through from Edinburgh to Uphall on the Glasgow road. Then in the moonlight I saw the curtain moving. . . .

It was Ma who came and sat beside me. She griped at Pa, standing there bleary-eyed in the doorway in his pyjamas,

39

because his mother had given me nightmares (she said). Pa looked sheepish and said he never thought it would harm the laddie. Ma held me to keep the darkness away, and asked, what was the matter?—And I said that I was sure I had seen the black-hearted Tories who had killed uncle Willie lurking behind the curtain, and the black-hearted Germans who had killed the Old Man were there too; the room was full of monsters just waiting the chance to kill me; and would it hurt to be killed, I asked, and would the elfin girl take me away to the land-under-the-sea for all that I wasn't bonny like Conla, and a prince?

The light was on in the room, and Ma held me and began telling me a story to send me to sleep.

'Listen now,' she said.

Listen now: how often I heard those words. When I was a bairn they bandaged me with stories, listen now, they said; fantastical stories about witches and seal-folk, Celtic Conn of the Hundred Battles, the German King of the Golden River. And grim stories too about the hard lives of grandfathers, great-, and great-great-grandfathers born in poverty, about the injustice of wars, the beauty of Sutherland, and the cruelty of its landlords. And it was all a story, a tale that I listened to in that pre-television age, vanished nights when the sea was lashing the shore, or the street noises were about.

Just like the inhabitants of such a story, my mother's folk had come out of the sea—or, more accurately, from a land over the sea, for they were Flemings from Flanders in centuries-gone-away days when wool merchants took the round-bottomed ships they called caravels out of Antwerp, voyaging. And at some remote point in that flux of time some remote Flemish man called Jan or Willem settled in Edinburgh's port of Leith, perhaps as agent for a shipping house, and he learned English, the 'sudron tongue' which Edinburgh ever spoke; and some local girl married the Fleming, and his son, or his grandson, or great-grandson, all of them exclusively English speakers, forgot the Flemish name that had been carried in the hull of the wallowing caravel from distant Antwerp, and became known and knew themselves simply as Fleming; and as Fleming they begat whole generations of Leithers. And behind them was the mass of Edinburgh—palace, town, castle on its high rock—and before

40

them was the mass of the trading sea from which came security for the shopkeepers and wealth for the burgh.

'And those years?'—were all a tale, Hughie, a tale. After the brave, vengeful Highlanders—your Pa's superstition-ridden ancestors among them—were pushed back into their glens by the red-coat soldiers, then burnt out of their glens by the clearances and chased overseas to Canada, to Australia, to India, to wherever in the world their sad progeny today attend Burns Suppers and plan camera-clad holidays back to the old homeland of kilts and white heather—after the affliction of this wasteful Highland disorder had been raised from them, peace at last reigned for the lowland shopkeepers, and Queen Victoria, like a good shepherd, led them into the golden age of trade, industry, and imperial splendour. Then it was that the gentry sported on their magnificent horses, that pipes and drums led a hundred proud red regiments to waiting troopships in bunting-bedecked and flag-waving ports, then that they voyaged off on the tunes of glory to fight with the Zulus, the Fuzzy Wuzzies, and the wild Pathans in the great cavalcade of Empire. Oh, a grand time it was to be a peaceable lowland shopkeeper, a rare time, those days before the year 1914 when a shot was fired far away, and the ships sailed off to war against an enemy who had machine-guns. Listen now, said Ma. Listen, and I will make it better, to this story of once-upon-a-time before machine-guns were invented, and the Germans were still our friends. . . .

In those days before we came to Edinburgh, my parents waved over my head like two grand trees, my Pa a majestic oak, Ma the slender birch. She was a gently religious woman, for all that Pa was so hot for the revolution, and like most such all her political instincts were conservative and left redemption to the Lord and the hereafter. I don't quite know how they came to marry, save that Pa had nearly lost his sanity in Hitler's war, and she had lost her Polish lover to the torpedoes off the North Cape of Norway. I suppose they were both lonely, and working as they did in the same office had seen the need in each other. At all events, marry they did, and between his politics and her religion was a peaceful coexistence that was often strained, but that never seemed to break completely.

41

Me: Ma, is it right that there's a land under the sea where there isny any sorrow or suffering or death?

Ma (at the ironing board): It depends on how ye look at it.

Pa (reading the newspaper): Ach! Filling the bairn's head with rubbish!

Ma: It depends on how ye look at it. Some say there is and some say there isny.

Me: But if there is, how does God no just tell the ones who think there isny so they'll ken?

Pa: Ha! That's a good one!

Ma: You just have to have faith that there is without knowing.

Pa (laughing): Bollocks!

Ma: Donald! I'll no have you using words like that in front of the bairn!

(Pa silenced)

Ma: It's like there are lands *beyond* the sea we dinny know are there, but we can still believe they are there because men we believe in tell us so. I dinny *know* if Heaven is there, but I believe it's there because I believe God and God tells me so. And the land under the sea is just another way of saying Heaven.

One Christmas in that village the snow came and drifted up to our windowpanes, and Pa lit a paraffin stove in the henhouse that all the hens sat round warming themselves at and clacking away like a gaggle of happy old women. And I breathed on the window and rubbed a peephole through the frost, and the yard outside was all one great whiteness, and the hedge wore its snow and ice like a coat. The land beyond was glowing blue in the moonlight, and the stars came out, and Ma said, 'Look, God's lighting His Christmas tree for us.' So we went back into the room to do the same. But our tree was a real one, a pine that Pa came tramping back with every year and set up in a barrel that he covered with red crepe and placed beside the kitchen hearth. And it was all my life's hope and ambition to decorate that tree the week before, standing on some giddy height of the ladder helping Ma drape the little green flexed lights among the branches and tie on the decorations that were made of paper and foil, but which I thought were treasures beyond anything the world could hold. So great was my belief in those treasures that I spent the whole year dreaming of seeing them again when the next Christmas came, because then we would be together once more, the three of us, in this same warm room with the cold beauty of the winter night all outside, and the electric light switched off, and the fire glowing and flickering and sending its armies of shadows galloping to all corners, and Ma and Pa both smiling at each other, and at me, and school a nightmare I had woken up from, and daylight when it came coming heavy with more snow and the frost that made your breath dance on the air before you. And the presents!—the soldiers and guns and knights and cowboys, the train set, the plastic Airfix ships, and the wigwam I could hide within in the unseen corner behind the toolshed! And then everything was all right, and no wrong and no hurt and no harm existed anywhere in the world.

But on the twelfth night the lights were extinguished, and the magical tree was as though it had never been. . . .

When we moved to Edinburgh—for the good of my education, said Pa—we lived in a flat high above Leith that was reached by tenement stairs, and on the top of the stairs was a darkness. At night, sometimes, Pa would scream in his sleep, 'Get off the bloody beaches!'—and I didn't know why. And Ma, sometimes, would weep in her separate bed, and I would hear her say, 'Stanislaus . . . Stani—'—and again I didn't know why. But their unhappiness and my not knowing upset me so much that Ma had to come and tell me go-to-sleep stories, or lift me to the high-up window and point to the lights from all the thousands of houses we could see, and tell me that there too wee boys just like me were having bad dreams.

And so the years passed, and each got colder than the last; and the city grew and grew with all its noise and its anger; and then a day came when she went away, my Ma, and I never saw her again, for when I came back home from school my Pa was sitting there, who should still have been at his work, and he was sitting there alone, and the room was cold and dreich and there was no fire in it, and he said:

'I've got bad news for you, laddie. Your Ma's deid.'

And I never saw her again, for she was only a box of wood that strange folk came and greeted round, and old women with hats and handbags kissed me on the cheek, and old men in suits patted my shoulder, and one wifie said consolingly to Pa:

'Och, but she makes a bonny corpse.'

And then they were driving her away, and we were following, and the rain was hitting the windscreen, and the black hearse turned a corner and we lost sight of it, and Hurry, I said, they're taking Ma away. And then it was a room full of staleness and solemnity, like the Sunday-morning kirk, only worse, and we were singing hymns, and the minister said, In My Father's House are Many Mansions, and he said that Ma had done a great work for God's Church, and it was surely a great and joyful consolation to know that she was with the Lord Jesus looking down at us from Heaven and smiling; and I thought:

—It's a lie. There is no God. There is no Heaven.

And at the door the minister came and held out his hand to Pa, and his face was round and his smile was soft and rosy, and Pa, who had said not a word the whole time, took one look and clenched his fist and banged him one in the mouth, and fairly caused a scandal.

The Old Man is standing on the dark shore looking over the waters, near invisible, the moonlight only catching the white crests as they come thundering in. Pa is standing beside him, looking, and I am between the two of them, looking, and their hands are on my shoulders—the one cold, the other warm, the one fish-wet, the other earth-dry—and we are looking for what will never be. And so I go back late at night, and it is cold, and Pa is angry, and I go to bed hungry and he doesn't come; and I lie awake waiting for him, but he doesn't come, and Ma doesn't come, and when I sleep I have nightmares and wake up in a terror—and there is no one there.

Darkness

The Redheugh smithy was on the other side of the road from our schoolhouse, weedy with ivy and so near hidden with hedge that cars in the night could speed past it without knowing it was even there. Outside the door a great water butt stood on a pile of bricks, its top well above both my father's grey head and Bob Purves's flat battered bonnet, and the brass tap at the bottom went *drip drip drip* and let a little burn trickle over the roadside. In hot weather, when the rain was scarce, Bob said he plugged it with a well-chewed wad of baccy, whereat I pulled a face that sent him chuckling, because his tobacco looked and smelled like burnt tar. Between the butt and the door was a mossy wooden bench long enough for two to sit on, and there Pa and the smith that was sat long that late summer of 1962, and I could hear their voices sometimes, but other times they would just sit with their pipes in a warm fug of smoke, saying *Aye, Aye* to each other like bells telling the quarters on a steeple clock.

Bob's house was small and timbered and dark as a cavern. It smelled strongly of Condor Slice and Navy Cut and all the dung and glaur of the countryside that seeped through the rickety yellow-stained windows. On the loose, I searched it, looking for a radio, and found a big shite-coloured thing called a wireless that Professor Quatermass could have invented, and that was marked (how long ago this seems) with the Light Programme, the Third Programme, and the Home Service, and it played *Forces' Favourites* and *Music While You Work*. So I fiddled with it on the track of Elvis, or at least Tommy Steele (am I really as old as that?), or somebody who could rock and roll convincingly—for, yes, I was ten years old in '62, and wore blue jeans and wanted to have a cool guitar and my own rock and roll band, and only unkind nature prevented me from ducktailing my hair properly and looking mean. But, alas, I failed to find any of them.

To keep me quiet, Pa bought comics off the newsagent's van that came daily with milk and rolls, sweets and gossip. He bought the ones he approved of, or at least saw no harm in, like the *Topper*, *Hotspur* and *Beano* where Farmer cashed Foxy with a blunderbuss and fired nails into his backside, and bright coloured wee boys with heads like balloons went *Aaaaargh!* and *Eeeeek!* and blew Teacher up with barrels of gunpowder—which I suppose led Pa to the conclusion that it was all serving a revolutionary purpose in the ranks of the young proletariat. And then there were the ones he didn't approve of, which I got him to buy anyway, for a while—*Commando* and *Action* and *War Stories*, where blood like ketchup squirted out of Japs and Nazis as our lads ripped them open with long blue knives—until the day he opened one, *Commando* I think it was, and there was the Iron Sergeant, with a face like a berserk robot, firing a flamethrower into a hut full of Japanese monkey men, shouting 'Try that for size, Tojo!' And the yellow monkey men were leaping and howling, tearing off their burning skins, exploding in mid-air blurbs of red goo, which I thought was fan-tas-tic; till Pa, his mouth quivering with anger, snatched it out of my hands, collected all the other comics he could find, and made an indignant bonfire out of the lot in the kitchen hearth. How mad I was with him!— though he told me that the American pilot who had atom-bombed Hiroshima had been brainwashed with this kind of stuff. And I said, So what?—they Japanese aren't human, I mean they're no like us. And he looked at me and said that the German gunner who had killed the Old Man had probably thought the same way.

The days Pa spent sitting with Bob Purves, I lived between the two houses, and explored both, finding a broken window in the high loft of the schoolhouse where old pigeon nests lay around in a smell of stale droppings, and where, with the days shortening, I could see the first fiery lights of the sunset and the blue-black shadows of the coming night crawling inward over the sea. And in the darkening hours, with Pa still clocking the papers for signs of the nuclear apocalypse, I would pad cat-like in search of secret turrets and passages; until the black night owl of the nearby tree sent me fleeing with his *Hoooo*, Tam o'Shantering down the stairs in a clatter to land bang on my dowp at the bottom: only to hear Pa's inevitable rage and curses at me for playing away while the world tottered on the brink of destruction. So the next day I would wander over to Bob's, and in the smithy that was, robbed of my comics, I would read the ones old Bob slyly bought for himself; while outside the window loomed the back of Pa's head and the back of Bob's head, amidst the smoke and the clack. And occasionally one disembodied head would turn, move, or twitch —always with an *Aye!*—but more often the two would just sit there near motionless, looking straight ahead for hours and hours like Buddhas in the tobacco fug, while I lounged feet up on Bob's battered leather armchair with half its stuffing spilling out, fuelling my brains with Batman, then running outside in a whoop to fight the foes of Gotham City down to the garden gate.

'And what does that signify?' said Pa, pointing to the sign on the butcher's van which said *Gladly My Cross-Eyed Bear* with a picture of an amiable teddy whose eyes looked at each other over the top of his button nose. The man at the wheel grinned and stroked his many chins.

'Well, sir,' he said, clambering down to look at the cock-eyed grizzly, 'it goes back to when I gave my wee girl here'—he gestured to the cabin—'her first teddy: the creature was cross-eyed. The teddy, ye ken. Well, I thought nothing o't, and that Sunday we went to the kirk same as usual, and when we got back home she telt me she had a name for her teddy—Gladly! Gladly? I says, what's Gladly got to do with it? Well, she says, we were singing about him—Gladly my cross-eyed bear! "Gladly my cross I'll bear",' he explained. 'And so I painted it on the van. I bet there's no many teddy bears have got hymns written about them—is that no right, stookie?'

A girl jumped down on to the road beside him. She was the girl from the valley.

'Och,' she said, seeing me. 'It's you.'

'Oh aye then, and what's this?' said her father. 'It's him,' she said. 'He's a right heidbanger.'

The van driver laughed and turned to my Pa to say something funny, but he saw Pa's look and said nothing. Pa snorted and said:

47

'Give your girlfriend a kiss then, son.'

His face threw an ugly sneer at me, the like of which I had never seen before: and, taking me by the neck, he shook me and said:

'Go on, kiss her then!'

His face was down close to mine. It was wizened, red and angry, thin and sharp, and his breath smelled bad. I turned my head away, but, fascinated, I could not take my eyes from him. I could not believe this ugly mask was my father. Then the mask snarled something, and spittle struck me in the face, and over the top of my head he said to the van driver:

'You see the way he treats his father? You see the sort of respect he has for his old man?'

And turning back to me, he brought his mouth up against mine, and said:

'Any more of your lip and I'll bloody murder you, ye hear? I'll give you the biggest leathering of your life, ye hear?' said the mask. 'Ye hear?'

I tore myself away and ran from him, and from the astonished staring eyes of the van driver and the little girl. I ran. Down through ocean-sized fields full of corn blowing like water, I ran—and ran, until over the fields came the sound of the sea to meet me, breaking on the rocks at the foot of the cliff.

Conla, it said; *Conla* . . .

(And to Conn, the King of a Hundred Battles, Kernann the wizard said: Your son is already lost to you. It were better that you let him go to the land of the ever young. But Conn of the Hundred Battles answered him and said: Never! He is my son and will do as I say. I will not lose him to some banshee!)

'Ach,' said my Pa sarcastically. 'Filling the bairn's head with nonsense!'

(And plunging down seaward through the corn, I seized the magical sword, which all but the seventh son of a seventh son thought was a dried stick in an old fence, and I shook it in his face.)

'Ach,' said Pa bitterly, through his teeth. 'Filling the bairn's head with nonsense!'

(But I too was bitter in my way, and wanted to live in the place

48

of myth, at one with the creatures of legend in my longing for the land that has no suffering because it is beyond time.)

'Ach,' said Pa, his mouth twisting in a spasm of pain, 'ach! Parsons' lies! God, heaven and the soul! Lies, all bloody lies! She's dead and burnt to a bad smell and a pile of ash, and that's it finished with!'

And that day, when we got back from the crematorium, he took the tie off his dark suit, sat down at the table and opened the newspaper. And there in it was all about Macmillan and Kennedy, De Gaulle and Khrushchev, hopes of peace, threats of war, and pictures of war somewhere, with armoured cars in the desert raising clouds of sand. Pa stared numbly at the dirty pages, and I stared at him, and thought of the minister he had knocked down at the chapel door, and the scandalized relatives, and the whisperings and the tuttings: and I realized then, finally, that there was just the two of us now in all the world.

I began to sniff. I was sitting near him, and I didn't want to move away and be alone in the cold. So I tried to stifle my sniffing, because I knew Pa hated 'greeting-faced bairns', and failed. I swallowed, and tightened my fists till the bones were gleaming white, while he stared at his newspaper with its dingy print. I held my tears, and held them till I couldn't stop them any longer; and so I just put my head down and wept with my face on the dinner table.

Pa screamed at me and flung the paper at my head.

'Stop your fucking snivelling!' he shouted. 'We're all Shite, ye hear? I'm Shite, and you're Shite, and it's a lot of Shite, the whole fucking thing, and we'll all be dead and buried in our boxes before long!'

And he stormed about the room, saying that this was Shite, and that was Shite, and it was all Shite to him, and that I was Shite—*Shite!*—nothing more, and he was black ashamed to have dropped such a useless lump of snivelling dirt as me into the world—and why hadn't I just killed her when I was born and been done with it? *Why?* he repeated, shaking me violently: *why?* And at last I managed to speak, and I said:

'She doesny have a box. You didny even give her a grave. You just burnt her up—you miserable fucking liar.'

And then he hit me, hard. For the first time.

49

Midnight

Time, time, tick tock, the hour glass and the cowled reaper. . . .

The hands of my watch say midnight, and it is getting cold here, walking back and forward on the shore with only the moon lighting my footsteps, knowing that behind me the city is settling down to sleep, and in the South Atlantic men are burning, bleeding, dying (. . . *with the scythe*), their blood on the water.

While all this city bleeds is damn history.

Back in the Ice Age, when all warm-blooded creatures had fled for their lives, a moving glacier struck an already ancient volcano here on the coastal plain of Lothian; and the ice split in two on the iron-hard rock of the volcano's core and flowed around it, slowly, painfully, carving out great gashes of land on both sides, and leaving a long tapering ramp of earth, as a river flowing past the pier of a bridge might leave a sandbar on the downstream side. Edinburgh.

And then the ice departed, the sea withdrew a little, giving to the plain areas that one day would come to be known as Stockbridge, Canonmills and Bonnington, where gardeners would mutter at the sandy soil and puzzle vaguely over the fossilized creatures their spades threw up. And ready, waiting, purpose-built by the vanished ice, dominating the whole plain between the Pentland Hills and the waters of the Forth, the first people who returned found the great rock crouching there like a stone lion. So they build their first settlement on its summit and called it *Dunedin*, 'the Fort on the Rock'. There the painted tribesmen looked out over a sea of trees, for great forests grew hereabouts, all over this land, the Pentlands were muscles encased in tree-flesh, and the Water of Leith was a mere silver singing in the green shadows of the place. And as they looked, the tribesmen realized that they could raid where they liked at their leisure from this safe lair.

So the rock became desirable: for the Romans trudging north, the sore-footed legionaries billeted on the coast who raised an altar to the gods of their own distant homeland and carved on it MATRIBUS ALATERVIS ET MATRIBUS CAMPESTRIBUS COHORS II TUNGRORUM POSUIT ('The Second Cohort of Tungrians erected this to the Alatervian Mothers and the Mothers of the Plains'); for the Northumbrian English cavalry riding north who took and named the rock after their king, Edwinesburgh ('Fort Edwin'); for the Scots sweeping south who took it from them. Desirable down the centuries as though made of gold was the castle town of Edinburgh, for Scot and English, Scot and Scot; and they made it bleed history with their battles, betrayals, burnings and murders, it wept slaughter from its very stones. Tick tock, it wept.

But now the time is past midnight, and quiet the city sleeps, its ancient stones layered over with plastic and neon. Now the anonymous daylight din of engines has faded, and small individual sounds punctuate the stillness of the hour. The tyres of a late-night car on Granton Road, the low growl of a distant lorry, the step of the lonely homewalker, the somewhere kirk steeple chiming mortality to those who no longer listen; and somewhere else sudden drunken voices singing, shouting harshly, and someone kicks a can *clatter clatter clatter* along the asphalt stones. The tramp I saw this while back hunching for sleep in a doorway, is he asleep now, is he snoring—*grunt!*—in the land of nod?

Listen, my fellow watchmen, do you know I am standing here while you yawn in your huts on the building sites, while you pace round the mesh gates of docks and warehouses, settle uncomfortably in armchairs not made for sleeping on in managers' offices, or lie on a bed of coats and cushions on the staff room floor in factories, galleries, gleaming nickel-bright banks? In your streets too you hear the walkers go, the unknown ones who have no conceivable reason for being out at this hour, but are out nevertheless. The policeman smoking in a corner, wearily stamping his feet. The glue-sniffer, dazed into another world, who has forgotten his home and how to get home. Those who have no home. The drunk, the subject for jokes, the 'blootered', 'pissed', 'half-cut', 'boxed', 'steamed', 'half-seas-over' wretch lying uncaring and uncared for in a dark place with urine drying around his unopened trousers. Oh the dark night owls, how they fly! And the girl whom I saw once and so briefly months, years ago, combing her dark long dark and lovely gypsy hair that night in a bedroom window, and whom I have remembered ever since because oh she was so beautiful. I have heard the chimes at midnight, gypsy lady.

Midnight, quiet hour sliding towards a cold morning. This side of the Castle on the rock, beyond the hollow the ice carved out these twelve thousand years gone by that is now the Gardens with its bandstand and floral clock, the closed shops of Princes Street, how beautifully their windows glow, each one like Aladdin's cave, a land of furs and elegance guarded by snap-down steel shutters. Two gleaming bookshops, their windows groaning with the weight of identical hard-back novels and tartan trash, Royal Deeside and the (wait for it)

Latest International Blockbusting Bestseller
As Seen On Television And Soon To Be
A Major Film!!!

(Wow!)

Oh stale bread, stale stale bread.

Look. There is the St James Centre, looming behind the ugly bus depot like some even uglier Ministry of Love, where weird glue-sniffers hang out, and muggers, and pushers, and the arse-end of a disco fight, some sad hard boy aerosoling swastikas on the wall, some drab run-away-from-home girl waiting for a fix—all in the shopping precinct where the steel-shuttered windows glow with *etcetera*.

Listen. Here come the genii of the forbidden treasure caves. Private security guards with armshields, policemen, police-women, all in midnight blue. Batter batter batter go feet hitting the concrete in all directions, over the pedestrian footbridge, along the corridors, down the subway tunnels; and out in the street waiting blue lights revolve in the dark.

And then once more it is quiet. Quiet beneath the Calton Hill where medieval kings held their jousts; quiet in the classical New Town; quiet law offices, quiet banks, quiet insurance companies. Quiet on the Royal Mile, the long ramp itself, the earthbar that formed in the lee of the volcanic core when the ice moved.

Quiet. *Hush*.

The place of ghosts: the High Street, the Grassmarket where the gibbets once stood, whither they hauled men from prison to their deaths, Montrose and Argyll the patriots, Major Weir the warlock with his black stick, the burglar Deacon Brodie; Canongate, the ruined Abbey, Holyrood's haunted palace, tragic Mary Queen of Scots and David Rizzio her murdered valet, stabbed to death for the love of her. Past midnight now in St Giles, its weathercock and its dome, John Knox's grand high kirk, mecca of the northern reformation—but the burning bush of the presbyterian faith has long burnt down to cold ashes. Long past midnight in the place of neon boutiques, littered pavements and plastic signs. Black morning in the place of death.

Cold, these early hours here. Edinburgh isn't Hamburg or New York; Edinburgh isn't a swinging city. No brazen raunchy hookers proposition you on the pavements, no all-night glitter-domes throb with heavy sounds, no sinful sex-parlours showing non-stop videos of girls taking their clothes off. A port without rollicking sailors; a capital without a debauched ruling class. In this city lust is furtive, private, frustrating, and utterly lacking in style. In the wee wee hours Edinburgh flushes herself silently and morosely down the drain.

Silence of a cold, wet, wind-blown city. Silent the grubby amusement arcades with their fantasy murder machines, the space invaders, star wars and he-man lasers, those electronic hell holes, silent now, switched off, black. The discos at last empty. The pounding beat of the box finito. The yodelling millionaires, Johnny Horrible and the Heidbangers, Total War, s.c.u.m., the Gestapo, have all slid off into unplugged nirvana.

The night closes its eyes and Edinburgh is become a city of statues. There along Princes Street they stand, the open-eyed dead men—Wellington the soldier, Livingstone the explorer, Guthrie the philanthropist. Down the High Street, round old St Giles—the Duke of Buccleugh, Charles II, John Knox. Round the New Town—Alexander the Great and his cuddie, Gladstone

53

and Pitt, another King, an Admiral this, a General that; big, solid, imperial men. And the war memorials, both bygone colonial skirmishes and recent global strife—the huge metal sentry on the Mound, the heroic little battle scene on the North Bridge above Waverley's trains, and the World Wars' dead in every cemetery below silent stone angels. Even the cold dock cranes here at Granton and Leith stand like the threatening megaliths of some primitive religion.

Now nearly everyone is asleep: even the early morning cleaners, their alarms haven't jangled at them yet. Hardly a sound on long Leith Walk, longer Ferry Road: hardly a sound anywhere. A yawning boy in soldier's uniform has closed the Castle, and a police car moves slowly through the sleeping streets. At Leith the darkened ships groan quietly, tethered to the quay—and suddenly I remember that rusty merchantman with the Soviet flag I saw today called *Ivan Susanin*.

And suddenly it is so cold.

When I was a boy I used to dream of running away to sea and sailing off on such a humdrum ship as that to wondrous warm islands and adventure: and as I look, I seem to see the boy I was standing on the prow of that phantom ship. *Come*, he waves to me, *come* . . . Those of us who watch the night, what heroic dreams we have! I have felt—as the police patrolman has felt, as the boy sentry has felt, as every insomniac and the watchman by the dock gate has felt—that I am the only one awake in this world, that I am guarding those who do not know and do not care for me; that I, like a vigilant knight, like the child who saved Holland, like the sentry at Pompeii, am on guard against the powers of evil, selfless I, faithful onto death, hello.

IVAN

Over the sea and over the snows and across the forests of the north, quite near my Noroway o'er the faem, sits Ivan. In Arctic Lapland, in the place called Kola, between Archangel and Murmansk. A remote place, like Sutherland; depopulated and very beautiful, like Sutherland; wrapped, like Sutherland, in legends—about the swan of Tuonela, and brave prince Vainamoinen, born of Luonnaaotar, the mother of the sea.

54

Enough of legends. Kola is now a military base bristling with the ballistic missiles of the Soviet Strategic Rocket Forces.

America's nearest equivalent is Nebraska where the Minutemen are.

Europe's nearest equivalent is Scotland.

And there they live, the nomadic thousands and tens of thousands of Russian and Ukrainian, Baltic, Siberian, Caucasian and Central Asian boys who are driven each year by plane, train and lorry to prefabricated men-only towns, their virgin bodies shrouded in army khaki and navy blue. They serve the nuclear submarines, cruisers and destroyers of the Soviet Northern Fleet; they guard the bases of the missile system, the forest clearings where the missiles sit like evil giants in their underground silos; they make sure that the few remaining Lapps will not, like the crofters of Sutherland—or the Sioux Indians—stage the last great uprising against the tide of progress.

And you see, I think one of these Russian lads is my friend Ivan.

I picture Ivan as a fresh-faced boy with a snub nose and tousled hair. Perhaps he has the broad flat face and high cheekbones of the traditional Slav. Perhaps he has freckles. I think he is probably a corporal: at least that seems right for a fresh-faced boy who is patriotic and law-abiding in the main, and was good at mechanical things when he was at school (as I'm sure you were, Ivan). He is sitting just now at a panel of buttons and switches and he is reading a book, no the paper, no he is doing the crossword, he is sucking the end of his pencil and puzzling. Near him is sitting his sergeant who is playing the balalaika, no playing with himself, no looking at a girlie magazine smuggled surreptitiously over the Norwegian border. Near the sergeant is sitting his lieutenant who is etcetera, and near the lieutenant is sitting the captain who, and near the captain is sitting the major, and near *him* is sitting the etcetera etcetera, until we reach the place where orders are made, where is sitting a happily married old family man with grey hair and a wise face and humane ideals; and between him and Ivan orders will flash on the hi-tech *brring brring bleep bleep* and Ivan, dropping his crossword and spitting the pencil out of his mouth, no tucking it behind his ear (he's a neat boy), will finger —between Ivan and Ivan's finger—between Ivan's finger and the

55

button beneath Ivan's finger—the orders will—press—and . . .

Tick tock . . .

Tick—tock—time . . .

(There will be a blinding flash over Edinburgh, me, Rosyth, Faslane, Holy Loch, Sutherland . . . my cousins in Manitoba whom I shall never know.)

The cowled reaper with the scythe.

(Of course, in Nebraska Corporal Chuck is sitting in front of a control panel reading Peanuts, and his missile is pointed at Ivan—unless, of course, Ivan's friend Boris whose missile is pointed at Chuck hits his button first—in which case Chuck's friend Leroy, whose missile is aimed at Boris, will—)

Ivan,

we bleed history, all of us.

Ivan,

there is folly in this world.

North of the land of the capital city of hope, the world's first socialist country, the workers' paradise, the land of the Revolution my father so admired, of Lenin and the International, of troika bells and lovely Natasha Rostova, where the morning sun fills Red Square and the Kremlin domes gleam over Moscow river, the missiles bloom in Lapland.

Tell me

Ivan,

my brother,

whom I never knew,

tell me, what was your childhood like? Did you have a Pa like mine, and was he too an old socialist, one of those who believed and paid for it behind the wire; did he come out from Gulag camp or war wearing lines on his face and bitter eyes to make your life a misery with the leadweight of lessons? Or was he, again like mine, a dissident? Was America his land of hope, and did he sit alone at night trying to understand the why of its atom bombs and its belligerent pornography, the whywhy of it all, Ivan, when you were playing football in the street? And when you had nightmares, when the bogles were round your bed and their breath was cold and clammy on your frightened wee boy's neck, did you have a Ma who came to you once and told you stories, not about Stalin and the Five Year Plans, but about the wonder-land, the over-the-sea land, the place where Ruslan and Ludmilla are, and the peasants' tsar lives for ever on a throne of gold? And later did you too come knocking shyly on the gates of manhood (as I, now middle-ageing, did in the days of the Beatles) and go singing over the fields by the river making poems like Pasternak to the girl of your blue eyes, and was she too a gypsy lady like mine, in days when there was no pink glare of napalm on the Himalayan foot-hills, no machine-guns coughed at the cross-roads, and the world was all for loving—did you do those things then too, oh you beautiful stranger, my brother Ivan?

(Chuck? Boris? Leroy?)

Well, here we are. It is early morning now in your target area, Ivan, and I can paint no cross on my door so that Time, death's angel, will pass over me with his scythe. It must be a late spring or early summer dawn in Kola. At dawn, or thereabouts, when the first people start to move, there is a part of me that smiles gently, as the sleepless man who has watched the hours away by his loved-one's side sees her turn and blink slowly in the morning light, and thinks—I have guarded you through the darkness, my dear, and you never knew. . . .

We have both heard the chimes at midnight,
Ivan.

Cold, so cold.

What The Thunder Said

That afternoon I lay on top of the redstone cliffs ('They call it Redheugh,' said Pa) and the sea wind was in my hair, and the sea was all a shimmering brightness under the late summer sun. The sky looked like a field of gentle clouds that grazed on the hilltops and drank from the far horizon beyond which lay Norway and all other lands: and I lay and muttered into the rough grass—*I'll fling myself over the cliff and die, and then he will be sorry!* Nothing heard me. To a cricket chirping nearby, and to a tiny spider running up a ladder of grass, it was just another dry, sunlit summer's afternoon.

Seek and ye shall find, said the Word (you Sunday Sabbaths spent sitting beneath the pulpit's overhang!). Look and it shall be revealed onto you.

I pressed myself into the earth, my ten-year-old body burrowing into the long grass until the grass was over my head, till I was a swimmer in a green sea, a lone walker in a cloister of yellowing stalks; and there was a smell of salt and gull shit, of tangled roots knotted in the red sandy soil, and my hands parted the waves before my face, diving down, down like some old Celtic hero to that land-under-the-sea.

—Welcome, Hughie. Welcome to the Happy Island where the fate of man is spun.

Was that a voice? I listened. On the horizon I heard a rumbling as of distant thunder, and I looked at it, and the summer sun was overcast.

—There, do you see me? said the thunder, rolling in over the sea.

On the horizon where the white clouds are.

Where Norway is.

To Noroway, to Noroway, to Noroway o'er the faem.

And the grey ships of Jutland with ensigns white—the Germans' white with a black cross, ours white with a red—throwing the creamy bubbling foam over their prows, while the shells from Midland and Ruhr factories scream. And the white water trees leap heavenward to greet the shells, and I hear the screams of jagged metal caught in their branches, and the screams of men within. . . . Do you see?

—What are those?

Those are bodies. They float until they swell, and then they sink. And when they sink, if you look carefully, you will catch the moment when out of the war clouds comes a woman who is clothed with the sun. . . .

Ah, she was fell religious, that woman who was my mother, and Pa would often send me out on Sabbath days to play football because he knew it would hurt her—which gave him some strange pleasure in turn. How often, sitting underneath the carved pulpit in the plain-lit barn of a presbyterian kirk did I hear those chanting rhythms of blood and lust that folk still took, even in the rock and roll TV-watching Pepsi-Cola fifties, to be the good Godspell of Jesus. And yet the haunting poetry of it, and the strange wonder in the words, were a fascination to me, for they cried out that *there appeared a great wonder in heaven: a woman clothed with the sun, and the moon under her feet, and upon her head a crown of twelve stars. And she being with child cried, travailing in birth, and pained to be delivered.* And I would close my eyes on her travail in that stifling kirk amid mothballed suits and Sunday hats, and I would see that Woman walking towards me, all naked and lovely she was, and in the stained-glass light beyond the swell of the organ where the sun fell among the elders on the green dais of yon Edinburgh kirk,

> I
> beheld
> a great wonder
> on the sea

—yes, a woman walking from the midst of the battle, and she was with child and cried that he might not be butchered in battle as his Pa was being butchered. And I looked at the woman, and I saw on her nakedness the blackness and the oldness and the brown knitted shawl I would see, and only once, in Marchmont.

'Are you the Old Lady?' I asked.

And, Aye, she said in her look; hers indeed was the mouth that would whisper forty years into the future tales of olden times, and warrior kings and heroes and such, to hide the cruel and awful reality that was Jutland. And there on the prow of the Ship now sailing from the Forth (over these very waters!), the great dreadnought Ship, the fine Ship with its guns, the pride of the greatest navy the world had ever seen, the Old Man her husband stood like a Viking chieftain before the mighty gun turret, and the white ensign of Nelson and Rodney was snapping in the wind; till hooded Time with his scythe came out of the muzzle of a German gun and proclaimed twelve hundred lives at an end. Then the guns went down firing their black smoke, and the mighty screws of the ship heaved cloudward, and the captain of that proud HMS *Queen Mary*—which had left the Rosyth anchorage and the waters of the Forth and seen the lights of Fife and Edinburgh, or such that shone in the First World War blackout, fading in the haze of that same morning—tumbled to the bottom of the sea with his telescope in his hand, and twelve hundred men came to lie round his feet, and the heart of each and every one was a many-threaded tartan, the red of hope and the blue of dreams, of suburban villas and crumbling tenements, school desks and initials and 1066 and ragtime and music-hall and dances at the end of the pier on fair summer evenings. And there they all lay under the waves at Jutland.

—Now look, look! said the thunder rolling itself back up into a black ball. . . . And through the swirl of smoke comes first a weathercock, syne a great crowned dome, and then slowly ridge upon ridge of grey tiled roofs, now in the turning twilight time between sea and hills and skies racing heavy with fire blossoms, like a running girl whose arms are full of red morning flowers.

Now from underneath the slate roofs appear the windows of Edinburgh—of Haymarket and Corstorphine with rooms full of sleeping citizenry, and of Bonnington and Fairmilehead and Leith, where the cranes are sleeping rusty metal dreams, and of Joppa and Gorgie and Grassmarket, where the tramps are, in the

Salvation Army hostel waiting for the public bogs to open, and of the New Town where hard lawyers slumber in soft beds, and Gayfield where the polismen are counting the minutes to 6 a.m. end of duty time and wishing they could arrest every one of them for idling, and Granton and Pilrig, Slateford and the Redford barracks where a soldier in puttees is stamping out a fag butt.

Edinburgh: Jesus, city of ghosts; *whooo* on the night wind, *whooo* in the closes of the High Street, Deacon Brodie and Major Weir tap-tap-tapping with his infernal black stick; and *whooo* down the via dolorosa of the Canongate where they lugged Montrose to be murdered, and the Marquis of Argyll is reputed to have leaned over the balcony of Moray House and sneered at him—*Ech, James Graham! And how can your braw king no help you now?*—and spat in his face, they say, and the crowd fair laughed; and then ten years later they were lugging Argyll up the same gait for to be murdered in turn, and a soldier sneered at him and shouted—*Ech, King Campbell! The mills of God grind slowly man!*—and spat him back, and the crowd fair laughed at that too; and they have put a great stony heart on the site of the Tolbooth execution cell where both men were taken to be butchered, and ever since it has been lucky to spit on it. They're full of spit, the folk of Edinburgh.

Listen. The city is waking. It is the 1920s this, because *(listen!)* the morning tram is rattling round Queen Victoria's statue from Constitution Street, and yon soldier waiting his relief is wearing puttees round his legs, and the polisman tramping up March-mont Road has boots and a tunic that buttons up to his throat and a helmet, and folk don't even have crystal sets yet never mind wirelesses. Listen! Tinny alarms are jangling and men with heavy moustaches are scrubbing their gaunt faces over zinc basins and shaving carefully with cut-throat razors, and women in dingy floral gowns are making strong mahogany-coloured tea and kippers on the stove; and in cold stuffy rooms ardent young writers who write pap for the *Evening Dispatch* are trying to write like James Cain is trying to write when he is not writing pap for the Los Angeles Thingumyjig; and if Robert Fergusson's wraith hears the aircock of St Giles crowing up there among the quickly fading stars, I hear the whistles that suddenly start blowing all over the morning town from Leith to Holyrood to

Portobello, and as the men in cloth bonnets and kerchiefs start trudging workward, others are fastening their neckties and angling their collars and wiping their bowlers, and trying to remember the rat that ran over their sleeping heads, and did it have a face like Ramsay Macdonald?—while out there in the street the Sun of Morning just opens his rainy arms and beams.

—Welcome to the first day of the rest of your lives!

Meanwhile in the sweetie shop at the corner Mr Mackenzie fumbles in his waistcoat for the door key, and walks into the dark cool room, lays the morning *Scotsman* on the counter (did my grandfather the drowned cabinet-maker fashion that counter? —probably) and hangs his bowler hat and jacket on the black stand, puts on the thin brown coat that he wears indoors, and inspects his big-bellied jars of boiled sweets in all rainbow colours, and caramels in paper pokes, and liquorice pipes, chocolate cigars, sugar men, candy women, toffee apples, dolly mixtures, copies of the *Boy's Own Paper* full of public-school English chaps knocking eight bells out the fuzzy wuzzies, and penny issues of a strange wee broadsheet full of smudged print and conviction called *Glad Tidings of the Coming Kingdom*. And rolling up the window shutters he greets the morning as his first customer.

'Well, my mannie, and what'll ye have?'

'Hey, Donald,' said the boy nearest the wall.
'Whit?'
'It's after half six.'
'Och.'
Silence. Three shapes lay under the quilt.
'Hey, Donald.'
'All right, I hear ye.'
Silence.
'Hey, Donald.'
'All RIGHT—fuck it.'
Don't I know yon voice though? Donald? The boy on the outside who is the eldest of these three brothers drags the sheets down off his face, yawns fit to swallow himself, and tousles a sandy mop with his fingers. I stand there invisible and keek at my father's boyish face. Heavens, to think he was once a laddie like

me! The Marchmont room is morning-lit. The huge black range stands there piled with all its black saucepans. Behind the sink is a clutter of dishes on a wooden rack, and my father clambers out of bed and hauls his short breeks on, and the water rattles in the iron sink as he scrubs at himself with his skinny hands, then fills a kettle bigger than his head with a huge wooden handle and a long curving spout, hauls brother Jimmy (later to emigrate to Australia and become a car salesman and never write) out by the feet, bang on his arse on the cold stone floor, and shakes brother Willie with a roughness that is also gentleness and asks, how's the bairn, and did he sleep well? And aye, says brother Willie who is thin and sick, I slept that rare I never heard yous all snoring. And while Jimmy is rubbing his nose and going one-armed into his semmit, and Willie is sitting up blinking like a wee white owl, Pa is away ben to wake the Old Lady—not so old then—with a cup of strong scalding tea and a 'I'm just away out, Ma' in the morning.

—And mind yer no late like yesterday.

'Aye, all right,' on the stairs.

And the sun from Japan crawling up over the Meadows sees Pa in his outsized tackety boots clattering along the pavement from Mr Mackenzie's with his paper satchel, and his long baggy shorts flapping at the knee, and his mouth knotted in a whistle:

> 'Ally bally ally bally bee,
> sitting on yer mammy's knee,
> greeting for a wee bawbee
> to buy some Coulter's candee. . . .'

And he whistles it again and again and again, a whine fair fit to make the windows stutter, syne home to his breakfast, his brothers both dressed—no sisters left, both of them that were dead in the Spanish 'flu that came at the war's end—terrible thing that epidemic, took one from every house in the street—and his Ma, the Old Lady, ladling out porridge into their four bowls—man dead too, in the war—and scowling at their dour faces.

—We're no gentry to be eating kippers every morning.

And off to school with all three of them, Pa and Jimmy in the senior school, Willie a primary bairn dawdling behind; and Joe

63

from upstairs catches them at the corner with a penny pack of jubejubes got from better not ask where, and seizing on a sardine can lying in the gutter Pa hacks at it with his boot.

'And it's five minutes into extra time—'

'The score is three wan.'

'See it on Saturday there?'—'Aye, great.'

Goal!

'Hey, Donald?'—'Whit?'

'Is it right we're no singing God Save the Hielan Fling the day?'

'That's whit we're telt.'

'How?'

'Wur teacher's a Bolsheevik.'

'Whit's that?'

'I dinny ken, but he's wan of them.'

Goal! . . .

Often on Saturdays there would be the Match, there would be the tanner matinees at the Picture Palace, cranky silents whirring in a flicker of white light, the laddies' eyes in the front row never leaving the screen as Rudolph Valentino bravely defies the Four Horsemen of the Apocalypse, and Mrs Swallow from next door but one chases the action on the piano set up just under the screen, slinging in wee bits of Swan Lake and Beautiful Dreamer as the fancy takes her.

But when next I see them they are down at the docks sitting at the far side of the Martello tower with a great barricade of empty crates stretching the breakwater's length, and Imperial Dock, Albert Dock and Victoria Dock all grinding and cranking away behind them, while in front is only the green sea throwing up its hands over the Middle Craig rocks. Then friend Joe and Jimmy and Willie produce fishing lines that are long sticks of cane with bits of string attached, and Pa starts holding forth out of a tatty Communist Party pamphlet telling about how God is a pure invention, nothing more, of the bourgeoisie to keep the working masses all ignorant and divided just so these terrible White Guardists that are rampaging against the Revolution in Russia can come over and shoot them down in heaps.

—That's whit they Tories have got in store for us if they win the next election, said Pa.

Joe nodded his head—Aye, that's right—but Jimmy just

looked stupid and said, If they've got all they White Guardists just desperate to come and shoot us down in heaps, whit are they bothering to hold an election for? So Joe passed along a Woodbine and said, Och, that's just their capitalist cunning.

—Aye, it's all they big bankers and that, said Pa, raking about in his pamphlet and then quoting an incredible piece about how the bourgeoisie were that terrified of the workers getting into power, they were going to hold elections and let some workers get into power, so they could prevent the rest of the workers getting into power, 'cos the bourgeoisies wanted to keep all the power for themselves, dead clever brutes that they were. And that's your dialectics for you, said Pa, whose faith in the written word was already boundless.

—Oh I see, said Jimmy, and looked blankly at the sea beyond which was Australia whither he would one day emigrate and never write.

Then one night Pa walked there alone—no, him and Willie —along the breakwater without the dock gates. The lights on Commercial Street and Salamander Street were a dull orange; the dockers, the polismen, the whores were all away home to their suppers. The two walked in the gloaming arm-in-arm like musketeers; and Willie, who was thin and sick and cold and not yet ten, stopped Pa, who was now tall and strong and nearly twenty and in the flush of his first job, and they looked out together over the heave of the waters, and Willie said, soft-like,
—D'ye ever wonder where the Old Man is?
for Willie had no memory of his father, who had seen his youngest son as a wee squalling bundle wrapped in shawl on his last home leave; and they never bothered to tell him otherwise, what with all the dying going on, but that his Old Man was killed in the war, like a dozen others in their street. And so Willie grew up knowing that war was a red-jawed monster that ate fathers and made mothers weep: but still he sat at his window and watched, and told tales to himself about the grand brave father who would come home to him one day on a golden ship, and every so often—though not so often now—he would ask his brother.
—D'ye ever wonder . . . ?
so that the Old Man would be alive a little bit longer in both

their minds. But Pa, who was right in the flush of his first job with his first wage packet jangling in his pouch, would have none of this creeping back to the cold shadows of the past. So he said,

—Och, it's a new world dawning when no man will be taken away from his home and family and friends to die in wars for capitalism. Capitalism is obsolete and dying out whether it knows it or not. It smothered in its own blood in the war, and the workers of the world aren't going to be taken in by all its guff any more. You'll see, Willie lad; before you're my age you'll be living in a good, clean, socialist state where war and hunger and unemployment have all been abolished, and all folk have the wealth of the land in common.

And he talked a lot more, did Pa, from the height of his twenty years, having been born in the Age of Hope that had never managed to digest the War and was now scouring round for a scapegoat.

Not that a man didn't need some dream to warm the cold shadows the future was flinging in front of it. When Pa lay in bed at night he fancied he could hear its boots come crashing down towards him, the boots of the blackshirt Fascisti in Italy, and of the National Socialists—some socialists they!—that yon damn lackey Hitler was getting to perform the same antics in Munich, dividing the working people into nations and mystifying them with chauvinist rhetoric. In the shipping office where he worked, polishing his dowp on a high hard stool, Pa took a keek at his brave red Party Card—felt better—felt *warmer*—and hid it away before any of the bosses caught him. The Loch Line were none too keen on having red Bolsheviks and troublemakers in their office there on Constitution Street with its row of fine banks, for all that they floated holds crammed with heavy machinery off to Leningrad on every going tide.

And so, while Ten Days Shook the World and Smolny was busy 'humming like a hive', while gunshots were going off in Berlin and in Chicago, while Mao and Chiang were tearing each other's throats out in China, and revolution was dancing the Charleston all over the place—aye, the big stuff happening everywhere but in Scotland—Pa polished his bum for the Loch Line, and tramped home every evening with a bag full of books from Leith Public Library, something in the way of groceries from a shop near the warehouses where bargains could be had by the knowing, and a tin of St Bruno and maybe a pamphlet or two from a wee newsagent's that slapped socialism and fags, Madame Blavatsky and Jesus all in a birn together on the counter. And meeting friend Joe outside Robb's yards the two would be off to the Waterman's to discuss what the *Scotsman* had said, and what the *Daily Worker* said back, and whether the proletariat could benefit from reading Shakespeare, and how long Reaction would last now that the General Strike was broken, and the coming (in their grandchildren's day, it looked like) of the Scottish Socialist Republic.

—But coming yet, for all that!

—Up the revolution!

—How's the man!

Clink of glasses.

Then in the evening, in the evening to the tent at the foot of the Calton Hill, put up by the Band of Hope to preach redemption, and daftly rented out to all prophets, reasoners and revolutionaries in need of a forum; there to debate the important things of life—the Means Test, the wickedness of all landlords, the possibility of miracles and reincarnation, the coming of the Revolution Antichrist Apocalypse Flood Free-Love Fascism Home-Rule Temperance Damnation, and the likely order thereof. And standing quite literally on a soapbox a heavy and devastatingly plain woman is shouting about family planning, while a Labour man and a Communist are busy punching each other, and an old man with a wee wispy beard is carrying a sandwich-board saying THE WAGES OF SIN ARE DEATH, and you telling him the word should be *is*, and the wee man getting all hot and bothered about it and quoting *Cassell's Popular Educator* to prove you wrong, and you quoting—

Ach, but night lies on Edinburgh, night, and out of scudding Calvinical thunderclouds comes the Edinburgh rain. The roofs of high Ramsay Garden glint in its fall. The bronze statues on the Castle Esplanade, the cold kiltie standing plinthed up on the Mound, King Geordie on George Street, all glint rainlight, pointing wet arms at the sky. And the shiny pavements with their glued-on leaves glint, and the parked thirties cars glint with their square cabins, glint with their running-boards and their funny wheels. The Water of Leith leaps and spits and gurgles through the Dean Valley, and the Cowgate glints its dark chasm where trampie-men shelter in cold doorways, boots laced with rough string, guts laced with bevvy; and black glass windows, and Granton rails, platforms of Waverley, hulls of Newhaven, all hundred thousand black chimneys and staircase gable-ends, all glint in the dreich dreich night.

And still comes the damnable rain, drooking Wellington the soldier, Livingstone the explorer, Guthrie the philanthropist, and all the other big stone and metal men who guard the sleeping city, washing the pigeon clart off their bonnets and green mould out their noses, refilling the beer bottles lying empty round their stone feet that wee boys will find the morn's morn and cart off to their glory holes to do with whatever wee boys do with empty bottles and old shoes and broken coat hangers and foreign coins and metal buttons.

And they all glint and shimmer in the rain, the bird-heavy trees of Hermitage, the iron railings of the New Town, the tenements of Abbeyhill where the rain runs in long green snotters from every broken rone, and sewers burble underground tumults to Seafield and Portobello. And throughout it all comes the maniacal sound of the sea's steady laughter.

Oh ghosts.

I am sitting with the sea in the Happy Island breathing his green air, listening to his laughter, and I mind the way we as bairns used to go yelling round the yards in afterschool hours *Ye canny shove yer grannie off a bus!—Ye canny shove yer grannie off a bus!—Ye canny shove yer grannie, for she's yer mammy's mammy—Ye canny shove yer grannie off a bus!* . . . And I think of my grannie, the Old Lady, sitting there beside me in old Marchmont gloom of iron kettles whispering me those magical dreams.

In the schoolyard we used to line up and sing with each other before having a fight a weird beautiful song that I never fathomed: *Have ye ony bread and wine, bread and wine, bread and wine—Have ye ony bread and wine, we are the rovers.* And wee Carol whom I fancied like mad (we were both about nine) runs up McDonald Road stotting her ball and jooking the pavement cracks going *One two three a-learie, four five six a-learie, seven eight nine a-learie, ten a-learie postman*—lifting her leg over the ball on each a-learie with a double hop for the postman, and a kiss for me if I haven't escaped in time: Carol who was to grow nice breasts and a taste for heavy rock music, and having got rainbow high one night to the throb of Jimi Hendrix and the smell of burning grass, would fly off the North Bridge thinking she had wings. Through the lacerated glass of the station roof below her entrails dripped on Waverley; and they sanded the platform and lowered ropes and hooks to pull her off. *Ten a-learie postman*: poor Carol.

And in that same line—*Have ye ony bread and wine, bread and wine, bread and wine*—singing it there with the rest of us—*Have ye ony bread and wine*—is my mate Andy—*we are the gallant sodjers*—who will become a Royal Highland Fusilier and get shot dead one nondescript afternoon in Belfast—*We are the gallant sodjers*. Aye, I can mind Andy when I walked my father's steps to the sea with him and Dougie and Eck, and we sat there on the clarty salt-smelling breakwater and looked out at the endlessness of it all, and at the big ships looking awful wee on it as they ploughed their furrows from Hamburg and Rotterdam and Bergen to Leith, and we talked—oh how we talked!—and where are they now? And the Newhaven fishwife I saw coming back with her shawl and her creel—already she was being pointed at as something very curious ('Look there! See!'). That was the day they ran the last tramcar all draped with Christmas tree lights down Leith Walk to grave at Pilrig. Oh Wee Macgreegor and Para Handy! Oor Wullie and the *Sunday Post* in glow of afterkirk noondays! O tempora, O mores!

Tread softly, ghosts.

—Listen, says the sea.

I am listening.

—Look, says the sea.

We are walking across the yellow sand under the upward soaring redcliff of Scotland, and the current is running its fingers over my feet which (I suddenly notice) are bare and bleeding.

—Come, come, says the sea in my ear, leading me to the cliff's base, and I stare at it in horror (underwater rocks are full of slimy squiggling things!) and look up through the willowing rainbow-light of the green waters, following the bubbles of my breath as they float questions to the invisible surface.

—Sea, where am I? I ask, but the sea grabs me by the neck and presses my head into the rockside, and astonished I feel the walls parting, splinters of primal stone float away down to rest in the sand with a slow-motion silent thud, and the sea lifts me by the breeks and floats me through into the waiting darkness.

—All the world is land, says the sea. You are walking on my land, the countries of the world are clouds of earth that form and scatter as I play with them.—And the sea lifts a huge boulder from Scotland and lets it roll backwards to the shingle bed, and small shells drift up and hover and return to settle on its back.—If I raise my hands, says the sea, there is no Edinburgh; if I raise my arm, Europe disappears. Look what I did to Atlantis!—But that was thousands of years ago, I say. The sea laughs, he chuckles like a pleased old man.—Really? he says. I thought I'd just done it.

—Look, says the sea.
I look. The yellow city lights of Edinburgh.
—Which is ours? I ask.
—Ours? says the sea.
—Pa's then, I say.
—There, says the sea, and he points, but I cannot see the one light among so many.
—Look, says the sea patiently.—There! Surely you can see it now?
Nope.
—Look, he says.—There! *There!*
He looks at me, and shakes his head.—*Humans,* he says. WIND!—And the wind comes running.
—Sir, sea-master? says the respectful wind.
—*Blow!*
And the wind blows.

Edinburgh nights when the rain is falling the wind bides elsewhere, away in the sunset land of visions and music, in the mountains like the mountains maybe of Styria where the Kingdom of the Golden River is; and that land is ruled by the sea, and the mountains are under the sea, as the mountains of Venus, unclimbed, mightier than Everest, are under the seas of the galaxies awaiting some future astro-travelling Hilary and Tensing to scale their giddy heights with great hopes and a little flag, and stand akimbo in the seasnow on the roof of the world wondering what next spectacular thing to do—and in the end burying a few chocolate bars in a little hole dug there with a scout knife. Yah! wind rustling the sailing seatrees, holding your aching sides!

Now blows the wind north, scald of remembered country, wild rider of legend, black furious horseman he goes galloping with this terrified child in his arms to the place of beginnings; his hooves yelling through the woods and among the jagged ruins of desolate crofts, round crumbling walls of the gentry homes and over cold hills of sheep; wind running through pale grass in the waterlight, singing joyfully amongst the rough heather roots: *Love this is my home, oh love this is my country!* And the Hebridean sunset burning like a Viking ship in the ancient distance where wind, lord of the icebergs, dances on the moony sea.

Hold me tightly, wind.

And south he gallops, traveller on reiver roads to the land of loot and roses, king of the field, knight of the open moorland, hovering in the whaupsong of Stevenson's gentle pasture (*Ah, wine-red moor!*) where green opulence now is in the place of lost battles; through the skeleton streets of Jedburgh and Melrose in the ashes of the forest and Berwick by the river of old grievances; the wind blows down all the ugly frontiers to a mere line on the road's tar. (*Never again let there be blood on this land, wind.*)

And suddenly he turns once more and runs west to where the wharves howl on the Clyde and the great ships cry, 'Give us steel for India! Give us coal for Montreal!' And on to the Atlantic breakers where ride the herring holds of the fishing, while under the same bleak swell roll the men who are the fishes' feast; wind who has seen it all before blows over the U-boat graves and over the galleons' wreck, chases the promenaders from Dunoon and from Largs, whips freezing deckchairs there on the Danes' bloody beach, sends trippers scuttling in their braces and rolled-up trousers for the pier picture palace to lose themselves from his almighty blast; and only ghosts can walk abroad in the uproar and find some consolation there.

Oh wind.

—*Whooo* finally turning east, to the heartfelt city, to the kingly town; wind *whooo* rattling the city's gates; and there I hear him after days and nights of rain and pissing drizzle as he rushes down the chalky hopscotched wynds and sobs in those since demolished closes between Leith Walk and the Calton Hill like the child I used to be; and—*whooo*—making a dance of slates and flowerpots in the air—*whooo*—now hammering the iron walls of the mission called Bethel—*whooo*—now snapping at the posters of the *Evening Dispatch*, Hitler rearms, Rhineland, Special—*whooo*—Salvation Army, we call this the sunshine corner, bash bash, praise the Lord!—*whooo*—Jack Buchanan now appearing in—*whooo*—Tam and Shug the Scotch comedians in—*whooo* cries the wind, sending the years rattling back down the close we lived beside to the sea that tumbles and leaps endlessly at its granite end.

So deep one night in the winters of the past I step from the wind's swath as the Tron clock tower is clanging its evening eight, and through the window of that Marchmont house I go into a familiar room with the beginnings of supper, and three figures, all dead now, drift to life and talk. . . .

'I must have stood in every puddlehole in the street coming back,' said Pa, pulling off his shoes. 'They streets are leaking.'

The heavy table was heavily set with stovies and bread and margarine, the kettle was nearing its boiling on the hob, and to brother Willie who was sitting looking a silent question at him over it all, Pa said:

'Nothing yet.'

'Aye, I kent as much,' said Willie.

'There will be one day,' said the Old Lady, dishing the stovies onto their plates.

—Aye, said Pa.—Aye, said Willie.

'Just a matter of turning up at the gates,' she said.

'Aye,' said her sons.

'It was that cold the day,' said Willie.

'Freezing,' said Pa.

What are they always on at me for? thought Pa, catching the look his mother passed to him which said, Considering the fact that you are the backbone, the very spine, heart, liver and kidneys of the office you work in, how can you no get your very own little brother a job?—Why are they always on at me? And he thought bitterly about brother Jimmy, one year younger than him, who had emigrated to Australia and was having a great time there, he supposed, though never writing. Why have I got to shoulder this? Why am I no out there in a fine new country instead of this dump? Why?—And as his mother heaped her sons' plates she saw him small-smile to himself.

What's he smiling at? she wondered. What's he up to? He hardly says anything these days. I wish he would. And yet she was also proud of her eldest son's reticence, his strong Highland silence. She had married a strong silent man in the cabinet-maker of Scourie: envy of all the lowland wives in the street she had been in those days, with her husband teetotal and calm and full of ancient wisdom, before the sea took him; so different he was from these weak southrons with their wicked drink and their womanish chatter. And she came to the contradiction she always reached when thinking of her eldest—He'll make some lucky lassie a fine man; and—He's got everything he needs here, I know he'll never leave me.

'See yon rain?' said Willie, munching away. 'Three days and never stopped. No real! Monsoon season in Edinburgh! There was flooding at Bonnington,' he said, and thought, Get's a job, you miserable bastard, like you promised you would. On a ship! No more counter work for me, thought Willie, who had had a position behind the counter in a wee chemist's shop before being sacked for daydreaming—I'm never going to bumsuck to those buggers again. And he chewed on a bit of potato which was hot, but not as hot as he wanted it to be (he felt there was chill rainwater trickling under his bones), and said silently, My brother's money bought me this, so what does that make me? Och, fuck it, he said to himself, fuck it, fuck it.

And fuck it all, thought Pa, scraping his plate. What are these people to me? He took sly keeks at the pair of them. My mother was the tube through which I came into the world. He quoted lantern-jawed Alexandra what's-it, Lenin's bird, Kollontai: 'Love is an invention of the bourgeoisie to keep women enslaved. The proletariat knows only sex, and the sexual act, stripped of its bourgeois mythology, is as simple as drinking a glass of water.'

73

There! that said it all. And what was a brother? In Red Spain, said the *Daily Mail*, brothers were shooting each other. He considered this gruesome fact with his last forkful of stovie, and tossed it away with a little laugh, knowing how utterly false it was, and false for him to consider it.

'No chance of any more casual?' he asked.

'Maybe,' said Willie, 'and maybe no.'

'Donald, your brother's no built for the labouring,' said the Old Lady.

'No built for anything,' said Pa, and put his fork to his mouth.

'I canny help it,' said Willie. 'I've done labouring when I could get it—haven't I, Ma?' turning to her.

'Of course, pet,' she said. 'Willie, will ye no have some bread, hinny? Donald, pass the marge over to your brother.'

Oh God, she thought, how feeble that sounds. Don't taunt the lad, she demanded, covering her panic. Don't tell him he's too sickly for man's work. Why no? Pa glared, it's the gospel truth. He knows it better than either of us, responded the Old Lady, and there's mercy as well as truth in the gospel, or I'm mistaken. Well don't expect me to hump him around like a haversack all my life, said Pa. (These words they signalled silently to one another across the supper table, each understanding the other perfectly.) Just look at him, she thought, as her younger son began breaking his piece of bread up into little rolls. Willie, don't do that, she screamed—but Willie's eyes refused to take her message. It was a long habit of his. Her man had done it the same way. She had first seen him do it in her folk's croft when he had come courting, all young-polite and shy those many years ago. *Willie!*

Pet, hinny: Willie, fuming, turned these words over and over. She still thinks I'm a bairn! Christ, I'm a man of twenty, and she is still talking to me like that! Is it my fault there is no work? I'll show them, I'll show them all, thought Willie, whom the dock gate polis had already apprehended doing his level best to run away to sea. Oh Captain Marryat! he cried, Joseph Conrad! Richard Dana! Perhaps Conrad had had a mother in Poland with brimming eyes and apron strings tough as barbed-wire. *All I need to do is walk out that bloody door!* . . . All I need to do, he repeated. But with no ship taking inexperienced men, and no chance of getting experience until a ship took you—forbye sarcastic grins from the old dockers who all knew about the whey-faced boy (he said these words bitterly) with his daft dreams of the sea. They all grinned at him, he was sure. He heard them snickering whenever he turned to trail away back.

If he goes on a ship, thought Pa, it will be the death of her. If he goes on a ship he might as well put a gun to her head and pull the trigger, he might. (He asked for, and received, the margarine back down the table.) I've got to tell her sometime, that's for sure. How will she take it? Better be now, he decided, looking at her over the bread he was eating, but her eyes were glaikit. She's away someplace, off in a dwam. Where? Well I know where. How can I tell her? How? he begged. And he looked at his mother again, wondering what feelings were hoarded behind her placid, buttery face.

She had gone through the looking-glass; she was drifting in that dreamland which was a Sutherland croft thirty years syne when everything was quieter and folk were in less of a hurry to do this and that, or get to some place that in the end wasn't— wasn't just. . . . Och well, but other things had driven them out, like it or no, and they had come south to find a living, and her man was gone, and her croft, she imagined, would be all a ruin now, untaken, and the fields . . . Och! It is night and this is Edinburgh and there are thousands and thousands of folk all around, and I am a daft old woman, she thought, thinking on like this.

'Willie, hinny,' she said. 'A scone? I made them special.'

He accepted it furtively, like a man receiving stolen goods, and spread it in silence. (She offered nothing to her eldest son who, after a time, stretched down the table and helped himself.) A still lasting quality of innocence—a breath, in fact, of something akin to immortality—the Old Lady, who was now old in her own eyes as well as in everyone else's, detected in this younger son of hers who could not remember his own father. Where does memory begin? she wondered. On the day of the Victory Parade, perhaps, when she had made him a little sailor suit that had buttons with anchors on them, and he kicked the big washtub in the back green that Donald had christened Kaiser Bill, and shouted 'Kaiser Bill's deid!' Still there, yon washtub.

(And her elder son, who understood perfectly, ate his scone.)

Willie, twenty years of age with a big brother to look after him and a mother to fuss over him, accepted her attention out of habit, and resented it too. Thinks I'm a bairn, he grumbled, coping with the scone she had forced on him like one of those Roman priests handing out communion wafers—thinks I'm a snotty-nosed wean, he repeated, munching a bite out of its thick side (crisp brown without, soft gold within), watching her begin the long ritual of pouring the tea. Yet I too can suffer, he said. What do they know about it? I'm no as soft as they think.

Go ahead then, ignore me, thought Pa. No matter. Why should I care? No, I don't care at all. I only earn the money that keeps you, but don't let either of you worry about that. You're eating my sweat there in your precious scones, like you've been eating it for years. Christ, he said in a mouthful of crumbs, I'm thirty! He had said it that very day, out loud, scowling amongst the ledgers, cursing the bosses. I'm thirty! What have I done with myself all these years? he asked of Lloyd's Shipping Register. What have I got to show for it? And he keeked again at the now dog-eared and dingy red card in his pocket where the words were still so beautiful: Communist Party. Better leave that behind. The Gestapo. . . . Head cracked open once in Edinburgh High Street was bad enough. Once these German polismen got to work on you. . . . He shivered. (Hadn't he seen Willie shivering when he came in?) Hitler's state—grinding his teeth—fascism, militarism, the rule of the beast. (And of course it's all lies, lies the stuff they print in the *Post* about Russia! Comrades would never—could never. . . . Lies!)

And there was a great parade in the Meadows, the Old Lady remembering it all so clearly, the pain of the returning men, she whose man had not returned; and she standing there with the cheering faces and her two boys, one hand in each of hers, and the Provost's speech—'A million British lives have been spilled on the altar of this terrible struggle. They did not grudge the sacrifice, those men who died for us. Now the awful offering is finished: it must not begin again.'—And one boy's hand in each of hers she stood there, a woman without a man, and saw the folk waving their flags and heard them cheering as the soldiers in khaki and hospital blue marched past, and Britannia, a fat girl in a flowing white robe carrying what looked like a pitchfork, rode on the local fire-engine pulled by two horses, and Willie was

76

happy, but Donald just stood silently staring. Oh one day they two will have children, she thought, and the circle will be complete. I will have achieved my purpose. And she said,

'You eat your scones, they'll put hair on your chest. That's what your father would say, God rest his soul,'

to the table at large. For she wanted them to ask her about her man that was dead, so she could talk about him (she wanted so much to talk about him); and she waited for it, but neither did.

I suppose she wants me to speir after the Old Man who's been dead and gone, damn it, those twenty years, thought Pa. Well, I winny. There's something wrong with a world that thinks more of the dead than for the living, something far wrong that can only be righted when true socialism comes, when we rise with the ranks, no from the ranks. She's dreaming, he thought, but she doesn't know I have my dream too. He rubbed the crown of his head. (She saw it and knew why.) God, that bastard hit me hard enough that day! They came on us like a fucking cavalry charge, they great teuchter polismen high on their saddles, their batons stretched out. What do they think they are, the Scots Greys? —think this is the bloody battle of Waterloo or something? And the crowd on the High Street yelling outside the City Chambers ('*Give us work, ye Tory bastards!*') broke and ran, scattering down the wynds, jooking behind St Giles (the doors were locked), and two polismen rode for friend Joe who was carrying a red flag, and I grabbed one of them by the leg and he came off his cuddy with a howl, and I pushed Joe out the road under the Chambers arches ('*Gives the flag, ye daft eejit!*') and turned to clout the other one with it, but he—WALLOP—he was—WALLOP—too fast, he— WALLOP

    WALLOP

       WALLOP . . .

         One day,

said Pa inwardly, one day I will work miracles. One day I will astonish the world. One day. You'll see. All of you.

'Any tea in that pot?' he asked.

The two brothers went over to armchairs beside the fire, while the Old Lady began putting dishes into the sink. (She would never never let them, or her man when he was alive, interfere with her Woman's Work.)

I don't want to ask about the Old Man, thought Willie, I have my own own dream!—who had his dream of his father as a heroic sailor carving bold lonely trails across the unknown oceans of the world. Ah, if only I. . . . That day. The rain had pelted the gleaming streets solidly for three days and nights past, and the breakwater was that slippery, and he had walked there with his hands in his pouches, and the sea had leapt and shouted at him, and he had walked there listening to the sound of the sea, feeling but not heeding the freezing wind that whipped his coat tails and tore at his unprotected neck. And walking there in the storm's gloaming with his thoughts far far away, his foot had suddenly caught in a tangle of seaweed the waves had thrown up on the high stones, and the dockmen shouted and ran as the sick-looking boy went headfirst into the sea. . . . His brother had seen him shivering. 'Ach, it's nothing,' he said. His mother had seen him shivering. 'Ach, it's nothing,' he said. This laddie has got the sea in him, he said. And he countered with a question, 'You all right, brother?'—for he had seen his brother Donald rubbing the crown of his head, and knew why.

Friend Joe from upstairs had pulled his daft brother away off the pavement with the blood from the baton crack running over his ear and down his cheek. That night Donald lay in the bed yonder—blood—and his mother wept and prayed old Gaelic prayers. Then she sobbed on Willie's very shoulder—'What will we do, Willie, if he dies?'—his brother unconscious all the while, and him thinking maybe he *would* die, and God what then? And so he ran to the chemist's for iodine and a wrap of bandages. Brother Donald was delirious all that night, and Willie and the Old Lady took it in turns to sit by the bed. That next morning he went down to the Loch Line office on cold Constitution Street with a wee note: my brother got thumped on the head by one of they wicked Red agitators; no, he just happened to be passing. And to the sour-faced manager Willie beamed a smile of school-boy sweetness, pleading underneath it all—please dinny give him the sack. And, thank Christ, they didn't. Donald, his big brother, who meant more to them both than either of them could put into English words, he wanted to tell him so—so much he wanted it—and—

'Ach, I'm fine,' said Donald, and stared off into the fire.

78

And Willie stared into the fire, shivering.

And the Old Lady at the sink kept her face from them.

And Pa was thinking: Germany! Which land he loved for the music of Beethoven, and the pages (in translation) of Goethe and Schiller, and as the birthplace of Karl Marx, home of the educated proletariat; and on free weekends, striding across the Pentland Hills with a pocketful of apples and a thirst for its singing burns, he would laugh to himself (he had no company), and slash at long thistles with his stick, and whistle the Ninth Symphony chorale,

> *Freude, schöner Götterfunken,*
> Joy, creation's happy fire,
> *Tochter aus Elysium,*
> Oh daughter of paradise. . . .

While the Old Lady was thinking of the man who had gone from her, who had stepped out of this same room and out of life itself, and gone to find his home in the sea. And she thought curses on the cruel sea, what was it to them?—from crofting folks, both of them, her man a cabinet-maker. Oh Willie, so like him! She scented danger in his daydreams, in his poems she never understood but thought that impressive—funny way to spend your time, writing poems. For beneath the sea and all the fine words and stories she read about it, she always saw her man's drowned face, bloated and torn at by fish and crabs.

And I would liefer die like that, thought Willie, than live a life that's no life at all. Set keel to the sunset sea, I will! I'll quest the far horizon and the green islands where strange creatures cry, and the trees bend over to kiss the virgin sands; and the wandering herring gull shall know me on the distant swell, and with Drake and Chancellor, Cabot and Columbus, I shall voyage on for ever.

And I will be free! told Pa to the night.

And I will sail! cried Willie.

And they will give me their children, murmured the Old Lady, dallying by the sink. . . .

And my cold face all this time was watching them down through the fires of the past, while the rain spattered on the window, and the sea-wind crashed and howled and wept in the dark world outside.

Sons And Brothers

'And whit happened to Willie?' I asked.

Pa sat beside me in the small warm light of the bedlamp and looked at his hands. He stroked back his hair, though it was short and scanty enough, and coughed, looked at the far-away wall, looked at the carpet, looked at his feet, looked everywhere but at me. The branch of the owl-haunted tree outside tapped at the windowpanes and asked to get in.

Through in the kitchen I heard Bob Purves moving. His chestnut face had been round the door ('And how's the laddie keeping?'—to Pa), a gentleness of lines, creases and stubble. His hot toddies had made me drunk. Pa sat helpless, looking at me. I had felt his hand on my forehead as I babbled, but hadn't been able to open my eyes.

'Whit happened then?' I repeated, as he stared vacantly at that far-away wall.

'Eh?' he said (he had heard). 'Aye,' he said. 'Well,' he said. 'My brother—your uncle—he died,' he said, 'of the cold, of the rain, while I was away in Germany. He was that like you,' he said, 'you were so alike, when he was your age and I was twice your age, he and you'—he crossed his fingers—'like that, ken? Just like that, the two of yous. You know,' he said, 'I often wondered how you were so close. I mean, how come you're closer to him than to your own father, eh? I mean, look at all I've given you! I know you didn't ask to be born, but, Christ, nobody can say I didny work hard these forty years, and then—and then, with your Ma dying . . . and you know, I come home at night and maybe you're out playing, and the house is that cold and dreich and empty, and och Jesus I just sit down in my coat and wonder what's the point of it any more . . .'

'Pa,' I said, 'I never kent him.'

'Eh?' he said. 'Aye,' he said. 'I was forgetting. Getting carried away.'

He gave a shy wee smile and was silent for a bit. Ben came the sound of Bob scouring dishes in the sink.

'Ken your uncle,' said Pa, 'what a laddie he was! A dreamer, a born dreamer. We all are, of course, but with him—! Ach, he could have been anything, any number of things, ken? Could have been a lecturer in the university, a doctor, a writer, anything that he put his mind to; but he just wouldny apply himself. That was the whole source of his problems—he just wouldny work consistently at any one thing. Ach. Of course,' said Pa, 'I'm no pretending that I haven't often thought much the same, ken? —thought how fine it would be to be my own boss and come and go as I wanted and make my own hours; but—ach—it's no in this world. Don't let them fool you, son; you've got to work, *work!*' he said. 'It's like Lenin said—ye don't work, ye don't eat, and that's it. It's awful easy to be thinking how grand it would be to be dreaming all day, and forget about the poor bloody workers who are breaking their backs to keep you in idleness. Work,' cried my Pa ferociously, 'is the only thing that makes a man, and that's why I'm hoping you'll get yourself a first class education and go to the university and get yourself a job that has good career prospects, and no be at a dead end like me after forty year of it! But Willie,' he said, 'oh Willie wasny for it! I told him, and nobody can say I didny, but would he listen? I got him a job, a fine secure job too, behind the counter in a chemist's shop, nine till half six five days a week and every other Saturday morning. There were four million unemployed men would have cut an artery to get that job—but no, he didn't want it; it was *corroding his soul*, he said, so he had to go back out onto the street looking for work because I couldn't keep him for ever on my salary. And it rained and it rained and it blew—ach, you know what the Edinburgh weather's like—and then one day when I was away he came back home shivering, and that night the Old Lady had to put him to bed like a bairn. But he got colder and colder, and she heaped blankets on him, and coats on top of them, but he just cried out,

Oh Ma, get me a doctor!

81

'Well, in those days, laddie, you had to pay for your doctor, there was no state money for a health service: there was plenty of money to build bloody battleships with, but no for a health service, oh no. So Willie just lay there underneath all those coats and blankets and shivered and greeted for a doctor. And the Old Lady said to him that it was just a touch of cold and it would get better, and no to greet. But Willie got colder and colder all that night. And then he died,' said Pa, 'just like that. And I wasny there. I just got told about it when I came back. And he was just twenty,' he said. 'Can you imagine that? Just twenty and dead through looking for work, and all because there was no money for a doctor.

'God knows,' said Pa severely, 'I suppose there are some good Tories—there was Churchill who was a Tory and saved our bacon right enough in 1940—but mind if any Tory tries to tell you different about those days that were nothing but a time of misery and hunger and fascism rampant, you just clout the bastard in the face, because that's all those years were, a hell on earth!

'Jesus,' said Pa, 'Jesus. Willie. You know, that next week the landlord's man came round trying to get the rent off us twice! We've paid you already, said the Old Lady, I've got it in the book here. And she showed him it there in black and white—RENT PAID. Oh well, that's just business, Mrs Mackay, he said, putting his wee book away. Tried to get the rent twice, and him a Wee Free, the bastard. That's where our money went. Dinny let them tell you anything else,' said Pa. 'Be a Socialist like I raised you to be, and forget all this stuff about the sea and bitches in grass skirts and whatnot. That's what Willie was for. He loved the sea because he couldn't bide looking at people. He filled his head with rubbish out of novels—golden beaches and coral islands! Ach, what's on a coral island that's different from here? Some poor bugger of a native worker getting a boot in the face from a capitalist. That's why no real Socialist can be a seaman,' said Pa strangely. 'Coral islands, indeed! Reality's on the earth, on the hard dry here-and-now where folk live, no in all this daydreaming nonsense. And golden beaches. *Golden bloody beaches!*'

(As he had said to me that night of Ma's death, the two of us

82

walking down Laverockbank in the gloaming, in the on-coming of a darkness that would bring a morn with no comfort: 'Be brave, Hughie. Don't let them push you around. Don't know any master, and don't master it over any man. Rise with the ranks, no from the ranks. Be the Socialist that I raised you to be.'—The very words, I do not doubt, that he had said to his ten years younger brother who died of pneumonia in 1936. And all the time the sea tossed and battered on Newhaven shore.)

Be Brave . . .

I lay and thought to myself. Be brave, Hughie. Be brave, young Gluck of the Golden River. Be brave, Conla. And the shadows were murmuring to me *be brave*, and the white sea-horses were whinnying *be brave* around the sandstone cliffs of near Redheugh, and *be brave* whirred my film heroes of the old Leith Walk Playhouse, valiant sahibs of *The Drum*, valiant whistling prisoners of *The Bridge on the River Kwai*, valiant patriotic John Wayne and his cavalry troopers in *Fort Apache*. Be brave, Hughie—be a man! And I lay and stared at Pa who was so strange as he built up the fire and put the guard over it,

—'Good night, sunshine'—

and at the flameshadows dancing ceilingwards after the door was closed, and I thought,—What is it to be brave? What is this never-ending struggle?

I had strange dreams the nights after Pa found me lying on the high clifftop, or maybe they were memories of things I had heard him speak about, and then forgotten, and they had lain there and lain unknown for years, and now the sound of the sea was playing them like a flute.

The Magic Flute

Whose sound is on the night wind; which must be greeting the first cleaners now, their alarms must be waking them about now (I cannot see my watch: I could never read the stars). Now they must be shuffling floppy-slippered about their neat, their innocently pretentious wee flats, these hard-working women in their curlers and dressing-gowns, brewing themselves scalding tea and rubbing their eyes (men snoring asleep next door), wondering—Is it worth it? Knowing, it is worth it for all that—this night I have pled sick (liar), this night I am too sickened to face work, to obey rules, to do my routine check of the doors, tick my assignments off the work sheet; this night when I can take no more, they are ready to face it all again. And they think of the burning sailors, the futility of war, all these big things, with simple sorrow, and are still patriotic and honest and law-abiding, hard-working women whose men are near retiring age, whose children are on the burroo. And about Ivan they think not at all beyond their sorrow—neither Jessie from further along Salamander Street, nor Mary from Restalrig, nor Rita from Lochend—for they cannot really believe in something which is so big and so bad and which should not be.

So they sit, each one in her own lit room surrounded by whole acres of darkness, lighting the morning's first cigarette, stirring a tea bag in a cup of boiling water. And Jessie's son-in-law from the same stair will drive her yawning in his wee Fiesta (for she is afraid of muggers), and Mary and Rita will meet at the corner underneath a street-lamp, where forty years ago they dated soldiers and hummed Lili Marlene, and walk together (for they are afraid of muggers); and at their destination the three of them will sit together in the staff room for twenty minutes maybe and blether, waking themselves up with yet more tea and another fag or two. And this they do six nights a week, forty-six weeks of the year, as they have done for ages. As it is done in every office, centre, institution and place of daylight labour in the land.

Night is the name of another country. If you wake to work in a silent house, if you know that you will never see most of those for whom you work (for they are at their typing desks when you have gone back to bed), there is a certain tingle that comes to you, a certain note played somewhere within you, that moment when you are sitting with an empty tea-cup cooling in your hands and no excuse to put it off any longer, the going out into the darkness of it all. It is then when the first horn sounds over the echoing wastes, when the first smell of land comes to the voyaging ship, and even the dullest and weariest (yes, even I) feels like some ancient creature of the deep taking that first tentative step upon unanimaled land, and shares, if even for just a second's flash, the excitement of Cortez or Columbus seeing the vision of a new world. Brief, of course, that excitement, and yet lastingly true.

Streets of night—oh my Americas, my uncharted land! Day belongs to humanity, and to the tame tribes—to the sparrows, pigeons and starlings, to the dog on lead and the cat sleeping on a windowsill in the sun, to them the city world, the concrete and bricks, the hedges that soak sunlight up like a sponge. But in the night a new world awakens: when humanity sleeps, other cut-throat carnivores, perhaps less rapacious, maraud around the frontiers of their bloodstained empires. In the absence of the now roosting birds new insects appear, like the moths that flutter to the yellow and white street-lamps and electric glitter of the evening, the bats that emerge from ruins, attics and hollow trees to hunt them there. The mice too, and the rats—the brown rats, for some reason called Norway rats, who go scavenging over the rubbish tips as their ancestors once came scavenging out of Asia in hordes near three hundred years syne, rat-conquerors leading, Attilas and Genghis Khans of rodentdom, vast rat hordes following their tails; and they scavenge today amongst our bright-coloured droppings while human Asia starves for want of those spilled chips and chicken legs, hamburgers and Chinese take-aways.

And in dockland here around me some of the old black species cling to the hawsers, the rats who brought the Black Death to Europe, killed a third of the human population in eighteen murderous months between 1348 and '50, and set the hysterical survivors killing each other to free the world of sin . . . My God, had they world revolution even then? And the feral cats, born in the city wild, who howl shatteringly down the dark closes, in the yards and back gardens, a couple of whom I can hear howling now near the dock gates beyond which are the warehouses and the crates with their strange visitors, the snakes, scorpions, tropical spiders who come clinging bemusedly to banana clusters from the oppression of Colombia, and survive against all odds except human fear and madness in the northern cold. And the frogs in the Water of Leith who croak in chorus in the place aptly named Puddocky. And the rabbits who warren in Warriston Cemetery among the crosses; and the badger in the Botanics whose tracks you can see when the grass shines with frost or with dew; and the foxes, bright eyes in the dark, whose dens are in waste places, like this railway embankment, and who come out at night to roam the city streets,

—where my father saw one, even in Trafalgar Square, that one London night.

London.
The train.
A steam train it would be in 1936—'The Flying Scotsman' perhaps—puffing and chuffing its way on that interminably long haul from Waverley to King's Cross, through deep embankments where all there is to see are slopes of harsh grass speckled with rubbish, and *chuga chuga chuga chug* goes the train.

And sometimes there are fields, flat lush green English fields spreading out voluptuously on either side of the tracks with little farms and crisscross hedges and no sign of the moorland and desolation of the north (*chuga chuga*); and on past incurious cattle and distant copses with more fields beyond, and no sign of the sea either since Lindisfarne, the heart of a rich country is this; and the midland cities and the pottery chimneys like huge black Guinness bottles, and past cul-de-sac streets running into brick walls at the foot of the embankment; and the windows, the windows you pass and repass at the end of those streets, the windows the

86

commuter waits for and identifies, the one with the red curtains, the one with the orange light, the one with the bedroom mirror (the one where I once saw a beautiful woman combing her long long hair . . .); and past all the people I do not know and will never know, *chuga chuga* says the train, *chuga chug*. Past other stations, Newcastle and Darlington, Northallerton and York, Doncaster, Peterborough and Stevenage, to the place itself, the great noisy shunting palace of King's Cross and the rattling trolleys and the kepied dark-skinned porters, and beyond them, and beyond the sliding doors, and the bustling bookstalls, and the waiting taxis, and the strange high-pitched accents, London waits.

London.

Metropolis.

'You should have seen it in the old days, sunshine!' said Pa.

Before it got bombed, 1936, as he passed through it en route to Germany, that heavenly country whose name would become sewage and foulness in his mouth within the next few years —London in those days, he said, was worth seeing. Not now, what with all the traffic and pornography and darkies (he used the word), but *then* (he used that word too).

I wonder. He hated London. The one day he had been in it he had been very lonely, he said.

(So would I be.)

He had taken a room in a crumbling hotel somewhere near the station—in Caledonian Road, I think—and though it was a summer's night, the iron radiator in the room was boiling and gurgling and could not be switched off, and the window was jammed shut with old paint and could not be opened, try as he might; and from outside, it being a back room above a warehouse roof, Pa could hear the night music of the city, the noise of many cars on the nearby street, the hum and whirr of unresting machinery, the city sound so much louder than it was in Edinburgh, only a fraction the size of this huge city world was Edinburgh. And Pa lay in his bed and he turned and he turned and he turned, and the sweat ran from him and he could not sleep, so eventually he got up and dressed and went out, away from the hot noisy room into the night.

He wandered along Euston Road.

He asked directions of a polisman—wandered on.

Marylebone saw him, and so did Baker Street as he strolled down it, vaguely wondering about Sherlock Holmes and cabs and gas lights. He leaned on the railings of Kensington Gardens and wanted to rest his feet on the grass, but the gates were locked. The night was warm and stuffy. It was unpleasant. There was no breeze off the Pentland Hills, there was no fresh wind from the sea. (He remembered from his mental map that London had neither hills nor sea.) He passed Buckingham Palace in time, where a Guard's sentry was talking to a girl through the railings. He walked the Mall and came to Trafalgar Square—and there he saw the fox.

Trotting, circling, here and there, nose to the ground, stopping to eat something, probably a dropped ice-cream, just beside one of the big stone lions. The only time he had seen Trafalgar Square, apart from favourably angled photographs in guide books, had been on a cinema newsreel. The British Union of Fascists was holding an open-air meeting there, and socialists attacked it and broke it up. The fascist speaker had been a slick young man with shiny hair and he had stood beside one of the lions and one of the socialists had flung a brick at him and knocked him down. Pa approved of what the socialists had done. The fox eyed him and kept out of his way as it sniffed about the rubbish in the Square. On the steps of a kirk with a spire and of a palatial-looking building on the north side a lot of tramps were sleeping. They roosted there like pigeons on a roof. A polisman shook one of them awake and asked him questions. The fox trotted out of the Square and passed under Admiralty Arch.

London was so big and Pa felt so small.

Day takes longer to come up in the south in summer than it does here. The sun took ages to rise on London that day. Pa was dithering about beside the Thames wondering what to do with himself when the sun came up in his face. He wished he was a fox: he wished he had a place to go to in the earth. He felt like a big, clumsy, unhappy animal in the midst of all this hot stone and stagnant air. The first street-lamps began to go off. A bright red bus passed him with an advertisement for Bovril on its side. It showed a Highland cow and a beautiful blue loch and a rosy-cheeked smiling woman holding a wee jar of Bovril. Crowds came swarming out of the underground. He nearly got run over on the Strand.

All that day he wandered about, killing time before he could join the ship that was to take him to Germany, passing a lot of famous landmarks and tourist sites which seemed pathetic somehow and disappointing, surrounded by all the rush and roar of the traffic. He walked through the City proper that was going to be pounded to rubble in four years time by falling bombs, and past all the little churches with pretty names that were going to be burned to empty shells. He found a tea shop that secretaries went to, and ate some thin sandwiches. He sat around. He passed the Tower of London for the second time and sat down on Tower Hill. A Jehovah's Witness was addressing a couple of folk about the imminent coming of the Lord, and there were some buskers. One of the buskers was playing a flute. He had his cap on the ground and there were a few coins in it. Pa sat and listened to him. It was the first purposeful thing he had done that day.

The busker played *The British Grenadiers* and *Jerusalem*, *Colonel Bogey* and *The Red Flag*. The sound of the flute floated into the screaming traffic and barging crowds and drowned there. Then another speaker stood up and began shouting about the wickedness of the world and the need for revolution.

The flute put a spell on Pa. He went forward into a time warp. An aeroplane went across the sky over London and sucked up all the Blitz bombs that the Germans were going to drop. All the buildings came together again. All the roofs flew back where they belonged, and the steeples of the pretty little churches sprang back up into the air. All the concrete and glass office blocks that were going to rise on Cheapside and London Wall vanished and were replaced by quaint stone houses with rubbed steps. All the concrete and glass housing estates that were going to land in the East End vanished and were replaced by slums. All the folk who had been crushed to death by falling rubble, or burnt alive, or blown to bits, came to life again. 1936 jumped into 1946 and the Second World War hadn't happened.

Then a speaker stood up and began shouting about the wickedness of the world and the need for revolution. The folk who hadn't been crushed to death all died of slow painful diseases, or heart attacks, or something else. The buildings on Cheapside and

London Wall were demolished to make way for more traffic. The East End turned into ghettoes and got burnt down in riots.

So the flute put another magic spell on Pa and brought him back again, and there he was on Tower Hill in 1936, and there was the famous Tower of London behind him looking like an imitation of itself in some Hollywood epic, and the Jehovah's Witness was prophesying God's coming kingdom, and the other speaker was shouting about the wickedness of capitalism and shaking his fist—and Pa walked away whistling the tune of the flute which wasn't, but which in Pa's mouth became, the Ode to Joy in the chorale of Beethoven's ninth symphony.

Freude schöner Götterfunken . . .

And then the sad welling sound became the rushing of waters, and there was Pa leaning incautiously over the rails of a ship watching the hull smash through the charge of the waves, sniffing the air on the Thames expectantly for the first scent of the sea. And down the Thames they went, the small ship from the Pool, from the town that Dickens would still have recognized, whose crumbling lanes spilled into the river at Wapping where once pirates were hanged, and at Stepney, at Rotherhithe, Deptford and the Isle of Dogs, sweet Thames run softly past those places I would one day know and be so miserable in. And on they went, past Greenwich where they crossed the O'—and Pa knew, and swore that he could smell the first sea there, though he couldn't possibly—past Woolwich and Dagenham, past Erith and Dartford, past old Tudor Tilbury to Gravesend where the first big ships were, and Pa knew them. Then into the bend of the river called the Hope, which is near the beginning of the sea, past the Isle of Grain and the mouth of the Medway where the Dutch burnt the fleet in wars long ago, and Samuel Pepys wrote in his diary, *God knows what disorders we may fall into.—Home, and to bed with a heavy heart*: then to Sheerness and the Nore and Thanet and

then

excited

with the sea wind finally stinging his face, Pa clasped the rail firmly in both hands and laughed and shouted for the sheer glorious joy of it, because there

Tochter aus Elysium!

was the sea.

I live near the docks in Edinburgh, in a flat on a stair by the railway lines. At night I can hear the sea. I can hear the noise the passing trains make; I can hear the lorries, the great juggernauts, the refrigerator vans. At night the ventilation systems rattle and purr on warehouse roofs. On the stroke of twelve on New Year's Eve all the ship whistles and sirens blow, howling in the birth of the year in Edinburgh Dock and Albert Dock, Imperial and Victoria Docks, in the Western Harbour, in Newhaven and Granton, and there is no sleep for anyone in Salamander Street or Lower Granton Road that night. And I am growing old. Or let's say that the stairs are growing longer, for I no longer run up and down them as I once did. After dinner—which I make for myself to eat by myself, and being an increasingly eccentric bachelor I am very finicky in my ways—after dinner I doze in my armchair, feet out before the fire, the way Pa used to do. And *wheesht, wheesht*, Ma would say, *your father's sleeping*, as I gingerly assembled my toy soldiers to do battle on the living-room floor.

And always there was the sound of the sea battering at the walls of Leith. In those days I thought it held the thunder of the whole universe.

At weekends, when Pa had his two wonderful days of freedom and longed to do something different, to be away from school teaching and tenement stairs and the rumble of the roads, we would go walking—the three of us—on wet spring or cold blowy autumn weekends along the shore here, along the promenade from Musselburgh up past Leith, past the ruin of Caroline Park, past Granton Gas Works, as far as Cramond to see the white yachts leaping on the choppy water.

And in winter, when it was altogether too cold and wet, and the spray lay frozen on the creels and dangerous wee ice rinks pitted the promenade, then we would go to one of the art galleries, to Queen Street maybe, or to the Mound, or better still to the Castle high up on its rock, built in the very clouds; and there I would stare at the great claymores in the banqueting hall, and the pikes, at the cases of Waterloo muskets and the thick tough red uniforms the soldiers had marched off in when folk came out to wave their flags. I would stand and stare at them, little boy, so fascinated by it all.

There were other cases where they kept the model ships that

the French prisoners had made in the years of their long confinement. And seeing those ships I would be glued to the case, my nose pressed to the glass for an hour at a time maybe, till Pa, who had tolerantly been wandering back and forth the while, cried out at last that he just *must* fill a pipe, he would die without one—or Ma cried that she just *must* have a cigarette else she would die too—and out we would go then into the open to the same favourite spot beside Mons Meg cannon by St Margaret's Chapel that has stood there these nine hundred years; and while Ma lit up her cigarette, inhaling long and thankfully, and Pa stuffed the briar into his mouth, and filled it and puffed at it in contentment, I would spend a pocketmoney sixpence in the slot of the long telescope that stood on the battlements there, craning northwards to the Firth of Forth and the hills and trees of Fife beyond, and eastwards to the sea that was its own horizon.

Sometimes when summer came we migrated southerly out of the city with a hamper on the green SMT bus to descend at Flotterstone or Ninemileburn or Carlops, little villages on the slopes of the Pentlands, and walk inward into the hills and be surrounded by the green waves of them, and tread without knowing it the site of old battles of the Pictish folk long since, and of the Covenanters who had died at Rullion Green, and of their conventicles in the lonely moorish places.

Then we would climb, up to the spilling water of the Logan burn by the spot called Lovers' Loup, and wait for the late summer moon to bring the ghost owls out to ruined Howlats' House by the reservoir of Loganlee. Or we would climb again, over the shoulder of Fairliehope Hill and Wether Law to the Cairn Muir and the glen of the Baddinsgill burn where another walker was never to be seen, and we had it to ourselves, knee-deep in heather—I shoulder-deep nearly—and the rabbits watched us curiously from the tumbled boulders, and the whaups cried overhead that we were clumsy strangers in their strange land. Then climb again perhaps, climb further up those treeless slopes to the mysterious piles of ancient stone erected on Carnethy and the Cairn Hills, or stand on top of wind-swept Scald Law, the highest point in all Lothian.

And there I would see the water again, away in the distant north beyond the smudge of city—and it still looked so huge, though at that distance the massive girders of the Forth Bridge arcing over to Fife looked delicate and thin as hairs, and the ships out on the sea were so tiny they could hardly be seen at all, and Fife looked like a mere island floating on the water when the sun smote the Forth and the very bridge sparkled. And turning round on the summit there I would look to the south and see the green masses of the Moorfoots and the border hills that led into England turning blue in the falling evening shadows.

When the long holidays came we would sail over to Fife on the ferry, passing under that same Bridge, now so gigantic, and I craned my neck upwards, upwards to it, yon great leap of steaming engines across the sky, and stared, clasping the wet iron handrail, at the white waves rushing the great stone piers that held the Bridge, wondering when they would collapse, and could they?—And then *Look! look!* cried Pa, and all the folk were looking and pointing, and I looked too and saw, briefly, just (did I?), the flat black head like a bonnet floating there beyond the piers between Inchgarvie and Inchmickery isles, and then it was gone, the apparition that Pa said was a seal. I tugged at Ma to tell me about them, and so from there to the Fife shore, and on the bus, and at dinner, and all that night she told me about *them*, the seals, the selkie folk and their shape changing, and the songs they sing to each other out in the sea. And there those holiday midsummer days spent at Pittenweem where King James had burnt the witches, or Aberdour where *half-owre, half-owre*—on those beaches where I played in the waves with a dog called Bobby, I was thinking about them and longing to meet them, the sea folk. And in the castles I built on the slimy shingle which, oh, seemed great grand towers above a plain of gold, I paced the battlements in the body of a pocketed little plastic soldier: invincible and impregnable those towers were, yielding to no one, while I was on guard, the sentinel whose waiting eyes stared hopefully over the sea, and the shouting of it,—Which would wake me at night in the small hotel room where I was alone, and I would press my face to the cold glass of the window and stare out there to the place which is beyond language, and the awful darkness of it all, straining to hear the song, hoping to see that light.

—Which waits for the unreturning ship, through the door that is open to the sea's noise, where the woman who does not yet know herself a widow sits fondly knitting that warm jersey for the man who is dead. And what images of kindness and longing do they see, those women who wait by the tossing shore? Don't they too see magical creatures walking to them over the waves?

And so I lie on the yellow bed and have strange dreams here at the bottom of the sea, I Conla, Gluck, the magical boy over whom a counterpane of torrents has been drawn, a quilt of blue-green waters patterned with peacock-coloured fish. I lie there on the depth of shells and hear every sound from the surface world of the past that murmurs and echoes down.

—Listen, listen, listen, says the sea. Listen to the sound of all that has been before you.

Listen to Mr Rain lashing the watertop, tiny spin of water bullets stuttering over the huge carnage of the ocean. Listen to the soon-to-be widow women standing on the dark shore, that raft of stone on the waters. Listen as an old fisherman in the cottage by the sea extinguishes a tell-tale light before drawing aside the curtains over the Forth or Weser, fisherman of Fife and New-haven, fisherman of the Jade and Bremerhaven, curtains over Scapa Flow.

Listen. Here come the steaming smoking dreadnoughts of 1916, the big big battleships, the ultimate, the very last word in scientifically engineered beauty coupled to imperial might; great ships that are a painter's dream ploughing through the night waters of the north into a bright and calm morning on the last day of May, the poets' month of flowers and love, German and British—and they were

us	them
Lion	*Lützow*
Tiger	*Derfflinger*
Indefatigable	*Moltke*
Princess Royal	*Seydlitz*
New Zealand	*Von Der Tann*

QUEEN MARY

And the white waves charged towards them like horses, heads down, nostrils flaring, and beneath them full many fathoms in the valley of their thundering hooves I heard them smash into the

94

iron sides, and the propeller screws churning and churning. Huge, expensive, and already obsolete though they didn't know it were these mastodons that cruised irrevocably towards each other on the last day of May (the poets' month) through the North Sea waves, by places where in Cromwellian times Robert Blake and Martin Van Tromp had fought each other for the dominion of the deep, said the nursery rhyme I once learned while sitting on a seesaw:

> *Van Tromp was an admiral brave and bold*
> *And the Dutchmen's pride was he,*
> *And he said, 'I reign on the stormy main*
> *As I do on the Zuyder Zee.'* . . .

And he tied a whip to his mast to flog the English upstart, did Van Tromp, and Blake tied a broom to his own mast to sweep the Dutchman off the waters and make the sea great for England, for he said, 'It is not for us (seamen) to mend state affairs, but to keep foreigners from fooling us.'—And he won, and for two and a half centuries thereafter the white ensign was the political sea and the red ensign was the commercial sea, and both carried the Union Jack at the hoist by grace of God and Robert Blake's artillery.

So now they came again, the great-, great- (how many times) grandsons of those mariners, while the great-, great- (as many times) granddaughters of their women waited in the ports from which the dreadnoughts steamed towards each other in clouds of black coal smoke, British Beatty (for us), German Von Hipper (for them), standing on their respective bridges like models of the stone-eyed statues they would one day become. And the ships passed the joyful-sounding islands: passed Scharhorn and the Isle of May, passed Wangeroog and Helgoland, leaving the shore of fair Pomona far behind in the flap and snap of their valiant battleflags—to meet off the hazy coast of Jutland where the flickering glow of Horn Reef lighthouse sent its peaceable signals over the wastes.

That day, in the boiler room of the *Queen Mary*, my father's father, the cabinet-maker of Scourie, was labouring with his shovel among the coals, stoking the vast furnace that drove her 27,000 tons at 28 knots and over, when the two fleets first spied each other off Jutland. Then orders were shouted through the holds below as above the bugles blared 'Action Stations', and while the great gun turrets swung round to face the oncoming battle, and the long guns were loaded and their muzzles raised to maximum elevation, the call came down—'More speed!' In the hold the stokers bent to their shovels; and the Old Man, the country cabinet-maker who had come from distant Sutherland to make fine furniture in the big city, and whose hands had crafted whole poems out of pliable wood, thrust his shovel into the coal heap and turned to the furnace door,—

While in Edinburgh the Old Lady lived among children and old men and young ones drilling in khaki on Marchmont Meadows and anxious women, and she didn't know her man's life was in danger yet,—

While in the German Ruhr, in a Krupp factory that made heavy shells, the furnace-master smoked a long pipe and thought peaceful thoughts, while women workers in the sheds counted the shells and marked them on the conveyor belts, on the waiting trolleys, on the ammunition trains, and thought of their men in the war,—

And more speed! more speed! cried the orders howling through the hold, and smoke belched from the funnels, and gunnery ranges were counted down from the finders—20,000 yards, 19,000 yards—the captain stolid on the bridge, binoculars to his eyes, the waiting gunners in the turrets, the waiting marines,—

While far below in the bowels of the ship the stokers worked, their shirts sticking to them now, shovelling coal from one steel chamber to another without a glimpse of daylight, feeding the red furnace door,—

While in Edinburgh the Old Lady lived among children and didn't know,—

While in the Ruhr the women who worked the shell factories, whose men were in the war, waited among trolleys and thought about,—

While in Plymouth,—While Bremen,—Waited, waited, thought,—

Then at 18,000 yards the signal flag 'Open Fire' sped to the yardarm and the great guns crashed out on the *Queen Mary* and the *Lion*, crashed out on the *Lützow* and *Derfflinger, New Zealand, Seydlitz*, crashed along both mighty lines of those 1916 warships, great and powerful and prestigious as Ivan's and Leroy's missiles are today, sending the Sheffield- and Essen-made heavy shells hurtling over to one another, and the spray flew, —

While in Edinburgh Pa came home from school with his satchel and his sums, and the Old Lady took out her knitting in that Marchmont flat where all the black pots and pans hung, and the black kettle hissed on the range, —

When the battleflags flapped and snapped outside in the world they could no longer see, —

And the Old Lady counted the rows on the red jersey she was knitting for her man, —

While the spray flew high over bridges and the green water tumbled onto decks, while the white water spouts went dancing, —

Pa sat doing his arithmetic homework at the kitchen table and his thin dirty wee boy's legs dangled free above the stone flagged floor, —

As the *Queen Mary* scored her first hits, crashing two shells home on the *Seydlitz*, crumpling a gun turret and burning its crew to death, —

Whose wives were waiting in Hamburg and Cuxhaven, Wilhelmshaven and Kiel, Emden, Bremen and Stettin, waiting, —

And the naked bodies gleamed in the red hot light, in the heaving, gasping coal rooms and the coughing choke of the dust clouds where the shovels plied, —

As they did to the furnace factories of Essen and Sheffield, —

By hands made to make poems of flesh and wood, —

As the Old Lady plied her needles on the red wool, —

As Pa did his ten-year-old's sums and pummelled his nose, —

In Edinburgh, —

On the last day of May, —

Then three simultaneous direct hits struck the *Queen Mary* and God knows what happened exactly, for all the appalled observers saw from ships astern was a tremendous flame of dark red burst from her, then a veritable Hiroshima pillar of smoke rise high 800 feet high into the air as she was torn apart by the detonation of her magazines. And the great ship broke in two like a child's toy. She threw her stern into the air with propeller blades still revolving, then another—underwater—explosion shook her—the steel walls of the stokers' hold tore open—men falling, somersaulting in the darkness, burning coals spraying out of the broken furnace door, and the shriek of steam, and the screaming. . . . Syne the water came and killed them all, and 1266 men and bits of men tumbled slowly in slow green motion down-down-downwards to sleep so suddenly and yet forever in the yellow bed,—

While the lighthouse on Horn Reef blinked its peaceful message over the North Sea from Jutland.

Half-owre, half-owre . . . Because . . .

Sleeping Plymouth, where are your sons now?

Look. Listen.

On the sea's depth I can see them, through the green swirl of the water, the keels and bodies that float down to be with the sediment of time, the Saxon and the Viking longships, the Antwerp caravels and the fighting sail, the trawlers and the merchantmen lifeboats could not reach—the lifeboatmen who died trying. All before and after recorded history's British beginnings when the Celts ghosted in from over the sea, when the continents heaved in the days of ice and lava and great vanished creatures, when the drilling rig Alexander Kielland turned turtle in the age of superoil 1980 and drowned its crew in six minutes flat,—I on the sea's bed can see it all, the passage of empires, strivings of English and Dutch pirates, American and Norwegian oilmen, amongst whose misty domains the lighthouse winks and winks.

Ivan, trained as you are to kill me, do you know that when I was ten years old I lay on the sea bed looking up and saw the lights of heaven flickering there on the surface of the waters, heard the sounds of the angels they used to tell me about in kirk, all those dreary men with their dark suits? And, Ivan, I stood staring at my heaven which they knew nothing about, and I walked in it when I was very small and Ma and Pa waved over me like two tall trees, and ever since I have looked for it in places where there are silences, and listened when lights shone in the darkness, far far away lights. And the sea was my great darkness,

98

Ivan, the place where love once was, and I sought the light of that blithe love as Columbus once sought his fabulous Indies. For there is an ultimate light which never was on any sea, though the horizons of all seas suggest that it is just beyond, and strange and illusory as I now know it to be, something of the truth is there, and I seek that light, Ivan.

As Pa sought it before me, that young wild adventuring father of mine who cried Byronically, 'Adieu, adieu, my native shore fades o'er the waters blue!' (he did, and a sailor thought him mad) as the ship from London Pool carried him over all the fated submarine strata of the past to—

The Land Beyond The Sea

It was 1936, the year of the Berlin Olympics, all Germany was wearing her party clothes, and as he walked through the swinging dock gates, which are the same everywhere, and entered the neat, orderly, *different* land that was Germany, Pa thought—

What? What did my communist father think in Germany that day back in 1936?

Two memories.
The first:

One winter—and I remember which one so well because it was the winter before Ma died—our teacher brought an Advent Calendar into the class. (Our teacher was a woman: women think of such things.) She didn't tell us what it was. Wordlessly she took it out of a brown paper bag and tacked it to the wall between the blackboard and a picture of salmon leaping a waterfall. She was a good teacher, she was always bringing in colourful things to decorate the educational dungeon with, and we all liked her for the picture map of Captain Cook's travels, the poster of Champion the Wonderhorse, and the blown-up photograph of happy girls in bright pullovers skating on a frozen loch. (We would have liked her anyway.) Now we all stared at the Advent Calendar and she asked us to guess what it was. None of us presbyterian schoolchildren had got a clue. It was a town rather like Walt Disney's Lilliput, all high gables and arches, cobbled lanes and funny pointed roofs. There was a castle, of course, with a drawbridge and a great gate. There was a great stretch of dark blue sky with lots of tiny silver stars, and there was one great eight-pointed golden star. And lots and lots of doors and windows. It was a picture of Bethlehem. It was twenty-five schooldays before the end of term and every day, said the teacher, we were going to open a door, or a window (they were numbered) —one by one. She got Carol to open the first window—and Carol, who would grow up to have nice breasts and an electric guitar and die horribly on drugs, Carol who then had pony-tails and ankle-socks and freckles and no breasts at all, opened the little cardboard shutters with her fingernail, and there was a woman with red arms and a rolling-pin making scones. Every day we got to open one, and there were folk looking happy and folk looking sad, a couple having a row, a bunch of lads playing football, soldiers in the castle sitting round a rosy hearth;.there was even a window in the clouds with a choir of angels behind it singing away. I got the door of the inn, and there was a good Dickensian scene of a bunch of beery punters getting plastered with mugs of frothing ale.

We all loved it, of course.

Then the teacher told us that Advent Calendars and Christmas trees were German inventions, and that was a sore shock because German meant Nazi, and the Nazis had tried to kill all our fathers in the war. We all went off the Advent Calendar a wee bit when she said that. Then she told us that the carol *Silent Night* was a German song, and we learnt a bit of it: *Stille Nacht, heilige Nacht.* . . . The girls at least thought it sounded nice.

When I went home that day, past all the windows and doors of McDonald Road, past the fire station and the envelope factory, I had a pretty clever thought for the wee boy I was: I thought, *Behind every window and door in the street is someone who is utterly different from everyone else.* And this thought had a brother: *Every day is utterly different from every other day.*

Then Ma died. She went away and never came back.

At night I lay staring at the face of the clock by my bed. It was luminous. Those green hands . . . ticktockticktockticktock . . . and all those seconds went running by like a bairn rattling his stick along some railings. I had discovered Time, and I was terrified.

That is the first memory.
The second one is this:

I asked Pa maybe ten million times what he had done in the war (we all asked our fathers that), and he told me the good bits. I asked him about Germany and he told me a little, reluctantly, in dribs and drabs—happily when he talked about the beer-gardens, the Harz mountains, the Rhineland castles; unhappily, knotting a pained brow, when it came to other things, goose-stepping soldiers, how he had once seen 'yon bastard'—Hitler—on the Rhine, how once when passing through lovely countryside on the train a little farmer's girl—'half your age, laddie, no more than that!' (I was seven or eight at the time)—had stood in the middle of a field and seeing Pa's face at the passing window had given him the Hitler salute. I asked Pa if he had kept a diary or written any letters from Germany, and he said no. Later on he said that he had, but that he had burnt them all. I learned that he had burnt everything from those days. Even two innocently pretentious pamphlets of verse he had had privately printed—he rooted out every single copy and destroyed them all.

My memory: We had a top flat and so we had the attic, a long gothic twilight place of crossbeams and dusty piles. We kept the Christmas tree lights there long after we had stopped getting a Christmas tree. One day I was raking around in it for some reason and among all the cobwebs and dust I found *a book*.

Plenty of books, actually. A chestful of them. If you have a long twilight attic under the slates you never get rid of anything, and there was all manner of junk lying there—sepia photographs of women in long dresses, an old HMV gramophone with solid 78 records, boxes of old clothes, a garden bench, a model ship. . . . And the book, a fat thick red book, 'Post Cards' written on it in faded gold. I opened it.

It had a hundred stout leaves, each one of which could hold two postcards, one on either side. It was full, there were two hundred cards. I took first one out, then another, sitting cross-legged in the dust under the weak yellow light. I climbed back down with it and took it into my bedroom, spreading the two hundred cards over my bed, and then over the floor. They were all addressed to the same person: my grandmother, Pa's mother, the Old Lady, in Marchmont Road. She had received them over the course of forty years and kept them all.

The order was simple, chronological. The first, a King George

V stamp, picture of a battleship on the back. *Dear*—it was from the Old Man, now in the navy, based at Rosyth. So were the next five. He was at Rosyth, a few miles away on the other side of the Forth. He told her he was all right, not to worry, 'keep on smiling', he said, he was 'in the pink'. The men swore a lot and he didn't like that. He read his Bible . . . There were Gaelic words here and there. One card was written entirely in Gaelic. I wonder why he did that? Was it to evade the censor? I got a Gaelic dictionary and tried to piece it together, but only got a few words here and there: 'Terrible war (something) I think (something) fire (something something) God's judgement (repeated) God's judgement on us (then a lot of somethings, and finally) vengeance.' Vengeance? In the sixth, last card is one phrase of the old language which I do know because it is a proverb: *Is e deireadh nan Gaidheal a bhi falamh*—'The fate of the Gael is to lose everything', he wrote. The postmark says May 1916. At the end of that month he was dead.

There follow a few dozen postcards from people I've never heard of. *Love, Annie . . . Love, Jeannie . . .* pictures of the Trossachs, Oban, the Lake District, London.

London . . .

Your loving son, Donald.

Dated 1936, month smudged out. King Edward VIII stamp.

Dear Hubbard . . . (Hubbard? Old Mother Hubbard?) *arrived yesterday in the big city. It is very big and noisy and the English are not very friendly people, but you would like the Guards playing their drums and whistles, you old tory you. Don't worry, I'll keep my mouth shut in Hitlerland. Sailing there tomorrow. Hope Willie is feeling better. Your loving son, Donald.*

The next postcard. Hitler's head on the stamp. Picture of the Bismark Statue, Hamburg.

Dear Hubbard, Well here I am in Germany . . .

Nearly every day of his holiday in Germany, Pa, thirty years old, sent his mother a postcard. At the beginning of each one he calls her 'Hubbard', and indeed thinking back to that one day so long ago when she quietened my greeting with the story about Conla and the mermaid girl, and minding the smell of her oldness, and all the black pots and pans that were about the place, yes, she was like that Old Mother Hubbard who lived in a shoe.

And at the end of each card he says, 'Hope Willie's feeling better, Your loving son—'

She had so many children she didn't know what to do.

There were twenty-three cards from Germany, then some more from various other Annies and Jeannies. Pa writes again, during the Second World War: *Dear Hubbard, Here is a picture of Naples which I'm enclosing with my letter. Give me Edinburgh any day. Your loving son, Donald.* King George VI stamps. Annie and Jeannie again. Then one from Ma and Pa on their honeymoon in Inverness, which they sign together. Annie and Jeannie. Queen Elizabeth II stamps. End of the book.

She had kept them all in the album. I don't think my father could have known of its existence, otherwise those twenty-three German cards would surely have gone into the fire. Inside the front cover is gummed a picture of a young man with a walrus moustache wearing sailor's uniform, and I know who he is even without seeing the letters 'Queen Mary' round the brim of his cap. Inside the back cover is a picture of Pa wearing baggy 1940s battledress with a lance-corporal's stripe on his arm. His eyes are very watery and he looks self-conscious. And I can see the Old Lady in wartime evenings alone in her room, blackout curtains drawn, hearing the guns on Corstorphine Hill firing at the bombers that fly over from Norway to blitz Belfast and Clydebank, and she is holding that fat wee book to her, wondering if even now he is lying somewhere with a splinter in his head and water pouring into his mouth.

Twenty-three postcards, all with pictures of Germany (a few in colour, most in black and white) as she had been in 1936; and on the other side, Pa's handwriting and Hitler's head on the little coloured stamp.

And as I read those cards, doors and windows began to open deep inside my mind.

I close my eyes and open them in Germany in 1936 in the shadow of the Bismark Statue, to the noise of clanking beer-steins, and a train—a clean orderly train with '*Rauchen Verboten*' on the doors—taking Pa to Berlin.

—Not to see the Olympic Games, in which he had no interest, but because, being in Germany, you are supposed to see Berlin.

And he passed through a neat and orderly land where slums in the British sense did not exist.

Pa's second postcard comes from Berlin. It is a picture of the Brandenburg Gate, six massive classical stone pillars holding a heavy mass of horizontal masonry on top of which is a beautifully sculpted goddess of Victory riding in a chariot drawn by four galloping horses. Victory holds a standard in her right hand—a pole capped by a cross on which an eagle is sitting with outspread wings.

Dear Hubbard—writes Pa. He is sitting in a little restaurant on the Kurfürstendamm, having just eaten, as every good tourist to Berlin must, an enormous helping of cream cake,—*Have arrived in Berlin. . . .*

And he taps his teeth with his pen. The table cloth is checkered white and green. The waitress is a plump young woman with a lace-up bodice and braided hair. How to put it all into words, these thoughts from the place beyond language? Here I am in the heart of western civilization—here I am in the sanctum of art and thought—here I am in the power house of the educated working-class,—

For Germany was all these things to him: the land of Beethoven and Marx, the great heart that had pumped its barbarian blood westwards against the crumbling walls of the Roman empire and avenged martyred Spartacus: the creators of a vital new order, the socialists of the dark ages were they, these marauding German tribes with their heroes and their eagle standards, their blood loyalty and their lust. The catalogue of German achievement was the drumroll of progress to a man like my father who had subscribed to *The Thinker's Library* and *The World's Great Books In Outline*, read William Morris with his piece and John Maclean with his dinner. Germany was the place even Lenin admired, who did not give his admiration lightly. 'What have we done to compare with the German comrades of the Spartacus League?' he demanded in his Swiss exile—and the answer was, nothing. Lenin sent the Red Guards against the Winter Palace to take Russia out of the *imperialist* war, to put her vast uneducated peasant masses at the disposal of the German revolution which was just about to happen in 1917 . . . but which unaccountably failed to happen.

Unaccountably.

Like every Labour and Communist Party socialist, every Fabian, progressive and Bolshevik, Pa believed that the German revolution was just about to happen.

Oranienburg concentration camp a few miles away was full of German socialists who believed that they would soon be free because the German revolution was just about to happen.

Even Stalin, of all people, had refused to take any serious steps against the admittedly unaccountable phenomenon of Hitler and the even more unaccountable success of that phenomenon, had refused to authorize the socialist-communist coalition that alone could have kept Hitler from power, because—

THE GERMAN REVOLUTION WAS JUST ABOUT TO HAPPEN!

But the German revolution had happened.

Hitler was the German revolution.

Pa had not yet discovered Time. Progress, for him, was an open book; its neat black print ran across neat white paper to a carefully worked-out conclusion. By this way of things, the working-class would triumph in the end, just like the heroine in a silent 1920s film who won her heart's desire against all odds. She won it because the film director had arranged it that way. He had arranged it that way because he wanted to entertain his audience. When Karl Marx wrote his books he knew that the working-class was going to win its heart's desire because History would arrange it that way. He knew that History would arrange it that way because all the books he had read said so. Perhaps Karl Marx hadn't discovered Time either, or maybe he was just entertaining the folk who worked away in the factories while he sat and wrote.

Ah well, it doesn't matter.

Marx got ill and died in a lot of pain just like Ma did. Ma died on a busy noisy weekday, and it didn't matter, nobody noticed. A whole world had blown up and nobody noticed the emptiness that there suddenly was in the midst of the universe, nobody knew that in the place where Love should be there was only this terrible emptiness . . .

Stop talking about her. . . .

Pa (let's get back to Pa) Pa sat in a restaurant on the Kurfürstendamm in 1936 and tapped his teeth with his pen and tried to put his thoughts onto paper. He was enjoying himself in this land of poets and thinkers and cream cakes even though it was unaccountably ruled by fascist monsters, and he felt uneasy about it. None of the Germans he could see seemed to mind being ruled by fascist monsters, and he felt uneasy about that too. And he knew that there were comrades imprisoned in Oranienburg concentration camp just a few miles north of where he was sitting and—

(What did they do with dead bodies in Oranienburg concentration camp, Pa?—They burnt them, shut up.)

And they burnt her.

(She was dead. What does it matter?)

They burnt her in the gloomy crematorium on the other side of the graveyard on a day when the wind was cold on Ferry Road, the traffic was awful noisy, and it was raining in between patches of chilly sun. They burnt her and left nothing—

Nothing.

Nothing.

Nothing.

Victory rolled over her in a chariot. The admiral on the bridge steamed over her in a battleship. Progress went screaming over her in a train. And they left nothing. They burnt the house where I belonged and left nothing, not even the ruined foundations for sheep to graze over, for the whaups to cry.

Pa didn't discover Time when he was my age, and I can't blame him for that, because his father died in a battle under shellfire, martyr of the 'bloody imperialist war' that gave Pa a reason for his continued existence—that lovely thing: an enemy to fight against.

But Ma died for no reason except that she had some rotten cancerous disease in her that didn't care if she was socialist or capitalist, conservative or liberal, whether this was Britain or India, whether the coal mines were nationalised or not, or what colour the fucking flag was. She just died because she died, on a bright bitter day with noisy cars in the street, and Pa—my father, who was so big and strong and wise and in all things admirable—cried.

Did I tell you that?

He sat on the floor and cried, and I put my arms out to touch his head, and then I cried too. There was nobody else there. Nobody came that night. Nobody phoned. And on the wind, it being high above Leith and the sea just on the other side of the road, all night between the occasional sound of a lorry and a car, I could hear the sound of the waves hitting the shore.

'I've got bad news for you, laddie . . .'

(Oh stop it, please . . .)

Your Ma's deid, he said. Your Ma's deid. Your Ma's—

(Stop it, stop it)

And the sound of the sea—

Deid.

And Pa sits in a restaurant, and a lot of comrades in nearby Oranienburg are already *deid*—and burnt—and he writes,

Have arrived in Berlin and just finished eating some of the famous Küchen which is a whole meal in itself! The weather is nice and sunny, and a German who speaks English has told me that the forecast for the rest of the month is good, so with any luck I will not need my brolly after all! I will spend tomorrow in Berlin as well and then get the train to Göttingen and begin walking in the Harz mountains! Hope Willie's feeling better. Tell him I am asking for him. Your loving son, Donald.

The Happy Wanderer

But listen: I see Germany in terms of one of those late-night foreign films on BBC2 where symbols clash and meaningful trumpets blare.

This Germany is a huge Wagnerian forest of beech and fir and linden trees, where the pale breath of sunlight only manages to steal amongst the topmost branches. Beneath the green roof great wooden stalactite trunks plunge down down down to the moist brown earth covered by centuries of fallen leaves and needles where no grass grows. Here are the *Freischütz* glades, the place of the woodcutter's cottage and Hansel and Gretel, for this is the land of tales where the path beyond the well dwindles away in a tangle of fallen branches; and in the *beyond*, which is so near to the firelit hearth and its thin thread of smoke, lie the terrors of a starless night. In those glades the heroes carouse like creatures of the swamp, brutal men with shaggy animal skins about their massive shoulders. They drink long and loud, they hold goblets made of hollow horn and wipe the foam from their yellow beards, they roast oxen whole over roaring fires, they eat the smoking meat from the tips of their dirks, that red-faced pack of killers in the forest night.

Germany is also a mountain, a vast majestic joyful mountain. Stalagmites of sunlit stone that soar up into peaks always head and shoulders above the clouds, where no bitter rain ever falls, just gentle refreshing rain, where free-born rivers spill down their torrents in the dazzling sunlight so that to the distant climbers they seem like rivers of gold shining in a fabulous land. And of course it is a fabulous land, straining itself away from the tentacles of the earth, raising its head upwards to the warm living sky, opening itself to the sun like a flower. The air there (they say) is so pure it has a voice and a melody of its own, and if you have the good fortune to hear it, it can teach doubt to you if you are foolishly faithful, and faith if you are truly seeking it and will not be content with less. For this is the habitation of eagles whose *beyond* is the rainbow bridge that sweeps to blue infinity. And this is the destination of the voyagers, the explorers of this lump of star that hurtles through space with its cargo of blood, that dances before Time in the veils of its brief glory.

And Germany, like all lands, is both forest and mountain, heart and head. For in the Ruhr enclosed by forests (*Wälder*), by Reichswald and Westwald, where ancient Hermann destroyed the Roman legions in the place then called the Teutobergerwald, in the Ruhr in their furnace-lit glades the dwarf folk work the factories and long to be where the mountains are, where the girls are beautiful and the boys are strong, and the sun shines so brightly over meadows and lochs, and there are ruined castles too, and wooded heights and ancient towns, and the poets and muses sing the romance of pure thought, and names like Schiller, Heine, Goethe and Beethoven dazzle the air like happy angels on Christmas Eve.

To this land now came the enchanted traveller, chuga chuga chuga chug, from Berlin where a band was playing near the station—

> *Freude!*
> Joy!

they were playing,

> *Freude, schöner Götterfunken,*
> Joy, creation's happy fire,
> *Tochter aus Elysium,*
> Oh daughter of paradise,
> *Wir betreten feuertrunken,*
> Drunk with love we enter
> *Himmlische, dein Heiligtum.*
> Into your holy place.
> *Deine Zauber binden wieder*
> Your magic reunites
> *Was die Mode streng getheilt;*

Nation and class again;
Alle Menschen werden Brüder
All men will be brothers
Wo dein sanfter Flügel weilt.
Around your eternal flame . . .

And brother Willie coughed in Marchmont—but Pa had forgotten about brother Willie, because this was Göttingen, beloved of Heine, celebrated for its sausages and university, the place from which explorers of the Harz mountains, ever since Heine (who was a Jew) committed his exploration to paper in eighteen-something-or-other, traditionally took their start. So Pa tramped into the Harz with his rucksack, stayed overnight in youth hostels, and left in the morning. (Picture postcard from Goslar shows the interior of a building called the Kaiserworth with the statues of eight Holy Roman emperors.)

Other walkers on the country road: hill-walking being as much a German habit as football is a Scottish one, there were innumerable others striding along, male and female, young and old, whereas in the Pentlands there was nothing save the circling birds and eternal sheep for company. And Pa talked to these walkers, for Germans talk to each other as we do not, and learned from the older ones tales of the Wandervogel, the migratory birds, the original 'youth movement' of Kaiser Bill's vanished days, who had walked the hills and forests singing, with guitars, sticks, rucksacks and comradeship, taken blood-oaths with the seriousness of boys and lovers, and vowed in the misty campfire-lights of forest clearings under the mountaintops and stars that they would create a new world, their ideas as misty as the fires, but no less warm and cheering—these young people, now older people, whose fathers were dead in the war called Great. As Pa's own father was.

And Pa quoted Goethe,

Über allen Gipfeln ist Ruh,
On all mountaintops is peace,

and they smiled and were happy because this foreigner knew their language, their poets. And Schiller he quoted (of course he did), and they all sang on the tramp (like the Canterbury pilgrims I see them),

III

Wem der grosse Wurf gelungen
All who have won life's great gamble
Eines Freundes Freund zu sein,
And true friendship have achieved,
Wer ein holdes Weib errungen,
All who have found loving wives,
Mische seinen Jubel ein!
Join in our song of praise!

Syne he mentioned Heine, the Jew Heine, and they were embarrassed, and Pa briefly didn't understand why.

To the Brocken, famous peak of the hills, where Faust danced with the witches on Walpurgis Night; and there (three different cards showing sights of the Brocken) Pa stood by his window in that neat room of the Brocken Hotel, listened to the hearty noises from below, and viewed the moon, as Heine had done over these same hills a century gone by:

'. . . Is there really a man in the moon? The Slavs say there is; his name is Klotar, and he waters the moon to make it grow. When I was little I was told that the moon was a fruit which God plucks when it's ripe, and puts it away in his big cupboard with the other full moons at the end of the world, where it is boarded up. When I grew bigger I discovered that the world is not so limited a space, and that the human mind has broken through the wooden boarding, and by help of a giant Peter's key, the idea of immortality, opened all the seven heavens. Immortality! Beautiful thought! Who first imagined thee? Was it some Nuremberg shopkeeper, who, with white nightcap on head and white porcelain pipe in jaw, sat some warm summer's evening before his shop door, and comfortably mused how pleasant it would be if this would only last for ever—pipe and breath never going out, to vegetate on for all eternity? Or was it a young lover in the arms of his mistress who first conceived immortality, because he then *felt* it, and could not help the feeling and the thought? Love! Immortality! . . .'

Ah.
Pa walked on, to Wolkenhauschen and thence down the

Ilsenthal to Ilsenburg—happy Ilsenthal, glen of the Ilse river fed on Brocken snow that curves its way so wonderfully through mountains sided to the very waterbank with beeches and oaks and birchen trees, while higher on the upper slopes pine woods stand against the summer sky. Neighbourhood folk, my father was often to recollect, say that Ilse is a princess who goes leaping down the mountainside with all the light laughter of untroubled youth, her robe of white foam shimmering in the sunshine, her diamonds sparkling. And the boys who fell in love with her! Why of course she was the only love of their lives, be they shepherd boy or the bold knight von Westenberg; or even Emperor Heinrich whose grand sceptred sworded crowned statue stands back there in the Kaiserworth hall, he, though he journeyed to Italy, was anointed by the Pope, and had the dominion of all central Europe laid at his feet, he longed regretfully for his tender-hearted Harz maiden who laughed and sang and ran barefoot over the meadowgrass one youthful summer morning.

The last Harz postcard comes from Wernigerode. *Dear Hubbard*—Pa writes. It is a colour picture of the Rathaus, the town hall, which is simply the most beautiful building I have ever seen in my life—white with dark chocolate brown timbers and orange bow windows fringed with flowers. The roof is high pointed and smoky blue, its windows detailed in green, and two slender spires and a cupola make it look like a cathedral. The clock on the roof (the very clock is lime green and boxed in red and has lemon yellow hands!) says 9.35 and the sky behind has the pale flush of gloaming, though whether of dawn or evening I do not know. The front door is red as tomatoes and encased in green planking. There are lots of little windows.

Pa ends the card with his customary *Hope Willie is*—. But Willie is not. Willie is not feeling better. In Marchmont Road his delicate young brother is coughing and coughing and still has no job. But Pa doesn't know. And doesn't want to know as in Wernigerode he boards the Weimar train.

Heine's Germany. Calm, happy, tolerant place, where good husbands have comfortable wives, and loving families live in cuckoo-clock houses, at peace with God and at one with all their neighbours. If on a winter's night a traveller had come to that

113

land, he would have found warmth and cheer and comfort there, and long deserved rest for his weary feet.

Weimar, says the postcards, belongs to Goethe and Schiller. They stand there on the stone pedestal with their arms around each other. The nineteenth century describes this as being 'comrades-in-arms'. The national theatre in the background is a serenely classical building. It doesn't mind the comrades-in-arms one bit. The national library doesn't mind either. The smutty works of the Jew professor Freud have been whipped away. The big sculpted men cuddle each other in public and nobody minds.

Classical serenity ruled in Weimar, in hilly wooded Thuringia with its many Swiss-like cantons, Reuss, Meiningen, Saxe-Coburg and the rest—names which conjure up pictures of alpine cows with little bells tied under their throats, and lush green pastures.

And Pa sat writing. *Arrived this morning in Weimar and visited Goethe's garden house. Saw a production of* Egmont *in the afternoon* . . . And omitted to say that in honour of the bard, party workers had paraded their banners outside the theatre doors, red flags before the classical serenity, black swastikas around Goethe's and Schiller's feet . . . *I didn't understand all of it, since it was in German, but Beethoven's* Egmont *music was great* . . .

He was in a beer-cellar eating bread and cheese. The band was playing Lehar waltzes. A picturesque if unnecessary wood fire was in the hearth: brass irons were hanging on the walls. And pictures of Goethe everywhere. Young Goethe, wild-eyed, surrounded by storm-tossed trees; Goethe in Italy, arcadian landscape, nymphs, shepherds, and gentle streams; old Goethe, stout and wigged, classical temple, fallen columns, the muse holding a lyre.

Goethe and Hitler. . . . Caption: 'The Man Of Thought —The Man Of Action'. Goethe, Bismarck and Hitler. . . . Caption: 'The Three Greatest Germans'. Oil painting of Goethe and Bismarck standing on either side of Hitler. Bismarck is saluting Hitler with his sword: Goethe is about to place a laurel wreath on Hitler's head.

Illustrations from Goethe's *Faust*. . . . Mephistopheles and pretty Gretchen. Caption: 'The Eternal Jew Seducing The German Soul'. Mephistopheles and Faust riding through the night. Caption: 'The Eternal Jew Leads Germany To Destruction'. Mephistopheles standing by the gallows, smirking—'The Eternal Enemy'. Mephistopheles cowering before an Angel with a burning sword—'Germany Awakes!' Angels carrying Faust's immortal soul up to Heaven—'The Salvation Of The German People'.

Hitler again: 'The Greatest German Of All Time'.

And I hope Willie is feeling better. Your loving son—. Pa finished his postcard and licked a stamp. Licked the back of Hitler's head, he thought with distaste. Bugger'll start sticking his arse on the stamps next. He finished his bread and cheese (the china plate had a dainty picture of Goethe's young lovers, Werther and Lotte, handing bouquets to each other). The band began playing *The Merry Widow*. He opened the book he had bought that day—'The German Heart', an anthology of verse and prose—and scanned the list of famous contributors. Heine wasn't in it. His poem *The Lorelei* was listed as 'author unknown'. Struggling with the spidery gothic print, he turned to Goethe and began reading:

Kennst du das Land, wo die Zitronen blühn.
Do you know the land, where the lemon trees blossom—

and laughed out loud because he had suddenly thought of the communist parody about rearmament:

Kennst du das Land, wo die Kanonen blühn.
Do you know the land, where the cannons blossom—

And folk turned and looked curiously at him for laughing, so he excused himself, saying 'Ich—Ausländer', and they left him to his foreign lunacy.

The firelight glowed romantically on the brass irons and on his face, it shone over the many pictures of Goethe and Hitler, and the band played—

'Vilya, oh Vilya, you nymph of delight,
Haunting the woodland, enchanting the night!
Vilya, oh Vilya, you witch of the woods,
Love me, and I'll die for you! . . .'

And the heart of my communist father was away waltzing with the Merry Widow in some classical ballroom.

What was this classical serenity of Weimar? A sense of the organic unity of all things? A desire for a tolerant universe in which even red flags and black swastikas could find their place?—Or simply the love of life which was full of loving? Urbanity replacing longing? Sensuality instead of desire?

In 1792, in that dawn of the French Revolution when it was bliss to be alive, a handsome middle-aged gentleman with a servant and the title of Herr Geheimrat (Privy Councillor) to the Duke of Saxe-Weimar, accompanied the curassiers of the Prussian army across the French frontier at Redingen. The commander-in-chief, His Highness the Duke of Brunswick, was marching on Paris to destroy the Bastille-storming revolutionaries, rescue the imprisoned monarchs Louis and Marie-Antoinette, and hang the damn sanculottes from the lamp-posts: for he wrote, 'Anarchy in France must cease, the King must have the security and freedom and legitimate authority to which he is entitled. . . . Inhabitants of towns, villages, and hamlets daring to defend themselves against the troops of Their Imperial and Royal Majesties and firing upon them will be dealt with immediately by martial law, their houses destroyed and burnt down. . . . The city of Paris shall surrender to the King forthwith and without delay. . . . If the Royal Palace should be attacked and taken by violence, unparalleled and eternally memorable vengeance will be taken; the city of Paris will be handed over to the military and razed to the ground.' And as the army of the old order poured on into France, marching columns of infantry raising dust on the broken roads, gaily uniformed horsemen jingling by on the sward, long lines of waggons and guns creaking along with their sweating crews—the gentleman from the privy council travelled with them in a light open coach, or sometimes rode ahead on horseback, and exchanged pleasantries with the aristocratic young officers of the Prussian cavalry. One day, meeting an old friend, the Prince of Reuss, the two men engaged stirrup by stirrup in a learned debate on new discoveries in the science of colours. Herr von Goethe riding to the wars.

What did he think of it all, this great Goethe, as the tired soldiers marched, as the expected hosannas of a liberated people failed to materialize, as even the prettiest peasant girls scowled at

the gay hussars, and snatches of the song of the Marseilles
volunteers was heard by the advanced posts—

> *Allons enfants de la Patrie,*
> Come children of the fatherland,
> *Le jour de gloire est arrivé*
> The day of glory is here.
> *Contre nous de la tyrannie*
> Against us the bloody standards
> *L'etendard sanglant est levé*
> Of tyranny are raised—

What did he think of it all?

> *Aux armes, citoyens! Formons nos bataillons!*
> To arms, citizens! Form battalions!

For now the red-caps were marching too: in their shirt sleeves,
but singing, the sansculottes came. In Paris the first blood stained
the guillotine.

> *La patrie est en danger!*
> The fatherland is in danger!

—said the declaration nailed to the trees.

> *La patrie est en danger!*

—and a man was shot for nailing it.

(Happy martyr to have died believing in a revolution! No one
in Europe can have done so with innocence since that day.)

Then it began to rain. Day and night it poured down, and the
rough tracks turned into ditches ankle-deep in mud. Germanic
curses of the marching soldiers in their heavy tight uniforms,
soaked to the skin. Curses too of the mounted officers, damning
this wretched country they had come to, damning the 'abomin-
able vermin', the 'scum of the earth', they had come to fight. And
Goethe's coach stuck fast, stuck and could not be shifted there on
the edge of Champagne, near a village called Valmy.

And there the army of the French Revolution stood waiting. A
cannonade was exchanged, which was no more than a skirmish
even then. A trench raid in the First World War cost more than
the 400 men who died at Valmy; a few hours casual dive-
bombing in the Second cost as many: and neither would merit the
briefest mention in the history books. Three times that 400 died

in seconds when the *Queen Mary* went down at Jutland, and it changed nothing, what they died for. Yet Valmy truly changed the world.

And there lay Goethe's 'classical serenity', for he, who was not a soldier, realized it when the men of arms did not. Realized that the cries of *Ca ira!* and *Vive la nation!* which swept down from the French lines meant something more than a tired tribal chant —meant that the resolute minority who had declared this 1792 Year One of the New Era wanted, yes actually wanted, to carry their Liberty, Equality and Fraternity at gunpoint and over piles of dead if need be throughout enslaved Europe, that kings and their lackeys might perish utterly and paradise be realized on earth.

Bliss was it in that dawn to be alive,
But to be young was very Heaven!

Said Goethe to the bewildered and defeated officers of royal Prussia that same night by the glow of retreating fires: 'Gentlemen, at this point and at this hour a new era in world history begins, and you can all say that you were present at its birth.'

Ah, classical serenity! Even then the dreams of the visionaries were choking in blood.

As Willie, gentle dreamer, was choking too in his squalid bed in Marchmont.

Goethe's Germany! A quiet, peaceful, and peacefully loving land, where the hours dance by to chamber music, and amateur savants enthuse about the science of colours. If on a winter's night a traveller had come to it, he would have found good cheer and comfort there, and pleasing peace for a troubled mind.

The band was playing when Pa left Weimar—Germany in 1936 was full of bands—and this is what they were playing:

Freude!

Ja, wer auch nur eine Seele
Happy he who can call
Sein nennt auf dem Erdenrund!
Even one soul his mate on earth!

Und wer's nie gekonnt, der stehle
Only the wretch who cannot
Weinend sich aus diesem Bund.
Will find no comfort at our hearth.

Joy!

There is a hint in Pa's next postcard (mad King Ludwig's dream castle at Neuschwanstein towering on a mountain above a sea of trees), a coy hint that Joy had suddenly become something more than that Wordsworthian pleasure in nature which sent him walking weekends over the Pentlands, drinking from the burns, feeling the wind in his hair.

Because of course there was the Girl. There had to be.

At night I could see the sea beyond Redheugh: there, on the Berwickshire coast where we had gone to escape from the Atom Bomb in 1962, the year in which they said the world was going to blow up. I could open the creaking window of the small room that had become my bedroom (Pa slept in the room next door), and there, beyond a line of trees flinging their arms in the wind, was the sea shimmering with moonlight, the waves breaking and joining, changing and rechanging the path of the moonglade till it looked like the falling footsteps of a white giant striding there across the waters. And the wind from over the North Sea blowing; and Pa sometimes away for a crack with Bob Purves the old smith in the cottage on the other side of the road. And as the autumn days shortened back then in 1962, the year the world was going to blow up, I would see their two heads blackly silhouetted in the brilliant golden glow of the living-room window shining out over the road, shining for miles. And I, who was supposed to be asleep, would lean my elbows on the sill of the little room and, with the window open, stare and stare out at it all; and the sea wind would be in my face, and sometimes rain, the sting and the spit of it.

Wind, tell me, how did I first come to know about her?

Go back to nights we spent alone, together, in that Leith flat after the wreath had been taken from the door and the scent of woman had left the bedroom, and the scullery was the place that men look after—i.e. a mess. Those were miserable hours when I used to go down after school and stare at the sea, sitting at the end of the Leith breakwater near the old Martello tower. 'Mister Martello played on his cello,' the girls sang as they skipped. The sea. I built plastic ships out of Airfix kits. I threw bits of wood at the sea and watched them float away. Sometimes I walked along the Water of Leith up to the Dean Village where the trees overhang it, and watched the leaves fall on the water and be carried away; and I would wish a message on those leaves that they might carry it over the sea to the distant shore where Ma now was, telling her that I was sorry for all the cheek I had given her, all the times (the many times, I was sure) when I had upset her or made her cross. Because she had died on a bright noisy day when no one should die. Because I missed her so. Because . . .

Because.

And one long night Pa came with me, down here to this same stretch of shingly beach between Newhaven and Granton, with the lights of Starbank and Lower Granton Road behind us, and over yonder those of Burntisland and the Fife shore; and he said, 'We are none of us ships of our own making, laddie'; and he said, 'Oh Christ, laddie! I miss her something terrible!' he said. And we walked here together in the darkness, and he was careful with me, that I didn't fall into the sea. And he talked . . .

Who she was, I don't know. He didn't want to name her, and I was too young to care. What she looked like, I don't know either. Was she beautiful? Was she a blond Gretchen? I will never know now. My father belonged to that male generation of Scottish socialists who had crept out from under John Knox's pulpit, and thought of sex with a snicker and a shudder, regarding women either, with unconscious humour, as 'comrades-in-arms', or as soft men, unreliable, and shrouded in a misty vapour of desire and carnality. Pa was grim-mouthed when he told me about the terrible things he had seen in the war, about the bombed cities, about the death-camp, about the two German soldiers he knew for a fact that he had killed at Salerno. He told me about these things sometimes when he was having nightmares: I will come to that later. But he *never* told me about sex, or about a woman's body, and how good it can feel. That would simply have been too embarrassing.

So Pa's German girl remains something in a poem. And he wrote poems about her. And then he burnt them.

Ah well.

But I can give you the date exactly. A postcard from Heidelberg, one of that telegram type which is a montage of little pictures with a couple of inches in the middle where you can write two or three words beside the printed captions saying *Arrived*—, *Hotel*—, *Weather*—, etc. This is what it says:

Feriengrüsse Aus Heidelberg

Angekommen: *Sonntag 16 Aug.*
Quartier: *Grand*
Essen: *Immer bangers n tatties*
Durst: *Hale*
Stimmung: *Hearty*
Wetter: *Bonny*
Geld: *Still plenty Weingeld!*
Absender: *Your loving son Donald*
P.S. Hope Willie is better.

No *Dear Hubbard*. On Sunday 16th August 1936, with the Berlin Olympics in full fling, and Spanish troops fighting round the Alcazar of Toledo, my thirty-year-old Pa had fallen in love.

Now then, what happened? It went something like this:

One night (Saturday 15th August?) Pa was out getting pissed. I think he got pissed, if you'll excuse the expression, rather frequently in Germany. At all events, this particular night after chucking-out time Pa and a couple of German lads he had never seen before, and would never see again, staggered through the complicated streets of Heidelberg with their arms about each others necks like the three musketeers singing '*Trink, trink, Bruderlein trink* (hic)', and vowing eternal comradeship to each other for as long as life should last. Syne a polisman came and chased them, and they ran and they staggered, they lurched and they bounced, they stumbled and they fumbled their way past walls that jumped out to ambush them, lamp-posts that tried to catch their legs in flying tackles, and even a parked car which came at them swinging its mudguards, till at last Pa found himself in a side-street of little cobbles, and the scampering footsteps and the shouting departed, and he was alone.

Alone in the middle of the night.

Alone and drunk in the middle of the night.

Alone and drunk in the middle of a town in Germany in the middle of the night.

Without the slightest clue where he was.

Enter the essential lady.

Or rather, enter Pa into the essential lady's bedroom, still without a clue. This was how it happened—

There was, near where Pa stood soberly erect, a door swaying slightly from side to side. For some reason Pa took it into his head that this door, among the several thousand doors in Heidelberg, was the door of his hotel. (It wasn't.) For some other reason he took it into his head that he had the key to the door of his hotel. (He hadn't.) He felt in his pocket, and, like Christian in the dungeon of Giant Despair, behold!—he found a key. It was the key of his front door in Marchmont. Pa told the night at large that he had a key. He laid it across a twig on the pavement and did a highland sword dance. The excitement was too much for his stomach. He hung his head over the gutter and was terribly terribly sick. He picked up the key and groped his way slowly towards the door. The door saw him coming. It stood still. Then it raised itself up and towered over him. Then it picked up the doormat and smacked him in the teeth.

Pa woke up after minutes or hours in a 'tired and emotional state'. He was utterly legless and was beginning to feel cold. He approached the door once again, patting it on the muzzle and speaking gentle words to calm it down. The door shied and snorted away from him. Again and again he tried. At last he got the key-shaped bit into the beast's mouth, but the mouth was so big the key shot right through and fell, clunk, hollowly on the other side. Pa pressed his forehead to the keyhole and began singing mournfully about how his heart was in the highlands, no here, and then he began to beat his head rhythmically against the wood crying out 'Allah!—Allah!—Allah!' muezzining the sleeping town that hung over him with all its high turrets and wood fronts, aye, quite the prettiest casbah he'd ever seen was Heidelberg. Eventually a window opened on the other side of the street and a voice bellowed at him to desist in the name of the Prophet else a watchman would be summoned to cast him into the caliph's dungeon. At least that's what Pa thought it said, for the voice bellowed in angry German accompanied by the slamming of the window, and it was all a strange noise to Pa as he staggered away weeping because the door still would not open for him.

It must have been near the outskirts of the town. In the backyards of some of the buildings domesticated animals were kept. Here a hen coop produced the odd squawk and flutter of wings invisible: there a horse snorted and scuffed at the hay in its stable. A rich smell of cow dung came wafting out of one arched alley-way. The fact that German cow dung smelled so like Scottish cow dung was a revelation to Pa, and he wandered wearily down the alley pulled by the smell of the shotten creatures. How he came to fall over the pig, he never knew. But fall he did—

CRASH

into the glaur.

He was on his feet in seconds, the outraged animal squealing behind him, his trousers in shreds, and the whole of his withers so bespattered with ordure that through the fumes of the beer even he could scarce stand the smell of himself. A *click*—*clack* —*clunk* of gabled lights going on, a *slip*—*slap*—*slamp* of windows opening, and—with a sudden torchbeam playing shamelessly all over him—a gruff authoritarian voice such as can only come from between the collar and the helmet of a uniform saying *Was?*—*Wer?*—*Schwein!*

Pa fled.

He woke to her laughter. 'Like the ringing of water on stones,' he said. 'A bonny sound.' He was in a byre, lying on a pile of hay and less mentionable stuff, and painfully, slowly, he raised himself up, feeling . . . well, yes, I know the feeling. And there she was. Early summer's morning and a cock crowing, and she was standing in dazzling sunlight in the wooden door frame wearing a pair of clarty rubber boots, and a thin raincoat, and nothing else (nothing else? how did he know there was nothing else?), and carrying a zinc milk pail.

(I think of that sight—which I did not see—and even now, standing on this shingle beach, I heave a sigh at the thought of her standing there like that . . .

(Wearing nothing else because of course she had just got out of bed. . . .

(Hold on!—how many fantasies like that have you heard in your time, and all of them lies? . . .

(Thousands, but my father wasn't a fantasizing man. She was standing there laughing in the sunlight, and beneath her thin flimsy raincoat she was lovely naked, and her breasts were . . .

(Stop. He couldn't have seen them . . .

(Unless her thin flimsy raincoat was hanging open! She is resting her left forearm high up against the wooden door, and her right hip is thrust out, and her knees are together, and . . . Oh, stop it

       stop it
       stop it . . .)

And whatever sense of these things it is that women possess was so appealed to by Pa sitting there, lost and ragged and covered in boke with straw sticking out of his hair like a collapsed scarecrow (he scarcely seems a very romantic picture), that this poem-girl of his, this woodland witch, wrapped him in her thin flimsy. . . .

(No, wait a minute, that's impossible—unless she was . . . !) wrapped him in a horse blanket/wrapped him in a piece of old sacking/wrapped him in a towel which she just happened to have handy. . . .

(But just imagine if she *had* wrapped him in her thin flimsy —which would have left her—*with nothing on but her rubber boots* . . . !

(The one thing that makes me believe this story is true, is that Pa was, by his own admission, too hung-over to do a blessed thing about it. It's difficult being randy when your stomach feels like a rabid rat had just crawled into it and died.)

Anyway, the point is that instead of just flinging a bucket of water at him and telling him to sod off, Vilya the witch of the woods wheeled him indoors and upstairs (somehow) to her bedroom (!), pointed him towards the bed, gave him a push between the shoulderblades, and he tottered towards it, collapsed upon it, and passed out.

The cock crew, the bells rang, the sun rose high over Heidelberg and crossed to the west—the *Abendland*, the 'land of evening'. Folk went to and came from work. In Berlin the healthy athletes pounded round the stadium, flung javelins, swam and jumped. In Spain the healthy soldiers killed each other. In Edinburgh Willie coughed and coughed. The sun set over the fantastic spires and turrets of Heidelberg, and Pa hadn't written to his Dear Hubbard, had forgotten all about it. At suppertime he ventured gingerly downstairs and relined his innards with turnip soup.

Turnip soup is scarcely the traditional dish of romance, yet it proved so for Pa, because over that supper table set for him by a family whose name he did not know until they introduced themselves German-fashion, standing and bowing and shaking hands above the dishes, he fell longingly and lastingly in love for perhaps the only time in his life. And under the table did their feet touch?—as Pa, so well brought up, praised the cooking and the kitchen work, and the big genial mother beamed at him over her many chins and made mental note of a man her daughter might wed. And under the table did their hands touch?—as Pa listened with more than politeness to the father's talk, for the bullet-headed stalky father was a member of the Party from pre-revolution days (red badge, number, black swastika proving it so), so Pa of course began asking about trade union affiliation, and pondered over whether or not the 'co-ordination' of unions and employers' clubs into a national Workers' Front might not, after all, have something to be said for it.

After all (her fingers slipping into his) there were no slums in Germany.

For this was also the land of Marx, Bismarck and Stresemann, of state-owned forests and state-owned railways, family planning, and Berta Krupps' hygienic housing estates for the industrial workers of the Ruhr.

And the workers of Germany (her knee now pressing his) had cheap holidays under Hitler, health care, 'co-operation' and 'team-spirit', planned garden cities, allotments, pocket money, and nice factories decorated with flowers.

It seemed (and her hair smelled of sun and hay) that the National Socialist Workers' Party was doing for Germany all that the Labour Party was still talking about doing for Britain.

And the bullet-headed father poked the tablecloth with his finger and talked about the 'true socialism of the people's community', and the genial mother smiled all around her plump substantial smile, and against his arm my socialist father (who was capable of reading the political press on his wedding-night and economic tracts on his honeymoon) could distinctly feel the curve of a warm young breast and hear the murmur of the mermaid's song.

A couple of days later (and after a couple of belated postcards sent to Edinburgh) the two of them set off on a journey down the Rhine. Well of course they did! No foreigner in Germany could possibly do otherwise. Besides, Pa, ever the word-boy, was quoting Byron—

> The castled crag of Drachenfels
> Frowns o'er the wide and winding Rhine,
> Whose breast of waters broadly swells
> Between the banks which bear the vine . . .

—and attempting to put it into his own erratic German, for the girl knew no English seemingly; yet as they voyaged down the river together on a white passenger ship, I daresay they spoke the language which is beyond words, and the Rhine gorge knew their love as it had known so many others.

Postcard showing the Mouse Tower at Bingen:

Dear Hubbard, They locked a bishop in this tower once, and he was eaten alive by mice! Think we should do that to the General Assembly! Having a rare time. Donald.

No *Willie*; no *Loving son*.

It was all.

A German Dream

The Rhine—whose Germany is that? Heine's, Goethe's, Schiller's? Schiller's, yes—a place of castles and robber barons, freedom fighters, nationalists, and heroic soldiers clasping battleflags. It is a river which partakes of the north. Days of mist and shadow, of dark hanging forest on the cliff walls. In such a climate Siegfried of the Nibelungs' song rode from Xanten to Worms in the days of dragons when Christianity had not yet sprinkled its holy water in all the forest glades. It is too a river with promises of the south, of the land of wine and roses, when the sun shines on the vine terraces and dances over the tightly packed roof of its little towns. North of Cologne it becomes the drain of the Ruhr and highway of the ocean ships, an artery of commerce as much as of myth with the big vessels steaming to Rotterdam over waters where Lohengrin once rode on the back of a snow-white swan.

But above all the river of castles. There they stand, dozens of them—for the Rhine was a merchants' highway back in the days of the Flemings and their Antwerp caravels, and each bend and mile of the river had its hungry warlord, there was not a hill, cliff nor island that was not lorded over by some freebooter or other in his stone tower. And their names have a fine roll; they sound gothically down the great river valley—Ehrenfels, Fürstenberg, Layen, Ehrenburg, Ehrenbreitstein ('broad stone of honour'), Rauschenburg, Rheinfels . . . Castles where once great love and cruelty dwelt together, where ladies waited for their knights to ride through the forest to the castle gate, where wretched prisoners howled unheard in deep cliff-set dungeons, places of plot and passion. Places where ruin now greenly dwells.

And among the castles and the fortified granges, the owls, the

127

ivy, and the little advent calendar towns, they came to Oberwesel, and stood on the cliff as tourists do to shout *'Wer ist der
Bürgermeister von Oberwesel?'* ('Who is the Provost of Oberwesel?'), did Pa and his German girl, and the echo dutifully
answered *'Esel'*—ass—and they laughed, and crossed to the
Lorelei Rock where the flat tabletop summit held an
amphitheatre 'Given by the Party to the People'.

Oh the castles, the castles that had for so long defended
Germany! Castle Katz above St Goarshausen village, built by the
Count of Katzenelenbogen, and its rival downstream, Castle
Maus above Wellmich—cat and mouse, literally—erected by the
warlike Bishop of Trier: Maus original and ruined; Katz a careful
gothic restoration of the original, because (says the legend)
in 1804, a few years after Valmy, a salvo of honour made
Napoleon's horse shy, and this so infuriated the French
revolutionary boys that they had the whole place blown up in
revenge.

—Why did they do that to us? said the girl, to whom Pa had
been expounding his theories about the rights of man. Why is
progress so vindictive?

Why?

And afterwards—after the guns had stopped firing, and the
shouting and the waving of flags had departed, and only the dead
in cluttered cemeteries marked the passage of the Revolution
—well, then the Count of Katzenelenbogen, whose name sounds
so cumbersome in English, sat there in his wig and silks in the
ruins of his home and drew pictures in the dust with his slender
cane: and he understood none of it, the Revolution with its
Liberty, Equality, Fraternity, its *Marseillaise* and *Ca Ira*; he understood only that some aliens had come into Germany armed with
progress and had burnt his home. So he told himself stories; and
because he was afraid of the present with its barbarous progress,
his stories were all of the old times when knights were bold and
ladies fair and gracious. And in this, yon German noble and my
ancestor Andrew Mackay, the Sutherland crofter, were very
much alike, I think, for they had both lost all that was theirs while
fighting the French Revolution; and in those same years the two
men who did not know of each other's existence both longed for
the place that had been their home, on a brae in Strathnaver, on a

rock above the Rhine. My ancestor was a poor man, and the law did not favour him. He took to wandering and crafting little things in wood. But the Count was a noble, and the law of the time smiled on such as he; besides there must still have been some gold in his pouch, for he took to craftwork too—a new castle in stone, as near a replica of the old as his memory could furnish and his workmen achieve. Stone upon stone his new Castle Katz rose up, Ivanhoe-land indeed with its burly keep, its slender towers, conical roofs and massive ramparts, where the Count hid himself in medieval knighthood, and kept the modern world, its steam-engines and its clamour, out.

Portents. But what are portents? In a beer garden, or beer cellar, in St Goarshausen some folk were singing that they knew not why they were so sad:

> *Ich weiss nicht was soll es bedeuten*
> *Dass ich so traurig bin . . .*

—the words of Heine's *Lorelei*, the mermaid lass, and Pa glee-fully joined in the singing of them. Clank clank of beersteins hitting the table-tops. Then Pa spoke out in praise of Heine, and was immediately shoved up against the wall by an angry wee man—a professor, he said he was, in some university, and he had indeed a bald head and eye glasses—who stabbed at him with his finger and told him that 'that Jew' Heine had done no such thing, 'that Jew' wasn't capable of writing such poetry, no Jew was, all 'that Jew' had done was to steal the words of some good gentile poet who had probably died of starvation, poor sod, and pretend they were his own—'a typical Jew trick', the angry wee man cried, which the 'Jew press' and the 'Jew so-called academics' had been foisting off on a gullible public ever since. What was Pa? the angry wee man demanded. A socialist? That was good. Did he love his country?—well of course he did! So what was he being taken in by the 'despicable lies of the international Jewish mil-lionaire press' for? . . . Pa disentangled himself somehow, and took no offence. Thought it was funny even, having been accosted by drunks often enough before.

Portents. But then a man can see no portents when he is in love.

That evening they climbed to the amphitheatre on the Lorelei

Rock, where, says story number one, Lore sea-girl sat combing her golden locks with a golden comb and singing in a voice so—so *wunderbar* says the German—that the poor sailors on the water below were lured to destruction on the cliffs: where, says story number two, Lore a lovely lass from a village nearby came to sit in the gloaming and watch the sun in the west and think of her lover who was killed in the distant wars. They climbed the rock to the amphitheatre where an orchestra was seated, and youths in brown shirts stood with the mouths of brass trumpets resting on their hips. They blew a fanfare. Then drummers, also boys, with long drums decorated with red leaping flame insignia appeared from the shadows. They beat a long drumroll into the setting sun. Other brownshirted boys stood holding burning torches in their hands.

Then the orchestra began to play. They were adults and obviously amateurs. Their middle-aged spread and thinning hair contrasted strangely with the muscular youths in brown: their domesticity with the medieval pomp of sunsets and flaming torches. They played with great sincerity, and the audience who were mainly locals and foreign tourists was entranced. A predictable medley: Wagner—Siegfried's Journey down the Rhine; Beethoven—and a choir, boys in brown shirts and girls in white, sang the Prisoners' Chorus from *Fidelio*; Wagner—the Ride of the Valkyries; Beethoven—and it was the Ninth Symphony chorale again, Schiller's Ode to Joy—

> *Freude!* . . .
>
> *Seid umschlungen, Millionen!*
> Oh you millions, I embrace you!
> *Diesen Kuss der ganzen Welt!*
> Let me kiss the whole wide world!
> *Brüder—überm Sternenzelt*
> Brothers—above the starry sky
> *Muss ein lieber Vater wohnen.*
> A loving Father surely dwells . . .

Pa didn't like it very much. Joy should be all of the midday and full glorious sunlight—and here it was slithering back into the darkness with the vainglory of drums and trumpets, and these macabre torches. . . . And children in uniform. He whispered in her ear, and she giggled. Did she blush, or was it merely the light of the torches? He whispered again, then chuckled.

'You're blushing,' he said.

She was blushing.

He took her hand and together they left the circle.

One night . . .

—are you listening, Pa?

One night, just before you got your separate beds—one night, after you had had one of your bad rows and you had stormed out into the rain—one night I discovered that Ma had also been in love.

You didn't know that, did you, Pa? She was once in love, and not with you.

One night, because your row had woken me, because you had stormed out slamming the door, because the television had closed down, because I was too scared to go back to sleep again, because there was no one and nothing else in our cold flat for her to warm herself with, one night she told me about him, sitting on my bed.

His name was Stanislaus. He was a Polish seaman. It was 1941. Ma was young, a girl just out of her teens and in her first job. She lived with her parents in Corstorphine where the streets were quiet and leafy, and the gardens had crazy pavements, bird-baths and terracotta gnomes. Every morning she came by bus along St John's Road and Corstorphine Road to the inner city. The anti-aircraft guns on Corstorphine Hill stood among the trees. She had a lot of girlfriends. They painted their lower legs and pretended they had stockings on. They put on a great deal of lipstick and stood for hours patting their hair in front of mirrors. They were all in love with Clark Gable. Before the Americans arrived, they all had Canadian boyfriends. Ma had a Canadian boyfriend. They went to the pictures, and before the main film came up there was music and the audience always sang along with it. They sang 'At Home On The Range' and 'Deep In The Heart of Texas'. All the girls tried to drawl through their noses and sound Canadian. Ma had a Canadian boyfriend. He was a fighter pilot. He got killed.

At night Ma took her turn firewatching on the office roof down Canonmills way. Very few bombs fell on Edinburgh, but everybody thought they were going to fall. German fighters didn't hold enough fuel to take them anywhere near Scotland, and unprotected bombers were easy to shoot down in daylight. A German bomber tried to blow up the Forth Bridge in the early days. He was shot down. Somewhere on the bed of the Forth half way between Leith and Aberdour fifty fathoms deep are the remains of that bomber with his skeletal crew. Then the Germans came by night, trying for the shipbuilding yards over in Clydebank, Greenock and Belfast. In the winter of 1940 and well into 1941 sirens wailed at night and the guns on the Castle and Corstorphine Hill fired at these flocks of Heinkels and Junkers and Focke-Wulfs flying over from Norway, and the searchlights would zigzag after them all over the sky.

Ma had a Canadian boyfriend, then he got killed. She went to the Pictures alone. The Ritz in Rodney Street was showing *Gone With The Wind*. She went every night. Then the same man sat beside her twice. It was the third night before she noticed him. Even then he didn't say anything. The fourth night it was she who talked to him. Stanislaus. He was shy and had very little English. He came from a place in Poland with an utterly unpronounceable name. He was a seaman in the merchant navy. He had a mother and a sister and an aunt in Poland, and he loved them very much (he said), very much. He liked the green countryside on the screen. Ma liked it too. Then, when Scarlett O'Hara began to pick her way through the wounded in Atlanta railway-yards, she began to cry. She couldn't stop crying. They left early. Stanislaus saw her home. At the door he bowed and kissed her hand. That was how she met him.

A seaman, and a foreigner, and a Catholic, he wasn't at all the sort of man she could take home to Corstorphine. Forbye he was absent much of the time. The convoys were sailing back across the Atlantic in those days, sailing from Halifax and Chesapeake Bay to Liverpool and the Clyde, retracing the route of the merchant and immigrant ships which had fed the young nations for so many years, sailing from the pilgrim waters of Nantucket and Boston, from Nova Scotia past gaelic Cape Breton to the old country, to the land of the Clearances, to fuel the fight against fascism. And Stanislaus sailed with them. Stanislaus was politically very naive. Folk who live securely today in posh wee flats in the New Town of Edinburgh and are members of the Fringe Theatre Club would not approve of Stanislaus. He thought that German National Socialism and Soviet Communism had combined to butcher Poland. When Stalin became an ally of the free peoples in the fight against fascism, the fight which was to bring peace ever after and a united democratic world, Stanislaus was perplexed, didn't understand it at all. He had a white Polish eagle tattooed on his arm.

Whenever he was on leave he came to Edinburgh. He and Ma walked in the Braid Hills. They held hands and smiled at each other,

—the way Pa and his German girl smiled at each other
—as they crept stealthily away from the circle of torches on top of the Lorelei Rock that night when the sun had slid westerly over invisible France to be a summer's sunset for the distant Atlantic and the shores of America
—to shine on the western face of Manhattan skyscrapers and Chicago skyscrapers, to make a loom of light around the lapping of the Great Lakes and the plain of Manitoba, washing the sky above the Rocky Mountains that stand in black heraldry, rampant like Scottish lions: and what Mackay farmer/rancher/townsman who does not know Sutherland (as I do not know Sutherland) is sitting on his porch this evening in 1982/'62/'36 sucking his pipe perhaps, smoking a cigarette in the calm cool of northern summer twilight, and wishing that this moment could last for ever?

For I love you, oh Eternity!

—As Ma and her Polish boy did, walking hand-in-hand like how many other young lovers in the midst of those war-torn years
—on the homely hills of Edinburgh, on the Braid/Corstorphine/Calton/Blackford hills where they walked away his leave those days when history was being so triumphantly made by the tanks and bombing planes

133

—which yet left Edinburgh shining like the delectable land, the very frontier of heaven were those quiet suburbs from Fairmilehead to Silverknowes, scattered like the fragments of a million years from the time of the Ice and the parting of continents; and still they find fossils there, in suburban gardens, in the pits of the Lothian coalfield, ancient dead creatures frozen in the black mud. But what young couple yet ever let such thoughts trouble them—for they know that they are all there is in the world, and that the present is for ever, and there is neither war nor pain, for the planet of Hitler and Stalin and all their death-machinery is merely the cinema horror of some film watched in the darkened Ritz.

For I love you, oh Eternity!

—As Pa loved his German girl, his Gretchen, his blond/brunette/redheaded but unquestionably very beautiful girl when they lay together that night in the ruins of a castle nearby the Lorelei Rock in the midst of the dark trees and a moonlit night

—as Ma loved her Polish boy, her Stanislaus, who was so big and shy and diffident with her, when they lay like a hundred other young couples (and all the boys in uniform) with no place to make love save in the open, in the grass, under the cloud-walking sky

—and I wonder, looking back to those contraceptiveless days, have I a half-brother in Scotland, have I a half-sister in Germany I do not know? For where am I in all this loving? A coughing cripple like Willie in Marchmont I, a watcher from the shadows of other people's lives who once saw a gypsy lady in a window, and have remembered her ever since. So standing outside the dwam of love I peek in through the curtains.

For I too love you, oh Eternity!

—I have loved you from the beginning, for then is the love which is beyond understanding, and it seems to me now that all our lives are no more than an attempt to fathom that which we cannot possibly fathom, for it is sea-deep: the most we can hope for is to come as close as possible to that which we once were before we knew it; perhaps before we knew anything at all.

—And I think of that wee girl I met once, twice, that summer at Redheugh, and the time Pa hit me and I hated him so—she must have seen and despised my futile longing, that girl with the raspberry mouth sitting on the green headland as summer turned to autumn. 'Have you got a girlfriend?' she asked, I being ten, she being ten also—and I shook my head and she laughed. Gladly my cross-eyed bear.

—Listen. Longing is kept locked in secret places; and in one such secret place this dark morning on the Granton shore I have unlocked a moment I have honestly not thought about since it happened, and it happened a very long time ago. Once, in distant aeons, the three of us went walking through a beautiful land. A white horse stood in a field, I remember it, and a cow was shaking its tail (now why should I think of that?); and we sat beside a running water, and I clarted there awhile, Pa holding me, while Ma set out a picnic on the grass, and there was sunlight, and a wind chapping in the treetops, and leaves falling. And thirty years later I am suddenly thinking of it, and there is a taste of salt in my mouth, for it now seems so terribly terribly important, yon moment that no one else knows anything about.

For in that moment I loved you, oh Eternity!

—I love you, says Ma to her Polish boy, who will the next day call at her parents' house with a bouquet of flowers and present them, blushing, unable to say a word.

—I love you, says Pa to his German girl, who will the next day present him with a handsome translation of Goethe's *Faust* and say, 'Donald, I am so very much fond of you, I think'—*Faust* which she has never read in her life, but knows that he will surely like.

—Flowers, which my mother always liked.

—I love you, they say all four.

—I love you, blood shaking my heart.

And longing kept locked in its secret place: the Thing in the room upstairs, the Creature in the dungeon below. Germany

was full of secret places, for a people used to oppression develop such places—in Mayerling where Prince Rudolf and his lover shot themselves; in Neuschwanstein where King Ludwig went pathetically mad in protest against nationalism, war and industry, and drowned himself in the loch below; in Castle Katz where the Count hid himself away from progress, war and industry, and read the novels of Sir Walter Scott; in Königsberg where Kant created his own world of pure reason with no revolutions, war or industry allowed in, and shopkeepers set their clocks by Professor Kant's measured tread falling on the street; in the happy islands of Zarathustra where Nietzsche created a new humanity of passion and song, Nietzsche superman who had a stroke when he saw a sadist flogging a horse. . . . And in Vienna where young Adolf Hitler tramped the streets one long dreich winter, and stood outside closed doors, and heard the gay music filtering through closed windows, and longed to be inside with all the joy and laughter
   —yes, even Hitler
   —yes, and even Stalin
   —both in dreamland
   —with all the future murderers
   cried

I love you, oh Eternity! I love you!

Hey, little boy blue,	In the morning of my life,
where are you going to?	building castles in the shifting sands,
where	when the minutes are so long,
are you	dreaming of what I cannot understand,
going	be patient with me—
to?	Love takes so long to unfold.
Where are you—	going to?

    The morning came, and they descended the hill, like young Gluck from that mountain in Styria where the King of the Golden River dwells, Pa with his German girl to continue down the river to Koblenz, Ma with her Polish boy to catch the bus into Edinburgh. 1936, 1941—Ma and Pa didn't know each other then, they were in love with other people, and history the bloody monster didn't interest either of them, though history was being made with a vengeance and people were falling over with bullets in them in various parts of the world.

Dear Hubbard—

(Greetings from Koblenz: picture of an old bridge—destined to be blown up in 1945.)

Weather still grand and having a great time. Some very nice folks. Beer's good too! Hope Willie's a bit better. Donald.

Portents. In 1936, of all years, when every socialist worth his balls was running round in circles pishing and howling and shitting hot blue bricks, when Spanish nationalist guerrilleros were still holding the Alcazar in spite of all the bombs, shells, grenades and bullets the republicans could lob at it, when Abyssinia was full of corpses and China was full of corpses, when every -ist who could get his mitts on a pen, pencil or typewriter was pounding out reams of stuff full of trumpets, hate, blood-lust, battleflags, boots and supremacy—when all this was going on, my Pa, Donald Mackay, Communist Party member number dot-dot-dot, one-time rioter in the High Street bashed on the head by the Edinburgh polis, was mooning along the banks of the Rhine, indulging in bourgeois lust and carnality with some wee whore/tart/trollop/scrubber/scrag/bit of cunt; and how often did they discuss Lenin's theory of revolution in the midst of all their damn fornicating? Not once! It was disgusting, just.

Thus the voice of the sneer machine: and I can see them, the craphounds, baying and slavering and snarling there on the carpet, leaping up and snapping their jaws at Pa and his German girl, those two pretty little animals loving together in a pleasant land within the bars of their golden cage. So beautiful is that picture that even Time the hound-master felt for them and gave them a week of eternity before. . . .

It was at Königswinter, on the east bank opposite Bad Godes-berg, just south of Bonn. For of course they were going to Bonn, Beethoven's birthplace Bonn—*Freude!* etcetera.

Königswinter is a spa, a favoured famous watering hole. Its shoreline where the passenger ships disembark is laid out with flowerbeds and the promenade is lined with trees. It has a wine festival. Bacchus dresses up with a crown of vine leaves and gives a medal to those who have 'quenched burning thirst'. It's a nice place, Königswinter.

From there you can take excursions into the Seven Hills and climb the famous Drachenfels Rock from the top of which, on a clear day, you can see the spires of Cologne cathedral downriver, and perhaps the roofs and bridge of Remagen up. It's a nice place too, the Drachenfels. And Bad Honnef—and Erpel. . . . Nice, nice places.

Naturally each one of the Seven Hills has got seventy legends.

Here's one about Drachenfels, 'dragon rock'—for there was a dragon who lived in the Rhine and stalked its great gloomy forests when folk were young, a fabulous being, epitome of everyone's ancient fears about the world beyond the woodcutter's cottage where a man's dim eyes and cloth ears put him at the mercy of anything going. And what was going in the German forests in those days, God knows it must have been bad for folk to fantasize this monster out of it—but fantasize they did. Being heathen, they made a god out of the dragon on the grounds that in a God-shortage anything will do, and the thing with power that terrifies and kills must be *it*. And this god killed all right. He demanded sacrifices, and not of dead chickens either. Living humans were offered to the dragon at the mouth of his cave on the rock, and oddly enough *something* always killed these victims, and that, said the priests, seeing the mangled remains of gnawed bone and entrail, was all the proof anybody needed. Well, came a time when, inevitably, two of the heathen princes fell in love with a beautiful Christian slave girl they had captured on a raid. They couldn't decide which of them was to have her, and since her opinion didn't count, the priest resolved their dilemma by giving her as a little delicacy to the dragon. So she was tethered to an oak outside his cave; but when he lumbered out snorting and slavering and licking his chops—BAM!—the girl whipped out a crucifix and gave the evil monster such a shock that he back-flipped splat into the Rhine and paddled away for dear life. Confronted with the miracle-working powers of the cross, all the heathens were converted to Christianity, the better-looking of the two princes married the girl, and the other one became a monk. End of film.

(Wait a minute. It's not a film. Stop being cynical. It's a legend, a myth, a fairy story; and we all know about these things, don't we? We know the Jungian and the Freudian interpretations of them, we know the chatter of the social anthropologists. We have these beautiful psychic butterflies well and truly poisoned, dead, and pinned to the board. Believe it? A dead butterfly doesn't fly again. Yet how I wish it could happen: that some maiden chained to a tree in Soviet Kola could suddenly work magic, make a sign, throw holy water at all those evil missiles lurking there in the forests and make *them* disappear, plunge downdowndowndown into the bottomless deep, never to trouble us any more . . .)

Here is another story, another dead butterfly from the Seven Hills, this one from the Löwenburg. It was haunted by the Wild Huntsman himself, Samiel, the Erl-King, the weird rider on a pale steed who is maybe the Devil, and maybe some damned soul like the Flying Dutchman or the Wandering Jew—or Britain's Herne Hunter about whom the old tale goes that he was a keeper in Windsor Forest whose sorcery made cows yield blood, and many other such fearsome things. Well, there was by the Löwenburg a noble cried Hermann von Hernsberg whose passion for the hunt was such that he defied all holy sabbaths and saints' days and went careering after the wild deer and the boar of the Seven Hills, ruining his peasants' crops beneath his flying hooves, and turning his dogs on any who dared raise fist or even voice against him for doing it. Came a day when—inevitably—knight Hermann became separated from his dissolute companions and lost his way in the woods. He had laid himself down to rest in a glade when, of a sudden, he saw an uncanny sight. A man, evidently noble like himself and garbed in outmoded hunting clothes, entered the glade and blew long and loud and high upon his hunting horn. No sooner had he done this than a horde of skeleton stags came through the forest, each with a human skeleton on its back, and this ghastly rout set upon the man with the horn, the stags buffeting him with their antlers, while the riders slashed him with their whips. So fearsome was this scene that knight Hermann, who had never known fear in his life, fainted dead away. When he opened his eyes again, the skeleton creatures were gone but the man was still there. In the forest light he explained to Hermann that he was an ancestor of his—now long dead—who in his life had been, like Hermann, obsessed with the hunt. When in the time of a great hunger some famine-stricken peasants were caught poaching deer from his forests, he had had them flung into his dungeons and left there to starve for a week, while his hounds too went hungry, and his foresters were sent to capture some stags. At the end of the allotted time the dungeon doors were opened and those prisoners who had survived were taken forth and tied naked to the backs of the stags. Then the hunger-maddened hounds were loosed on them, with what results need not be described, sufficient be it to say that the last stag and peasant had died together in this very glade. The cruel huntsman had died that very same night, and before the Throne God damned his soul to be hunted nightly by those whom he had slaughtered until the Last Day came, whereat the demons would hunt him for all eternity through the fires of hell. . . . Needless to say, with his ancestor's sorry example before his eyes, Hermann von Hernsberg mended his ways from that moment forth.

(Because it had to end like that: these tales are appeals for justice in the place where there is none, a hope that somewhere beyond the river of death there will be found the Court that should be in this cruel world and is not. And I wonder—will the burned of Hiroshima and Nagasaki ever come together again, will all these charred bones, boiled flesh and melted eyes come together again, and will they walk, these radiated zombies, through the green fields of Nebraska and the streets of Omaha as a dire warning? —And will the missile crews heed that warning?—And will dead butterflies ever fly? . . .)

Pa and his German girl spent a day or two in pleasant little excursions round the Snow White hills—for it was to the Seven Hills that the dwarfs brought Snow White to hide her from her wicked step-mother, and marched off to mine their jewels singing 'Aieee aioow it's off to work we go', the way a column of Hitler Youths was singing as they passed them on a country road, brown-limbed boys, girls with sunburn and freckles, striding out with spades sloped rifle-fashion over their shoulders. And did any of these Hitler boys look into the nine years distant future of 1945 when they would run into Snow White's hills to hide from the vengeful Americans who were pouring across the

Rhine at Remagen bridge with more tanks than anybody thought the world contained? Portents. In the early summer evening they returned to Königswinter.

They had missed the news, being in the hills that day. Down the lovely Rhine *He* was coming. Who? Hitler of course! Here? Yes! And the crowds rushed to the riverbank, old men and young, women and girls; shopkeepers closing early, bustling down the street, slipping their door keys into waistcoat pockets; holidaying professors from famous halls of learning, from Heidelberg, Tubingen, Göttingen and Berlin universities, experts in Kant's categorical imperative and Hegel's dialectic, historians of art, searchers for the meaning of the world soul and of existence, now clutching their hats and pressing through the throng, Excuse me, comrade, to the butcher, Excuse me, lady comrade, to the housewife, touching his brim. And she pulled him excitedly, Donald, Donald, I must see him, her face flushed all of a sudden (was she blushing again?), and to please her he used his shoulder to carve a way for her through the press. Excuse me, he said, excuse me *bitte*—I'm a foreigner, I don't understand— excuse me!

And at the bottom of the street they came to a halt for the crowd was standing there waiting, packed up against the riverbank, the promenade a solid mass of people, the *Polizei* guarding the precious flower beds, little boys clambering up into the trees. Pa looked and saw the trees creaking with their fruit, bare boyish legs and ankle socks, bairns sitting on their fathers' shoulders. And Pa looked and saw the windows of the timbered houses with the turrets and high gables and conical roofs, and at each and every window were faces, and on the balconies women were standing with babies in their arms, and old men with grey hair. And the crowd heaved once more, and Pa looked and saw a couple of burly polismen shepherding a class of schoolgirls into a position from which they could see the river, and Pa took advantage of this and saying gruffly *Polizei, Platz da!* brought his girl in close beside them.

There was the river, and a chain, and the schoolgirls, and Pa and his German girl, and the folk and visitors of Königswinter all around them; and polismen here and there standing with crossed arms, and everyone else pointing and standing on tiptoe, and bairns crying because they couldn't see, and tugging at their parents' sleeves. And *she* looked so beautiful, she was standing on tiptoe too, and Pa put his arm round her womanly waist to raise her up a bit, and she put her hand on his shoulder (his dependable shoulder), and he smiled down at her excitement and enthusiasm —but her eyes were all for the river.

Then the music started, though God knows where the band was in that rammy, and it played quickly and insistently *Deutschland über Alles Die Strasse Frei Die Reihen Fest Geschlossen Fridericus Rex Fest Steht Und Treu Die Wacht Am Rhein* and, yes, *Freude Schöner Götterfunken* it played, and it played, the brass sounds, pied piper music, the oompah ballooning over the thousands of heads.

And then *He* came.

'Oh can you see him, can you see him?' cried the girl.

But Pa could see nothing: he heard—

'Look, there! There! Yes he is! No. See him? Yes! No. Yes! *Sieg heil! Sieg heil!* Over there, see? As I see you. What a day! Wait till I tell auntie Sophie, she'll never believe. . . . What's that? There. There! Look! *Sieg heil! Sieg heil!* There he goes! That's him! That's our man! Just an ordinary working bloke like you and me—now he's leading the whole country. Yes, that's socialism for you. What a man! *Sieg heil!* Die for him I would, just lie down and bloody die! Do anything for him, anything! Daddy daddy lift me up! *Sieg heil!* All he'd need to say would be, Max (that's me), Max, would you give your life for your people?—and I'd say. . . Look look look he's looking at me! At me! At me! At me! *Führer! Führer!* . . . Do anything for him I would—'

'Ooooooooooh!'

—And his girl was crying, tears were pouring down her face and she was screaming, clenching her fists in front of her breasts, and all the schoolgirls were going delirious. Pa was bewildered, shocked. Never had he seen anything like this. Americans, groping for an explanation, likened it to the performance of the Holy Rollers at religious revival meetings in the Appalachians. Pa's nearest experience was of a football crowd bawling 'Kill the fuckin Fenians!'—but the crowd had been men, men and nothing but men, ill-educated working men and full of beer at that. These folk were different. These well-off, educated, sober folk were going out of their minds, and why and how he simply did not know. And the women! The women were the worst. He was shocked, *shocked* by the behaviour of the women, Pa who subsequently thought mini-skirts were immoral and that strippers should be banned for inciting lust.

Weialala leia.

Then he saw *Him*. A tiny brown mannikin standing in the prow of a little white steamer that went chug chug chug and vanished out of sight. And that was *Him*.

Wallala leialala

And he heard—

'Did you see him? Oh yes! As I see you! The greatest day of my life! The way he was standing there. So strong. So tall. So proud. So erect. It makes you proud! Makes you feel great! The centre of the universe! Oh God! I'm going to faint. The greatest day of my life! Die for him I would. Bloody marvellous! Just wait till I tell the folks back home! Die for him I would. Did you get a picture? Feel so proud. Greatest day of my life—'

And she was sighing and shuddering and her eyes were dreamy and distant, and Pa trembled when she touched him and moved away, but she didn't notice, she wasn't thinking about him, and Pa didn't want to touch her or be touched by her ever again—Pa who subsequently was to say that The Beatles were just a bunch of fascists.

All women love a fascist, he thought.

I don't think he ever trusted a woman again after that, not completely—not even Ma.

As the crowd was dispersing he saw the band. Brownshirt boys with those torches. The torches shone over the waters of the Rhine in the gathering darkness

burning burning burning burning

as the boys goosestepped off. Crash bang wallop. It's an impressive/repulsive thing, the goosestep—like the Red Square parade Pa always refused to look at on the telly saying that it was bad because it was bad, *and* bad because the Tories would use it as propaganda against socialism. And the schoolgirls who had just had national socialist orgasms for Hitler (one of them actually *had* fainted and was being carried away on a stretcher) looked

143

doe-eyed at the stamping boys, and the boys knew it, and they expanded their chests and stamped even louder.

—as they would stamp into Austria and Czechoslovakia and Poland, and the Second World War

—and the girls would love it and wave their little flags, their little red flags, and comb their golden hair.

<blockquote>
burning burning
All women love a fascist
la la
</blockquote>

Gladly my cross-eyed bear

burning.

Pa crossed to the west bank of the Rhine alone.

On A Winter's Night A Traveller

The year they started running convoys to Murmansk, they were showing Noel Coward's *In Which We Serve* in the pictures. Ma and Stanislaus sat watching it. She translated for him and he nodded. Noel Coward had given up his silk dressing-gown for a naval officer's uniform. He led his destroyer flotilla against the Germans. It was surprisingly good. John Mills and Richard Attenborough were among the crew. Richard Attenborough got killed. John Mills's home was blitzed by a bomb. Stanislaus nodded his head: yes, yes, he knew people just like that. Even when the survivors of the sunken ship, clinging to a raft, sang 'Roll out the barrel' he nodded: yes, yes, men did that. Ma trembled.

Outside, the skies were quiet, the streets were drab. The war was very far away from Edinburgh. The only vapour trails in the sky were British, there was no accompanying rat-a-tat-tat of machine-guns fired a minute before, no desperately wounded men drifting downwards on parachutes, though sometimes a limping vessel came in to Leith, a torpedoed minesweeper, a mined torpedo boat, a submarine battered by depth charges, and the ambulances would be waiting. German prisoners were kept in Donaldson's Hospital where other German prisoners had been kept the war before, and they were surrounded with barbed-wire and guarded by reservists with loaded rifles and fixed bayonets, because some of the Germans were fanatics who might do God knows what, though none ever did. And there were Italian prisoners kept out in the Lothians, and they were surrounded by farmyard mesh and guarded by elderly men not up to much else, because the Italians were amiable peasants with little understanding of the war, and local children came and sat

145

outside the mesh and pushed sweets through the wire to the Italians.

The first Americans appeared in Edinburgh in 1942, self-sure free-and-easy men, and more Canadians, and many more Poles guarding Scotland's east coast. And wherever they went, these foreigners, but above all the Americans in their smart uniforms, the imp sex would jump up, and the girls giggle at each other and at them, and, and . . . And, said the disgruntled British soldiers in their ugly khaki boiler-suits, it only takes one Yank to get them down. But the war was far away. There were only the closed and shuttered little shops, the notices saying 'No cigarettes', 'No eggs today', 'No chocolate', the big Victory V posters, a huge foot hitting a spade and a caption saying 'Dig For Victory'. And Ma took the bus every day from Corstorphine in to Princes Street, and from Princes Street down to Canonmills where the office was, and at lunchtime she went to the corner tea shop, now long gone, with other women from the office and nearby offices, and women from the munitions works in head-scarves and dungarees, and they talked about their men overseas, and about rations and babies and films and the wireless, and about their men overseas.

That year—because Hitler and Stalin had fallen out, and Hitler had attacked Stalin—they began sending convoys up round the north of Norway to Soviet Murmansk.

To Noroway, to Noroway, to Noroway owre the faem, to the place of snow and fir trees and the midnight sun, where German U-boats lay sheltered in fjords Viking longships had once known, bombers crouched in readiness on airfields strategically placed by the North Cape, and fearsome surface raiders with haunting names, *Scharnhorst, Tirpitz, Lützow, Admiral Hipper, Admiral Scheer*, lay in Tromso fjord and in Alten fjord waiting for the convoys to come. And as the convoys assembled in their various ports, in Chesapeake and Halifax, in Liverpool and the Clyde, as the destroyer escorts waited to take them into waters where it was an equal death to be burnt by a homing torpedo or frozen alive in the Arctic Sea, the chaplains of the ships and the ministers of the convoy and navy ports (Edinburgh's port of Leith among them) prayed 'For those who go down to the sea in ships', as their Latin-chanting predecessors had once prayed of a scourge from these same fjords, '*Ex furore Normanorum, libera nos Domine*' ('From the fury of the Norsemen, Lord deliver us'). But they were poor pale butterflies, these English prayers that fluttered over the oil-slicked waters, for the days of avenging angels were over, and if God's heaven ever did exist then it too was a shuttered shop ruined by the war with a notice saying 'No prayers answered any more' hung over the door.

What a frozen inferno they went into, those seamen who brought Sherman tanks and Ford trucks, crates of canned beef and bottled beer, to aid Stalin's Red Army, Ivan, though you weren't born then and neither was I. But your father, what was he doing? In his slit-trench in Stalingrad, was it, or at Smolensk, or perhaps before the very gates of Moscow, did he think the time would come when his son would be pointing missiles more devastating each one than all the bombs and shells of that whole war put together at the folk who had risked so much to bring him the bully beef in his stomach, the bullets in his rifle?

And did either of my parents foresee Polaris and Trident, the Holy Loch and Faslane? . . .

For landsmen soldiers and for soldiers' folk the war had moved away south and east, the threat of invasion receded until it was not believed in any more, and after the heroic year 1940—the exciting year of Dunkirk and The Few when people waited with pokers and with garden forks for the Nazi paratroopers to come swarming down—the cities of Britain became grey, careworn and depressed places. Patriotic cries now urged folk, not to fight them on the beaches and on the landing-fields, but to 'save fuel', 'save paper', 'save water' and 'waste nothing'; and while some soldiers and airmen were sent to the African desert or to the jungles of Burma, many more spent their time in scattered garrisons across three continents beyond the enemy's ken, or trained on and on interminably in gale-blown camps in York-shire and wandered their leave away in the streets of provincial towns wondering what on earth to do with themselves.

But not so the seamen. For them the war front was on the shingle beach—or as near to it as a U-boat torpedo could come. The war was very far from Edinburgh, but for the folk of seafaring men it was no further than the Granton and Newhaven shores. Small ships had died silhouetted against incautious

147

coastal lights, the mighty battleship *Royal Oak* had heeled over and drowned eight hundred of her crew less than half a mile from the hills of Orkney. Whenever a man was on the sea his folk had to wonder—would today be the death of him?

Then in 1942 they began sending convoys to Murmansk. Stanislaus went with them, and before he left on each convoy she wondered, sailor's woman, would she ever see him again?

It was in remote Loch Ewe that the Murmansk convoys finally assembled. Macleod of Lewis had once ruled the stony lands that curved round it between the Minch and long Loch Maree, disputing it with a Macdonell of Glengarry in times long gone. From there the coast sweeps eastward to Loch Broom, to Ullapool of the fishers, the herring and the mackerel hunters, syne north to Lochinver and Enard, Eddrachillis Bay, the slopes of Ben Stack, and finally Sutherland, the *Duthaich MacAoidh* there in the wasted north whence the convoys now sailed to fuel the fight at Stalingrad. Northwards ever northwards went those ships and all their men, past the Faeroes and Iceland, Jan Mayen and Bear Island, the southern tip of Spitzbergen (where the Snow Queen's palace is), to the Murman coast and Kola, and Archangel on the far White Sea. Richard Chancellor once sailed these waters in Elizabeth Tudor's time; his Muscovy Company brought goods to Ivan the Terrible. Now to Stalin went these precious convoys. And Stanislaus, a Pole who hated Stalin as he hated Hitler, went with them through seas high as houses and the glaring blue white and green of the floating pack-ice.

In the early evening Ma did her morning's journey in reverse, returning home to quiet Corstorphine, to the crazy pavements, bird-baths and terracotta gnomes. If it was not her fire-watching night, she sat knitting in by the hearth, and her mother sat knitting there too, knitting knitting, and her father sat smoking his pipe. Ma cried a little when she talked about her parents: they had both been killed the day after Hitler died in ruins because a lorry swerved to avoid a dog on Corstorphine Road. They sat there, anyway, and clack clack went the needles, and they listened to the wireless. There was Tommy Handley with the *ITMA* show, and London Pride has been handed down to us—London was still 'taking it' seemingly—the Brains Trust, German wavelengths (furtively) for good music, Lord Haw

Haw for a laugh, and Vera Lynn singing, 'We'll meet again, don't know where, don't know when—

But we're bound to meet again some sunny da-aay.'

And there in the armchair in warm, safe sleepy hollow, with a picture of Churchill on one wall, and a picture of the King and Queen on the other, and a grandfather clock tick-tocking somnolently in between, Ma thought fondly and anxiously about her Polish boy who, unknown to her, was already dead in his coffin ship at the bottom of the Arctic Sea.

On a winter's night of that year a traveller came to the door. He was also a Polish sailor. He told her about it. She hadn't known the details. 'Missing, presumed dead at sea', seemed gentle, almost—like falling asleep. He told her about the ship he had survived, and Stanislaus had not. 'But perhaps I should say no more,' he said, sitting with a teacup and saucer on his knees, sitting uncomfortably on the edge of the armchair by the hearth. She insisted. And so he told her . . .

In the stormy Arctic night the U-boats had attacked on the surface, and the Royal Marine gunners had fired and loaded, fired and loaded in the darkness, and the escorting destroyers had careered past them—nothing romantic about these ships passing in the night—and there was a chattering of machine-guns from somewhere, then a flash and a tanker leaping into flames. Then a destroyer had rammed a U-boat, and the submarine rolled over and sank in seconds—not a Hun got out of it, he said fiercely, no they were all trapped like rats in a sewer, struggling, screaming in the darkness of tiny upside-down compartments as the water poured in, and they tried to keep their mouths above the water, in the last few inches above the water, till the water reached the iron ceiling which was the upside-down deck, and they died, the dirty Bosches, they died.

—We give as good as we take, he said. But then . . .

The sudden crash of the torpedo sent men sprawling everywhere. The ship didn't blow up, no, nothing red and dramatic like that, because they (thank God) weren't carrying petrol or ammunition, they were carrying foodstuffs mainly, crates of bully beef cans, and chocolate and cigarettes from America; so

149

when the torpedo struck they didn't blow up, but it tore a terrible hole in the ship, and the ship shuddered, and things tore loose and fell crashing about them as tons of seawater poured into the bilges. Then the damage control party worked in the bowels of the ship, and Stanislaus was in that party, he said, wielding torches and axes and fire-extinguishers, pulling hurt bleeding men free of the wreckage, and hammering shoring timbers into place where watertight doors had cracked and jolted with the blow. And they were thinking, the Poles and Britons and Americans of the crew, they were thinking—We're going to make it, they were thinking—Supper tomorrow in Murmansk, they were thinking they were going to live after all, when the second torpedo came at them and then—

(They took the teacup and saucer out of his shaking hands) And then—

(He put his face in his hands; he spoke words in Polish; they didn't understand what he said) And then—

they thought they were going to live, but— there was this sudden flash up the sides and the iron plates from the hull flew inwards and it was strange because there must have been an explosion but he didn't hear anything he just saw the iron plates flying inwards in slow motion and one of the iron plates took off a man's head and the man's head flew away just as slowly and his headless body stood there spurting blood and then it crumpled and that was odd wouldn't you think because it must all have occurred within a second and yet it seemed to take so long and not until the headless body hit the ground did he hear a single thing and then—

They screamed. The steam lines were severed, and the engine room was suddenly full of scalding steam escaping at high pressure, and how men died in the engine room is best not known, but they screamed.

(At night I can still hear them screaming, said the man) and everything went dark inside the ship, and he was fighting his way through festoons of electric cables, over broken glass and crockery and splintered wood, and there was a door jammed and men were pounding on the other side of the door and couldn't get out, and the deck heaved, and he clambered up a ladder—or maybe it was down a ladder—and there were pools of blood, in the light of the burning he could see the red pools on the deck that were running towards the walls as the deck heaved—and the crates in the hold broke loose and tumbled over one another, and there was screaming and screaming as the crates smashed into men and crushed them—and there was a moment when he thought how silly it was, men dying like that under all those cans of beef and cartons of chocolate and cigarettes bound for Russia—

And then—

He was walking on the sea. Yes. And there was Stanislaus. Yes. He was walking on the sea too: with a face of ashes. Then the wreckage they were on sank, and Stanislaus sank, and he and another man held Stanislaus as they floundered in the water, beating the top of the undulating oil slick, trying to get free of the ship before she went down. Then there was an explosion, splinters came like flying sawblades, bodies were blasted that had survived so long, and with a hiss of steam and quenched fires followed by a hollow roaring sound as of a great waterfall, their ship went under in a welter of foam, and Stanislaus, who was already dead, went with her—the ship sucked him back like a jealous mother, and only a few survivors were left, clinging to splintered rafts and wreckage on top of the Arctic waves.

On a winter's night the traveller left, with their thanks, with their kind wishes, their regards. He goes out of this story. The three sat alone in the silence of their living-room.

Tick-tock, said the grandfather clock slowly. *Tick-tock*.

Ma said she was looking forward to the spring. She wanted to see the garden in flower again. She was looking forward to the flowers.

It was Saturday night. On Sunday morning the three of them took their wee black Bibles and went to the kirk as usual. On the way back Ma was still talking about flowers.

Her parents hadn't really approved of Stanislaus when he was alive. They were sorry now. 'He was a nice boy,' said her mother. 'A decent sort,' said her father. 'I'd like to plant grape hyacinths,' said Ma, 'along the edge of the path there.'

They went home.

They ate a silent dinner.

They listened to the wireless.

They went to their different beds.

Ah well.

Everything passes in time, everything. Even hurts as big as that one. Oddly, Ma didn't think of Stanislaus moving on that ship, fighting for life. She saw only his dead face—immobile. She thought about the German submariners choking as the U-boat turned upside-down and sank.

Ma went to work. She did her turn fire-watching. She went to the pictures. She talked casually to a few boys, but she preferred to go alone. She saw Johnny Weissmuller as Tarzan, she saw *Casablanca* and *The Maltese Falcon*, *The Scarlet Pimpernel* and *Pimpernel Smith*. She read romances by Georgette Heyer. Her girlfriends worried about her.

She listened to the wireless—and out of the crackling meshed box came the fruity voice of the BBC announcer telling her that we were fighting a Good War against Hitler and his Nazi gang, telling her that fascism and racism were awful wicked things that had to be FOUGHT, had to be rooted out, destroyed, wiped from the face of the earth, they were so wicked.

Listened again—and out came the honest man's voice of a Labour politician, pacifist in the last war, minister of heavy machine-gun production in this, telling her that pacifism had been all right when he was liable for call-up because the Kaiser's Germans hadn't been *that* bad, but it was downright sinful now that he was too old for call-up because Hitler's Germans were just a lot of dirty fascists, and fascism had to be FOUGHT, the Germans had to have the guts machine-gunned out of them for their own good, he said.

She listened again—and out came the timid and eager to please voice of some parson or other who said that wars were so awfully unpleasant and upsetting as a rule, but still this one had to be FOUGHT because the Germans were even more awfully unpleasant and upsetting, and God was really cross with the Germans, and it was rather nice to hear Our Boys marching off to the killing whistling Onward Christian Soldiers, and he hoped that they would remember not to have anything to do with loose women when they got there because that would spoil the anti-fascist crusade something awful it would.

And Ma heard all the good reasonable logical arguments that were put forward by decent men in favour of the killing, and she couldn't understand them, they came out twisted and ugly, because she only saw her dead Polish boy, and the German submariners choking as they drowned; and so she cried *It's all nonsense, nonsense! What has it all got to do with the likes of us?* And the wireless had no answer for her.

Her father, a Royal Scot of 1916, gassed at Passchendaele, said that Hitler was different, he *had* to be got rid of; but why boys had to drown in the sea to do it, he didn't know. Her mother thought it was all sad and miserable and hoped it would soon be over, when Britain would be a much better place and the lights would go on again all over the world with peace ever after, just like the song said. But these were wet coals, and Ma could light no fire with them.

What would you have thought of the Falklands, Ma, I wonder? Of the sinking *Sheffield* and *Coventry*, of the men who died on the *Sir Galahad*, of the Argentinians on the *Belgrano*? Of the battles for Goose Green and Stanley, and why they had to be fought? Would you have understood it any better than I can?

How Ugly He Is

On the west bank of the Rhine, opposite the peaks of the Seven Hills, stands the town of Bonn which in 1936 was no more than a small university city. On the east bank is the industrial suburb of Beuel. Tourists don't go to Beuel: they stay on the west bank and take photographs of the cathedral tower and the Kreuzberg kirk. Pa walked along the Rhine front past big big houses and palaces built by the aristocracy of the nineteenth century overlooking the river.

Bonn used to be a Roman army camp, Castra Bonnensia they cried it, Caesar's legionaries who came here to defend their empire and civilization, and to capture Germans for the slave markets in Rome. When God spake unto the Roman general Constantine and told him that He would help him win his battles and the coveted imperial crown and kill all who stood in his way if he became a Christian—and when Constantine hearkened unto the Word of God, took baptism, and did indeed win all his battles and became emperor in Rome over the bodies of those who had opposed him—then, legend insists, the new emperor's gentle old mother, Helena, built a Christian kirk in Bonn and dedicated it to Cassius and Florentius, two soldiers of the Theban legion, who had become Christians in the days of persecution and refused orders to kill and enslave because their new religion forbade it, and suffered martyrdom accordingly. Whether lady Helena meant any criticism of her bold son who was now happily killing and enslaving away in the name of gentle Jesus prince of peace, is not known. Every century or so Bonn is burnt to the ground by rampaging Christians who are affronted with the place. The worst burning to date was in 1689 when it was burnt, not by the French, though the French burnt absolutely everything else in sight, but by the Prussians because, while Bonn was anti-French, it wasn't anti-French enough: so they burnt it, and when the French got there with their matches ready for a bonfire, they found only ashes.

Bonn University in the nineteenth century heard the lectures of the famous German nationalist professor Ernst Moritz Arndt, who preferred the Prussians to the French because it is better to be burnt by bastards who speak your own language than by bastards who don't, he said. It also heard Schlegel who lectured on Shakespeare; Hertz who investigated radio waves; and Argelander who listed 324,198 stars in the northern sky. The day Pa was in Bonn, the university was giving a series of public lectures on the social, moral, cultural and hygienic inferiority of the Jews, proving, with a great deal of witty evidence, that Jews are actually a naked ape species who have no connection with the human race at all. These lectures were very well attended by students who spoke several languages and had read a lot of paperback books and magazine articles about politics and sociology.

Pa was on pilgrimage. He wasn't going to the cathedral or to the Kreuzberg, he wasn't going to see the Roman remains, he wasn't going to the university. He was going to the house of a Flemish alcoholic who had fathered Ludwig van Beethoven in 1770.

In the town of Bonn lived two young men—let me call them Fritz and Kurt. They weren't students, and neither of them had ever heard of Schlegel, Hertz or Argelander. They came from industrial Beuel on the other side of the Rhine and they were both socialists. Fritz was twenty-six. He had worked as a porter in the railway station, and then for a firm of decorators. He had once gone over to Bonn to hang wallpaper in a private house as big as a block of flats. The house had a balcony just above the river and the family who lived in it sat out there in the summer for their Sunday dinner, and the young ones played tennis in the garden. Fritz had never played tennis. The firm went bust in the depression and Fritz lost his job. He couldn't get another one. Neither could his mates. They hung about all day. The men went over the bridge to Bonn and tried to beg. Their sisters went on the streets. Fritz stood outside the railway station in Bonn. He shuffled his feet and kept his eyes on the ground. He said, 'Excuse me, sir, but can you give a fellow German the price of something to eat?'—and touched his cap.

Kurt was twenty-two. When he'd left school there had been no job for him. Luckily his Pa was still working. His Pa was a window-cleaner and some days he had to work over the river in Bonn where folk could still afford to pay window-cleaners. Sometimes Kurt took his Pa's piece over to him. The rich folk in the big posh houses by the Rhine wanted clean windows so they could see the Seven Hills. Kurt thought that all the rich folk were probably Jews.

One day, when Kurt was seventeen and Fritz was twenty-one, there was a meeting in Beuel. A speaker was standing on the back of a lorry addressing the crowd through a megaphone. He was surrounded by a group of tall, strong-looking young men, and each man was wearing a brown shirt, brown breeches, black leather boots, and a red armband—and each had a gun. Kurt thought they were the most beautiful sight he had ever seen in his life. The speaker told the crowd that these men had all been unemployed and apathetic and careworn, but at last they had decided to act; they had stood up, they now looked people straight in the eye, they had joined the revolutionary struggle of the masses against Jewish-capitalist oppression: they were stormtroopers. Fritz was impressed. He and Kurt both joined that same day. They learned military drill and discipline. They wore the brown uniform. They had red armbands with black swastikas on them. Girls, who had wanted nothing to do with them before, now looked at them admiringly.

Fritz married and his wife gave him two fair-haired daughters. He was longing for a son so they could go fishing together and play football, and things like that. He had a dog too. Some weekends they went on trips through the Seven Hills and people saluted Fritz in his brown uniform. He read his daughters to sleep with fairy tales about Snow White and dwarves in dark forests. He was a kind father, if a little rough. Kurt hadn't married yet, but he planned to marry a rich widow or something of the sort one day, and live in comfort in a big posh house by the Rhine. At present he was being a virilely unfaithful lover to about six different girls. One of them was pregnant, but he had no

intention of marrying her. When her father came round to
bluster him, Kurt stood with his brown legs apart in their
creaking, gleaming black boots, tucked his thumbs into his black
belt, and grinned. The cowed father slunk away. No one could
use shotgun tactics on a stormtrooper.

Eighteen months after they had joined the Brownshirts, phase
one of the National Revolution occurred. This was 'The Seizure
of Power'. On the thirtieth of January, 1933, Comrade Hitler
became Chancellor of the Republic—admittedly with the help of
some right-wing middle-class rubbish, but they were going to
get the chop pretty soon, as everyone knew. Stormtroopers from
all over Germany went to Berlin for the victory march. Fritz and
Kurt were part of the Bonn contingent. By torchlight they
tramped under the Brandenburg Gate and down the Wilhelm-
strasse singing the Horst Wessel Song—

> *Die Fahne hoch, die Reihen fest geschlossen*
> Up with the flag, close the ranks . . .

singing,

> *Wir sind die Revolution der Armen,*
> We are the Revolution of the poor,
> *Wir kämpfen um Freiheit und Brot*
> We fight for freedom and bread . . .

They tramped past all the big palaces and ministries singing their
revolutionary marching songs, and they crowed that soon there
would be no classes in Germany, just comrades in a people's
community. Kurt picked up a girl on the Kurfürstendamm. Fritz
did all right too. Then they got the train back to Bonn.

In Bonn and Beuel they were kept busy. They ate and slept in
the stormtroopers' barracks. They entered public buildings—
libraries, offices, hospitals, schools, things of that sort—saying,
'National Revolution, comrades! Jews out!' They went to Jewish
shops and took anything they wanted. If the shopkeeper objected
they beat him up, then took money and gifts from him not to beat
him up worse. They patrolled just like polismen, and when they
were on patrol they carried rifles. One day they beat up a trade
unionist who refused to be 'co-ordinated' into the new Workers'
Front. They beat him up with coshes and flung him into the river.

When he began to drown Fritz hauled him out, and they kicked him in the stomach until all the water was out of him. Then they swaggered off leaving him unconscious on the pavement with a notice pinned to his jacket saying PEOPLE'S JUSTICE. They did this in broad daylight. Nobody objected. Nobody did anything. Several people even applauded them.

On another occasion they arrested a schoolteacher who was a social democrat. He taught German literature and wrote verses in imitation of Heine. A girl in his class had told her parents that he had spoken highly of Erich Maria Remarque's pacifist novel *All Quiet On The Western Front* which was now banned, and her parents reported it to the stormtroops. That's why they arrested him. They kept him for three days in the barracks and made him stand to attention facing the wall. If he moved they beat him. They made him clean the lavatory. They made him clean it again and again and again until it shone. They made him wash his hands in the toilet bowl. When he began to cry, they made him stand at attention again and say by rote, 'Remarque's a pacifist scum. Heine's a Jewish louse. My mother's a whore, my father's a pimp—and I'm not worth a turd in the gutter.' And if he got a word wrong they would beat him. Sometimes Fritz would interrupt him and shout, 'What is Heine?', and the man would answer, 'A Jewish louse.' 'What is your mother?', and the man would answer, 'A whore.' 'Louder!' 'A WHORE!' 'What's the name of the dirty pimp that shagged her?', and the man would name his own father. On and on, and if he hesitated for as much as a second, Kurt would lash at him with his cosh. They made him strip naked in front of some streetwalkers. The prostitutes jeered at him. One of them wrote obscenities in lipstick on his thin pimply body. Fritz and Kurt both laughed until they hurt. Finally they got the man to sign a declaration saying that he had been very well treated in the hands of the People's Justice and that he had seen the error of his ways. Then they released him. The educational authority sacked the man that same day for 'besmirching the honour of the profession'. A few days later his body was fished out of the river. Verdict, suicide. When they heard, neither Fritz nor Kurt gave a damn. Almost certainly that night Kurt was making love to a new girl. Almost certainly that night Fritz was telling his daughters a story about Snow White.

Pa walked past a newsagent's with bright red advertising boards and turned into a little street called the Bonngasse and sought out number 20. It was a modest house flush on to the street standing beside Jos. Hesse, Watchmakers. Jos. Hesse had a large clock hanging over his door. The hands stood at 2.30. Pa crossed to the other side of the narrow street and stood looking at the Beethovenhouse. It had a big double door on the right hand side and a window on the left. The window had wooden shutters folded back against the wall. On the first floor were two windows, on the second floor two more. Two smaller windows sat in the tiles of the sloping roof. They had all painted wooden shutters folded back, and window boxes at each spilled flowers down the wall.

Pa thought that Beethoven was the greatest musical genius who had ever lived. Compared to him, Brahms, Bach and Handel were so many silly wee laddies playing on penny whistles, and the rock and roll I fancied was the howling of barbarians outside the gates. Beethoven and Shakespeare stood together on the pinnacle of human achievement, as far as Pa was concerned. He would tell me various tales about how the Tories—those wicked creatures—had tried to kidnap both men; of how they had claimed that Shakespeare's plays had been written by a Sir this or Duke of that; of how they had put it about (a deliberate plot, no less) that Beethoven was an aristocrat because of the 'van' in his name, though actually the Beethovens were Flemish peasants in origin and their name means merely folk 'from the beet fields'; of how the Tories had then claimed Beethoven was a bastard son of the King of Prussia. Pa roared with laughter and anger both when he told me that—Beethoven son of some pisspot king! 'They're afraid to admit a common man can have genius—and that's because they're down on the working people!' Yes, Pa.

Then Pa saw something else. Because of the sun, Jos. Hesse had the sunshades pulled out above his windows full of watches, and in the shadow of one of these shades an old man was sitting on the pavement. He was in rags and he had a white beard. He was the first beggar Pa had seen in Germany. You saw them often enough in Britain, but not in Germany. Pa crossed the street.

159

The man was a few feet from the door of the Beethovenhouse. People's Justice had not yet passed the law which would require all Jews to wear yellow stars. The law had, however, deprived them of German citizenship, it prevented them from marrying gentiles, it excluded them from public office, the civil service, the stock exchange, journalism, teaching, farming, radio, theatre, and films. And because they were no longer German citizens, they had no defence against those shopkeepers who hung signs saying 'No Jews Allowed' on their doors, 'Jews Not Admitted', 'Jews Not Wanted In This Shop'. A known Jew, and there were always those who knew you, might find that not only did he have no job and no prospect of ever getting one again, but that he had no income at all, no pension, no benefit—from all of which he, as a Jew, had been excluded—and no means of support except whatever savings he might have that had not been wiped out in the economic depression. Even then many shopkeepers wouldn't serve him. And when his savings were gone—? Why, he could starve. And the old man was starving.

Suddenly every horror story Pa had ever read about Hitler's Reich—and the British press had been heavy with them for years—came flocking back to him. He felt Gestapo eyes popping out of every window and door. Then he checked himself and laughed, there on the street. 'Ach, a load of blethers,' he said. He dug his hand into his pocket and fished out all the coins he found in it. He dropped them in the old man's lap. Furtively the old man keeked up at him. He wasn't rheumy-eyed and smelling of stale drink like a British tramp. He had the look of an intelligent man fallen on hard times, very hard times. '*Danke*' ('Thanks'), he said. A woman came out of Hesse the watchmakers. She began to talk angrily. Pa was in no mood to talk back. 'I'm a foreigner,' he said in German. 'I don't understand.' The clock above the pavement was at 2.37.

Pa went into the Beethovenhouse.

At 2.38 Fritz and Hurt swung into the Bonngasse from the other end. They were talking about the Olympic Games. Germany was harvesting all the medals, which was as it should be. Except for the dirty stunt the Jewish Yankees had pulled with that nigger, Jesse Owens. They had found him swinging through the trees in some jungle somewhere, given him a good shave, fed him up, and doped the poor chimp till he took off like a rocket and scored four golds. Fucking Yanks with their lousy fucking tricks. It was all because the Jewish millionaires who owned America hated the German Socialism ever since it had blown the gaff on their plot to rule the world. The capitalists wanted to make the whole world just one big America where the working folk lived in shanty towns and slums while the Jew bosses lived in palaces and raped workers' wives and daughters beside their swimming pools. That was what America was like, and it wasn't going to happen here, not if Fritz and Kurt had anything to do with it it wasn't.

They were neither of them in a particularly good mood. They hadn't been for the past month, despite the holiday weather. Not since the Troop Leader had paraded the lads one morning and told them that for the next few weeks they were going to be on their best behaviour. The country was going to be full of foreigners flocking in to see the big Games with their cameras and what not, so he didn't want any of his lads having a bit of fun with a Kike in the street and then some damn Yank tourist taking a little snapshot of it and saying, 'Gee, Wilbur, jest wait till we show *this* to the folks back home!', and then some damn Jew newspaper in Los Angeles or New York using it to colour up its next bleeding heart propaganda bleat against the National Revolution. So for the next few weeks they were just going to dance round the Jews like a lot of fucking ballerinas. They were going to treat them like they were made of bone china. It was going to be, Yes sir, Mister Jew, three bags full sir, Mister Jew—and that was national orders from The Man Himself, get it? They got it. The 'No Jews' signs came down. The 'Beware of the Jew, it bites', and other nice slogans they liked to paint on Jewish windows were washed off.

'They'll have us eating fucking kosher matzos next,' said Fritz to Kurt.

'Yeah, fucking right,' said Kurt.

Then they saw the woman on the pavement under the clock. She was waving to them. They could see her expression. There was 'outraged citizen' written all over it. Heigho. Both men quickened their step.

'Anything the matter, comrade?' said Kurt from ten yards away.

There was. There was a Jew on the pavement. The old man was crouched up shielding himself with his arms. The woman had been hitting him with her handbag.

'He tried to rob you, did he, comrade?' said Fritz hopefully, eyeing the old man.

'I saw a foreigner giving him money,' said the woman.

'Oh, did you,' said Kurt, prodding the old man with his boot.

'Just like that,' said the woman, 'in public! It was disgusting,' she said. 'I mean, what are the authorities going to do about it? Having some dirty old Jew lying about on the street with all his dirt and germs, and then some foreigner giving him money so he can just lounge around like that all day. It's disgusting!' she said. 'Disgusting!'

'And where did the foreigner go?' said Fritz.

She pointed to the door of the Beethovenhouse.

'Right. We'll take care of it,' said Fritz.

'I mean, I was just so disgusted,' said the woman. 'What is this, America or something? Dirty Jew!' she said. She spat on the old man.

Kurt grinned.

'We'll take care of it, comrade,' said Fritz. 'Just you go home now.'

He watched the woman until she was out of sight.

'Anyone coming?' said Kurt.

'Nope,' said Fritz. He turned and looked up the street. 'Nope,' he said.

Kurt kicked the old man savagely on the shins.

'Fucking Yid,' he said. 'Fucking dirty fucking Yid.' He kicked the old man again.

'Being paid by a foreign journalist, was you?' said Fritz. 'Telling him all sorts of lies about the National Revolution, was you?'

No, no, said the old man. He tried to shield his legs. Kurt kicked him again.

'Maybe he thought you was his long lost brother,' said Fritz.

'Maybe he fancies you,' said Kurt.

'Slipping him one, was you?' said Fritz.

'Giving him a wank, was you?' said Kurt.

'Let's see the colour of the fucking money then,' said Fritz.

'Stand up when you're fucking spoken to, Jewboy,' said Kurt. He dragged the old man to his feet and tore the coat off his back. The coins jangled onto the pavement and rolled about.

'Clumsy Jew,' said Fritz.

'Clumsy, clumsy Jew,' said Kurt.

The old man kneeled down and picked the coins up one by one.

'Please don't hit me any more, sirs,' he said. He handed the coins to Fritz. There was about ten marks in small change.

'Now you know what I'm going to do with this?' said Fritz in a very reasonable voice.

'Yes sir,' said the old man.

'Confiscate it in the name of the People's Community, ain't I?' said Fritz.

'Yes sir,' said the old man.

Kurt gave a snort of laughter.

'Aw, what a clever little Jewboy,' he said.

'And you haven't got anything bad to say about us, have you, Moses?' said Fritz. Kurt stamped on the old man's foot. The old man whimpered.

'Have you, Solly?' said Kurt.

'No sir,' said the old man.

'So fuck off, Jewboy,' said Fritz.

Kurt was still standing on the old man's foot.

'Why don't you fuck off, Jewboy?' said Fritz.

'Please sir—,' said the old man. He tried to drag his foot out from under Kurt's boot, and fell down.

The two young men laughed.

'On your feet, Yid, you're making the place look untidy,' said Kurt.

The old man staggered to his feet.

'Now fuck *off*,' said Fritz. 'And don't expect to be so lucky next time.'

The old man turned to go.

'At the double!' shouted Fritz. 'Huphuphuphup—'

The old man couldn't run, but he hobbled as fast as he could.

The two stormtroopers looked up and down the street. The

few pedestrians who caught their glances hurriedly looked away and walked on.

'I fucking needed that,' said Kurt. 'I feel a better fucking man.'

'Now let's sort out the fucking Jew-lover,' said Fritz.

They drew their coshes. As they went through the doors of the Beethovenhouse, Kurt began to whistle—'The Ode To Joy'. Quite coincidentally. He hadn't got a clue who the composer was.

The clock said 2.51.

Pa signed the visitors' register. He bought four picture post-cards at the little counter shop. He asked where the Birthroom was. He was told. He knew he would begin there.

In 1770, when Ludwig van Beethoven was born, three families lived in the house on the Bonngasse. On the ground and first floors lived that of Herr Clasen who owned the building and was a well-to-do maker of gold lace at the court of the Prince Bishop in nearby Cologne. Above the Clasens on the second floor lived the family of one Herr Salomon, musician at the court of the same Prince Bishop, whose violinist son, Johann Peter, achieved lasting and deserved rest in the cloisters of Westminster Abbey. This was the prosperous part of the house. Now there was a third family, and they lived at the back in a small wing of rooms built over the garden. Years before, in 1733, the then Prince Bishop, Clemens August, whilst on his travels, had stopped by a kirk in Flanders, the Flemingland: aye, and some say it was at Liege, and some say it was at Louvain, and there he heard a singer in the choir whose voice impressed him so much that he asked the Fleming to join his service. And so a certain young Louis van Beethoven, who came from a long line of quiet shopkeepers and peasant farmers scattered from Antwerp to the Forest of Arden, journeyed heroically to Bonn in Germany on a waggon piled high with all his worldly goods, like some poor Siegfried come to claim his modest bride, and he never saw his native Flanders again, I suppose. And now the entire house, in the poorest part of which he and his had once been hungry lodgers, is named after his grandson, an ugly runt of a bairn who became that great Ludwig van Beethoven whose bric-à-brac and manuscripts fill all the rooms, while the Clasens and Salomons and their riches have vanished behind the veil of time. And, had he not paused perchance to get out of the rain in a Flemish kirk one day, Clemens August, Prince, Elector, patron of the arts, Lord of the Lower Rhine, Archbishop of Cologne, Primate of all Germany, would be as a man who never was . . .

Beethoven. After the events of the next few years, Pa was to have many bitter things to say about Germany and the Germans, but in the end he could forgive them all for the sake of that one man.

The Beethovenhouse is a temple, and the Birthroom is the inner shrine of that temple. It is at the top of the poorest part of the house, the smallest room right up under the roof. Here Beethoven was born. It is such a wee box of a room, the ceiling so low-beamed, the wall so slanted, the space so tiny, that it is scarcely more than a cupboard. Yet no pious Catholic from the remotest island ever took the road to Rome with greater devotion in his heart than my atheist father felt as he stood there in the door of the little room. The day was quiet. The other visitors were in the museum rooms where once the Clasens and the Salomons had led their privileged lives. Pa stood in the place alone. A bust of Beethoven, some dingy laurel wreaths, and a shaft of dusty sunlight from the one window shared the silence with him.

And Pa heard the crash of orchestras, and the music that was all valour and freedom and living urgent joy welling up like ocean waves—and he heard

—Yes, I *heard* it, he insisted—

like a pure crystal of sound trapped inside a stone, he heard the very melody that had haunted him all these days—

Freude, schöner Götterfunken,
Tochter aus Elysium . . .

Pa gave me a novel to read once, in days when I was reading the *Beano* and Biggles and war comics and suchlike things. Pa didn't approve of novels by and large, held they were vain things, but he approved of this one because in it he found the spirit of the nine symphonies, of *Fidelio* and the concertoes, of Beethoven, Schiller, Heine, Goethe and Shakespeare all rolled into one. *John*

Christopher, the *Jean Christophe* of Romain Rolland, was a fictionalized life of Beethoven, a fantasia on the theme of human greatness. I found the book boring at the time and read little of it. I jooked his questions and hurt him with my obvious lack of interest. In those days I preferred war stories and action. This is how it starts:-

From behind the house rises the murmuring of the river. All day long the rain has been beating against the window-panes; a stream of water trickles down the window at the corner where it is broken. The yellowish light of the day dies down. The room is dim and dull.

The new-born child stirs in his cradle. Although the old man left his sabots at the door when he entered, his footsteps make the floor creak. The child begins to whine. The mother leans out of her bed to comfort it; and the grandfather gropes to light the lamp, so that the child shall not be frightened by the night when he awakes. The flame of the lamp lights up old Jean Michel's red face, with its rough white beard and morose expression and quick eyes. He goes near the cradle. His cloak smells wet, and as he walks he drags his large blue list slippers. Louisa signs to him not to go too near. She is fair, almost white; her features are drawn; her gentle, stupid face is marked with red in patches; her lips are pale and swollen, and they are parted in a timid smile; her eyes devour the child—and her eyes are blue and vague; the pupils are small, but there is an infinite tenderness in them.

The child wakes and cries, and his eyes are troubled. Oh! how terrible! The darkness, the sudden flash of the lamp, the hallucinations of a mind as yet hardly detached from chaos, the stifling, roaring night in which it is enveloped, the illimitable gloom from which, like blinding shafts of light, there emerge acute sensations, sorrows, phantoms—those enormous faces leaning over him, those eyes that pierce through him, penetrating, are beyond his comprehension! . . . He has not the strength to cry out; terror holds him motionless, with eyes and mouth wide open and he rattles in his throat. His large head, that seems to have swollen up, is wrinkled with the grotesque and lamentable grimaces that he makes; the skin of his face and hands is brown and purple, and spotted with yellow . . .

'Dear God!' said the old man with conviction, 'How ugly he is!'

He put the lamp down on the table . . .

Joy, creation's happy fire, oh daughter of paradise!

And Pa heard the melody again, heard the song of joy and freedom, heard it from a human throat, and that behind him, turned suddenly full of joy and longing once more, his heart fluttering to embrace this kindred spirit, and—

'Well, if it isn't the Jew-lover,' said Kurt, swinging his cosh in the doorway.

Pa blinked.

Kurt was swinging his cosh on a leather thong. He was swinging it with his right hand into the palm of his left. Smack, smack went the rubber on Kurt's palm. Kurt looked very big and strong and healthy, and he was grinning unpleasantly from ear to ear. Fritz was walking through the museum rooms in the main building. He didn't know that Kurt had found the foreigner just yet. Outside, the clock said 2.59.

'If it isn't the fucking Jew-lover,' said Kurt. Smack, went his cosh. 'We ain't got time for fucking Jews,' he said. 'We ain't got time for fucking Jew-lovers neither. Hey, Fritz!' he shouted down the stairs. 'I've got Jew-lover up here. Come up and talk to a real Jew-lover, Fritz!' Smack, went his cosh. 'Jew-lovers,' he said to Pa, 'ain't so very common where we come from. Fact where we fucking come from Jew-lovers are just trembling on the verge of extinction, they are, just trembling on the fucking verge.' He was really enjoying himself. 'Hey, Fritz!' he shouted again.

'Yeah?' came Fritz's voice from the bottom of the stairs.

'Jew-lover here wants his foreskin clipped off,' said Kurt. 'Jew-lover here wants to turn real Hebee. Don't you, Jew-lover?' —and he poked Pa in the chest with his thick rubber cosh.

Pa blinked again. Kurt was talking German, of course, and Pa didn't know all the words. He understood Kurt's voice though, yes he understood that all right. A hard man, a real radgie, and he's got a mate clumping up the stairs. He looked at the cosh in Kurt's hand. The place where his head was scarred began to ache urgently. *Kennst du das Land wo die* (what's German for cosh?) *blühn?* Well, this is it, he thought.

167

'—,' said Kurt. 'What's up, shithead, can't you understand fucking German?'

This is it, thought Pa. He took a step forward and punched Kurt right in the face. Kurt was enjoying himself with the Jew-lover. None of the Jew-lovers he and Fritz had worked over ever fought back—they had all just lain down and taken it, just fucking taken it. He expected the same this time too—Jew-lover would just fall to the floor and blubber, Please don't hit me, sir, and that sort of shit, so he had only drawn his cosh for effect, swinging it like that, it made him feel good, just like a torpedo in a Hollywood film, a real tough guy. He was enjoying himself, then he saw the fist coming. Fucking Jesus, he's going to slug me! Kurt jumped back and raised his arms, but he didn't move fast enough—Jew-lover's fist took him right in the mouth and Kurt tasted blood as he staggered back to the top of the stair. He swung out with his cosh and hit something all right, but then Jew-lover landed him another one, and Kurt took a step he didn't know was there, found nothing but space under his foot, and went arse over tip down the stairs *crash* into Fritz, and *crash crash crash* went the two of them and landed in a pile at the bottom. And Jew-lover jumped over them and ran.

And they ran too.

Jew-lover was running for his life.

But they were running for his life too.

'I'm gonna get you, ya fucking bastard Jewboy!' bellowed Kurt.

'—get you, fucking Jew cunt!' yelled Fritz.

And they caught Jew-lover near the public lavatories—

And Pa's head was a jumble of memories, Ehrenbreitstein, broad stone of honour, Joy! Joy! and a mountain and a forest, the Harz in moonlight, Siegfried the hero riding through the forest on a white horse—and a maiden sitting on a rock combing her golden hair . . .

I sat in my bedroom and looked at the postcards spread out there on the floor. The four black and white cards showing pictures of the Beethovenhouse in Bonn are all somewhat crumpled. One has nothing written on it and hasn't been stamped. It shows the Birthroom: a bust of Beethoven and some wreaths and a shaft of sunlight. It is faded now. On the back is a rusty brown stain. The second has nothing written on it either. It has been torn down the middle and sellotaped back together again. The sellotape is brown and brittle with age. It shows the street outside. The clock above Jos. Hesse's door is just in the picture. It says 2.30. There is nobody on the pavement, no old Jew, no woman hitting him with her handbag and spitting on him. The third is a view of the garden at the back. It too has nothing on it. It has been crumpled up into a ball and has been painstakingly flattened out and ironed. The photograph is all cracks. An outside view of the attic where Beethoven was born. A door at the bottom, and a wooden fence, and a tree in bloom. I don't know what sort of tree it is. Suddenly I see the cracked faded door flung open and Pa comes running out and jumps the fence, running straight into the camera like a man in a film. I see two uniformed men with armbands coming running out. They jump the fence too. I see their coshes. The fourth, last, card is the best preserved. It is another view of the street, taken from the opposite direction. The hands on Jos. Hesse's clock say 3.01. His sunshades are drawn down. A girl in a summer frock is walking past the door. There is a 1930s car in the distance. There is no sign of a man being assaulted outside the public lavatories by two brawny boys with rubber coshes who take him in turn. It has a Dutch stamp. There is some shaky writing on the back. It says—

Dear Hubbard, I've had a spot of bother and coming home. No money, but the embassy will help me. Don't worry.
And I think it says—
Germany's mind is very sane, but her soul has gone mad. But the handwriting is very shaky.

Hitler's Germany. And if on a winter's night, or any other night, a traveller had come there he would have been questioned, 'Who are you? Where have you come from? Why have you come here? What do you want? Are you an orthodox believer?'—and piercing eyes full of faith and stupidity would have nailed him to the door.

In 1936 Pa was flung out, persona non grata, over the Dutch frontier. Nine years later he ended his war in Antwerp. He never went back to Germany.

Yet he told me about it so often. And about *her*, his poem girl. Yes, he even told me about her once. For those few days in Germany in 1936 were his life's golden time—and he made a bright picture book of it, a story about a happy beer-garden land with trees and flowers and creepers on the orchard wall; he drew it from his good memories and kept it in the attic of his mind for winter telling . . .

I took down the atlas and opened it at the map of Germany, or more accurately the two Germanies, for the frontier between the Eastern and Western Republics now runs through Heine's Harz and communist guards with machine-guns patrol the barbed wire. Does the beautiful house still stand in Wernigerode, I wonder, and do folk still talk about Ilse the water princess in the shadow of the watchtowers, does anyone laugh and sing and run barefoot through the meadowgrass in those hills now?

There was a land on the other side of the sea—and before he came there, Pa had never crossed the waters, for we are a rather little island in the end, and the sea is all around us.

There beyond the sea—and it was from there the Angles and the Saxons once came heroically voyaging, standing in the prows of longships with crested helmets on their heads in the crumbling days of Rome's empire. And they came to the north, to the land of Lothian, and on the shore of the Firth they built their Edwinesburgh, their Fort Edwin, on the great rock, and gave us their Angle-spreche, our English tongue, and I have none other.

Beyond the sea—from there the legends come, about mountains above the clouds, and golden rivers, and little wise men with pointed beards, and monsters and forest giants in a place that smells of pine needles, where you might expect to find Christmas presents at the foot of every tree.

There was such a land . . . and in that land there was a forest, and in that forest there was a castle, and in that castle was a jackdaw's nest of all the things I have ever lost in my life.

—Maybe one day you will find it, said Pa as we walked along this very same stretch of shingly beach between Newhaven and Granton, with the lights of Starbank and Lower Granton Road behind us, and over yonder those of Burntisland shining along the Fife shore. Maybe you will be luckier than I.

Time Present

They say the night is always darkest just before dawn, but I do not know if it is so, or if it is only the thought that makes it seem that way. This is the dreich, the woesome hour, when you wait for a change that you cannot make to come any quicker, will it as you like; and you think, God, what a useless creature I am! God, what a scunner it all is! And if it is cold, then this is the hour when you will shiver and hug your jacket about you; if there is a spit of rain, this is the hour when it will come, the hour when the wind will blow. It does all three in Edinburgh, even in summer.

A city of wind and rain. A city with pleasant summer days that are so easily forgotten. A city with chilling winters whose memory lasts. ('A bit dreich the day.'—'Aye, but at least there's no snow.'—'Give it time. Give it time.') The road, the wynd, the close, the backstreet, the piss, the rot, the litter blowing, the cold cold estate. When bonny Mary Queen of Scots landed it was raining on Leith. My mother hung her plants in the air above Leith, they were a green rumour of lush meadows and trees and mountain water, and you could look up to our fourth-floor windows from the street and see the green leaves there away up above the grey stone, and it was as though the street was the bottom of a well and up there was the foliage of a better world.

Edinburgh is a city like the sea. Its bed has the contours of wet tower blocks. The crevasses are spiky with statues. And folk find ancient sea creatures fossilized in their gardens. A place full of ghosts, old warder of buried bones, living animal creatures tumbling down slowly in slow green motion down down downwards to the hospice and the eventide home, the cemetery and the crematorium.

Edinburgh, early summer treading in the shadow of spring.

Two hours before the office workers wake the dawn will come. Soon. Here and there the first birdsong is in the air. Soon—but for the while the sky is its blackest. *Brrrrring* go alarums here and there. The first milk and bread lorries are rattling. Delivery for the early morning shops, the open-the-shutters-at-six-o'clock shops, the milk crates are being piled outside their doors. *Brrrrring* go alarums for the dayshifts who must travel far to work, *brrrrring* for the second wave of morning cleaners. Jessie from Salamander Street and Mary from Restalrig and Rita from Lochend will all be mopping by now, scouring out showers, washing the linoleum of much-trodden corridors, pushing heavy vacuum cleaners round offices for secretaries whose legs are still in bed. *Brrrrring* the alarums will go for Dot and Maggie and Vina and all the second-wave starters.—And I can hear an alarum *brrrrring* somewhere behind me, and the clatter of the milk, and the first cars.

Magic flute whose sound is on the night wind, we listen to you, we watchful ones. The boy sentry on the Castle esplanade (seventeen, eighteen years old he is, like the boys in the Falklands); the crew of the polis car off to who but the crackling radio knows where; the watchmen on the building sites, office blocks, on the dock gate. Watching statues even, whom music they say can sometimes make to walk and weep, Burns nearby with his face to a pub and his back to a bank, Queen Victoria at the foot of Leith Walk whom I proposed to one night when I was very very drunk, the big kiltie on the Mound. And the black ships in Leith, the boats in Granton and Newhaven, and whoever wakes on them to hear the gull-cry over the Forth or the geese who fly in the gloaming and are called the Gabriel Hounds. And among those ships, the *Ivan Susanin*, and I wonder—Who wakes on her? Who are you, my Soviet brother? And I make the sound of the graveyard owl, and cry Who? Who?

Sea, you've set me thinking of them—

The Black Ships

I saw that morning in '62 when the storm came and battered the Berwickshire coast.

Through came the sound of Bob's heavy feet in the hall, the old smith who had shod his last horse perhaps before I was born. Every day we saw him, and Pa and he talked together, and I sat and listened to their talk, and they did not shoo me away any more, nor did I wish to be away when I could ask them questions about worlds I had not known. Such questions!—and such tales told in return by the smith who assured me that he had shod Napoleon's horse, and I believed it, until Pa couldn't stop his laughter any more, and then we laughed all three. (They have both gone into the darkness now, and I am here alone.) And another time he told me how he had seen Admiral Beatty's squadrons steaming from Rosyth, the *Lion* leading, the *Queen Mary* astern of her—and I don't know whether he really remembered that or only thought he remembered it, for Beatty's ships sailed to Jutland through the night many miles out to sea, so how could he have seen them? Yet he had, he said, he had seen the *Queen Mary* before her destruction, himself a laddie little older than me attending class in this very schoolroom where we were now sitting in the evening warmth: one morning, he said, when there was a light on the sea, the great ships had crossed the horizon outward bound from Rosyth on the Forth to the North Sea to do battle with Von Hipper and his Germans, and the bairns had all run out of school, and the teacher too in her long skirt and bonnet, and they had run down to the red cliffs and stood along the top of the cliffs and waved and shouted for the far-off sailors bound to their deaths at Jutland. So perhaps he had seen it after all—or perchance it was another battle they were going to, the Dogger Bank maybe, or the Helgoland Bight, for there were many battles in that war, and many men died in them.

Stories stories stories in that remote house between the hills and the wind and the sea. And it was 1962, the year Pa thought the world was going to end—and he was right, because a world ends with every creature that dies; but it was not his meaning; what he meant was the *whole* world, or at least a large part of it, ending in a collective apocalypse of bombs and missiles—and that threat which was so real for him, if not for us, but which we could still sense from his unease, made these stories very important all of a sudden. Yes, all of a sudden Pa began telling me many things he must have wanted to tell me before, but had been inhibited from doing by Ma's presence when she was alive, and by her very absence those silent wretched nights after her death when we had meant so much to each other but had been able to say so little. Now Pa began talking, sometimes in Bob's presence, sometimes when we were alone, and sometimes when I lay abed and the wind chirled at the panes or came yodelling down the lum. He talked and he talked about his own folks, about Sutherland of the mountains, about Edinburgh when he was a bairn, about his own youth and young manhood—about the war and War in general. ('What did you do in the war, Pa?' I asked, as every boy asks.) And he talked . . .

Summer passed into autumn. It meant nothing much to a city lad except a coldening of the weather and shortening of the day, but here it was a tawny shadow stretching over the lie of the land. For there was a road and a fence and a yellow field and the sea, and the yellow field was suddenly being worked on by big chestnut-brown men doing strange things: high up on proud red tractors they rode like captains on ships ploughing the yellow wave, and the earth wrapped its rich brown smell around them, and I wandered about watching in my pallid city skin.

Sometimes we walked together, to the ruins of St Helen's kirk girt with nettles, to the ruins of Fast Castle on a jutting promontory like a place that God forgot, to the narrow bridge on the valley I had gone clambering up, and the ruined tower beyond it. The wee girl was nowhere to be seen.

We lay on the blown grass in Fast Castle, in what had been the courtyard of the Bride of Lammermoor, and was now but a green hump on a sea-surrounded rock with a few bits of tumbled brown wall standing still like broken teeth in the face of the North Sea wind; and a fisherman came to the bottom of the rock, way below us, risking his neck on the slimy black crag to cast his line where the sea was shattering, and he came up with silver fish dead in his bag and said that he had heard a seal cry there below us. He was a red and healthy man and smelled of the salt of the sea.

We walked carefully around the nettles that congregated in St Helen's nave, one end only of the old kirk standing, and wondered whoever could have come to this place on the desolate coast, what folk from deserted homes, what folk from vanished villages that were ruins and bits of ruins had come here in days when religion had fire enough in its belly to warm them against the blast?

We explored the valley beneath the narrow bridge, and lost ourselves in the wood that was the valley's floor, that would seem a small copse probably if ever I went back to it, but which these twenty years syne was a grand primeval forest for the hunters and the trappers and the Red Indians, loyal Mohicans, fearsome Hurons in their war canoes paddling down the river that was here just a burn splashing over the stones in the deep-cleft glen that Cromwell's troopers had once crossed. Pa sat on a fallen trunk and smoked his pipe while I went my wargaming ways, stalking the cruel Hurons in their paint with my long musket, spying on the English cavalry from a low branch where I fancied I was invisible. Mind, I was Gluck then, Conla, the magical boy, and I saw these things so plain. Yet I did not see Ivan and his missiles in the forests of Kola.

Then we heard a vixen scream, for it was the mating time said Bob that night, but we didn't know what it was, horrible it sounded, like a banshee, like all the werewolves of Hammer studios baying at once, so I ran back to Pa who was standing like an alert sentry holding his glowing pipe, and we departed with what dignity we could.

Ruins and vegetation and stories of the past . . .

We collected driftwood on the beach below the red cliffs. It was getting colder and neither of us lingered at the job. Likewise the sea was getting rougher and the waves came further with their spray. The summer days when I could draw on the sand with a stick and find the drawing there undisturbed on the morrow were over.

Autumn, that end-of-the-world-year. Of the things that walked by night on the shoulder of the Lammermoors, I have no notion. Of those that walked by day, I saw only the eternal conventicle of sheep beneath the whaup-cry, and a rabbit once that a stoat had feared, that trembled when I put my hand on him, then bounded up the bare hillside; and Pa smiled. And the wind over the fields was colder and colder, and the sea was grey and ugly during the day, but at twilight, with the sun going down behind the hill, there was a while when the sea shone like blue glass sprinkled with jewels—bonny it looked, but cold. Dark shadows began to spill from the folds of the Lammermoors and the windows of the clachan lighted against the coming night. At least our window did—and Bob Purves's in the smithy when he had left us after an evening's blether. The green shed of the Women's Rural Institute was never lit. On a couple of weekends a light flickered in the old mill, but we never saw the owner. And sometimes, unknown to Pa, I would run out into the dark and the cold rain and look at that glowing light our house was throwing out to the sea like a very lamp of Scotland, and wonder who out there could see it.

These were incendiary nights when the driftwood fire crackled in my dreaming eyes as I sat there on the threadbare rug, with Pa in the battered armchair pulling on his pipe. And there was a wailing and a weird howling about, but it was only the wind. Syne Pa, who had been silent, would sigh deeply, take the hand from his forehead, look about and blink a bit, then tap the cold embers of his pipe into the hearth. And then he would take my hand, and we would walk together into the hearth, we would pass the black iron of the range and the blue and green tiles that surrounded it, and tread the fire, walking into the crackling salt-washed wood of ships and creels and broken cargoes to find the land of Germany, the streets of an Edinburgh I had never known, and the far country road that took us both back to the land of beginning, to Sutherland, *Duthaich MacAoidh*, the home of the Mackays, the sons of the sea.

Autumn. The sea wind came soughing among the ruins of St Helen's, it flurried the grass of the fallow fields so that magic-minded folk might tell their weans it was the Wind Man from the North Pole running over it with the skirts of his long coat trailing the ground. And then it was winter.

And the storm came.

For a whole week it raged. It began during the night, the wind rising about midnight, and when I woke up in the morning it was still blowing strong. Pa predicted that it would soon blow itself out, but it didn't. Our heavy metal dustbin had blown over and was rattling about on the road. Some branches had come down as well, and the wireless carried news of traffic accidents and polis warnings. And then there was no more traffic, so Pa walked down and found that a telephone pole had fallen and was lying across the road; but in the afternoon men came and raised it and Pa talked with them. They said that poles were down here and there, and nearer Cockburnspath a big tree was down across the road, lying there it was with its roots in the sky, and they were going to have to get an electric saw to cut it into moveable portions, they said. They didn't talk about Cuba and missiles and the Bomb. When Pa speired at them they said such things were terrible, terrible, but none of their business—what could they do?—they were the affair of the government. They were concerned with clearing the road and getting the phones back into operation. They said there was rain coming. They hoped they would get home to see the television that evening. They liked to laugh with Harry Worth and The Flintstones. They said the long-range forecast was for snow. Pa came back shaking his head. That was the first day of the storm.

I asked Pa if it was what the men had said that had upset him, and he answered that it was what they hadn't said. 'They canny see it,' he said. 'They just canny see it.' And he shook his head and stared at the fire and wouldn't say anything. Then the rain started. After a while it was drumming on the window like hailstones. I made our meal, such as it was. Pa stared at the fire and said he wasn't hungry. So I said I wouldn't eat unless he ate too. So he began to eat, grumpily. So we both ate. That was the night he told me how he had seen 'yon bastard'—Hitler—on the Rhine, and how the folk had cheered for him. And the rain fell and fell.

177

Then next morning there they were, the strange ships. Three identical black hulls anchored in a line in the lee of the promontory where Fast Castle stood. Of course I knew what they were—they were pirate ships! They were U-boats! I got into a good firing position behind the hedge and opened up with a piece of piping which was the barrel of a Bofors gun: *ack-ack-ack-ack-ack-ack-ack*—I sent a stream of bright tracer shells into each one of them, and one after another they burst into orange flame and pillars of smoke, and men screamed and plunged into the tossing sea, and they died, the dirty Bosches, they died. Then the rain started again and I ran to find Pa.

That night the sea shattered and shattered so loud that I lay awake listening to the noise of it. And I minded Pa telling me, sometime in the past, how he had heard the guns of the battleship *Warspite* shelling the German-held cliffs at Salerno, and the great roaring of those guns: and Ma telling me about the guns on Corstorphine Hill firing at the German bombers, how they had fired during the night and the window-panes had rattled: and myself in the ferry going over to Fife in the long holidays under the great red beams of the railway bridge, and a train leaping hundreds of feet over our heads like the zipper going up the fly of God Almighty. And still that night the sea was shattering on the Berwickshire coast, birling boulders around the beach, sending splinters of red stone flying into the air, and flinging daberlack weed and flotsam, sand and jellyfish up into the grass of the first landward field. And how long, I wondered, would it be before the sea had torn its way over the field and up to the road, how long before the spray would be hitting these rain-battered windows, how many centuries before a laddie like myself lay listening while the sea battered the ruins of Redheugh, and would he know that I had once lived there? How long before the sea reclaimed the world?

The three black ships were there the next morning and the next again. Pa borrowed Bob Purves's binoculars and pronounced them trawlers weathering out the storm. He could see no name, no inscription and nobody on any deck. There was nothing to say whether they were our ships from the Forth harbours or from Hull, or foreign ships, perhaps even Soviet ships bound for Ullapool. There were none of us fisherfolk, and the phone lines

178

were down, and the crews on the three ships remained below decks, and the waves dackered their hulls and the cliffs and cut moonscapes in the sand and shingle beaches.

Strange how many things in this world come in threes. I saw three ships come sailing by: I saw—the three musketeers, the three wise men, the three stooges, the three blind mice. I heard Moscow being called the Third Rome, communism being likened to the Third Age; and how often Pa told me harrowing tales about the Third Reich, and the Third World War which would kill us all.

Sea destined to reclaim the world, tell me why these ships made him so uneasy.

A black ship it was brought Pa home from Germany—a Dutch collier bound for Leith. He sat among the coal sacks in the dust of the coal and breathed painfully. His broken ribs were taped up, bandages were on his face and head.

> *Frisch weht der Wind*
> Fresh blows the Wind
> *Der Heimat zu.*
> To the homeland.
> *Mein Schottische Kind*
> My Scottish child
> *Warum weinst du?*
> Why are you weeping?

Why, Pa? Did you suspect that socialism's soul had gone mad too?

Any road, in the autumn of 1936 Pa came back to Edinburgh, no money in his pocket, starving, dirty, and in pain. He landed at Leith docks. He didn't have money for a bus to Marchmont Road. He didn't have a suitcase. His English translation of Goethe's *Faust* ('Donald, I am so very much fond of you, I think') had been confiscated—perhaps People's Justice thought it was a subversive text. In his pocket were three crumpled torn post-cards of Bonn, one with his bloodstain on it. It was a Sunday. He limped wearily up the road: past Kirkgate, past Queen Victoria's statue, up long Leith Walk. He flinched when he saw two polismen come out of the station in Gayfield Square. Little boy blue, where are you going? When he came at last to the Meadows, he lay down in the grass. There was a wind, of course; it had been raining, of course. He kissed the grass and loved it. He thought the troubles were over. He thought of Willie, his wee brother, coughing there in Marchmont. He could see the mouth of the road where his home was. He walked towards it.

He came in. Willie was dead. His mother, the Old Lady, put her hands to her face and cried out, *Heavens, laddie!* because his face was such a mess. Willie was dead. He took his jacket off and hung it on the back of the chair. But Willie was dead. He washed his face in the sink beside a clutter of dishes on a wooden rack. And beyond it was the bed where Willie was lying dead and would never waken. And Pa put on the kettle, yon same kettle with the wooden handle and the long curving spout, and said to the Old Lady

—Aye, then.

And said

—Aye, then.

And his brother was lying dead, the brother who was his only kin forbye the Old Lady, and Jimmy, who had emigrated to Australia and not written since; so Pa sat there and looked at his young brother Willie lying there so cold before him, and the kettle began to boil, and Pa's head told him that Willie was dead dead dead, but he couldn't believe what his head was telling him. And his mother, the Old Lady, was standing there mumbling through her now falling tears, telling him how Willie had coughed and coughed and gone pounding the streets looking for work, Haymarket, Granton, Leith, Musselburgh, but never a job was there to be had, and he coughed and coughed. And the night came, the night before last, and he cried out

—Oh Ma, get me a doctor!

—Get me a doctor! he cried.

But she was feared. There was the money, but how long would it last? Besides, Willie had always been sick, but he had always got over it. So she told him

—Wheesht, wheesht now, dinny fret

and she made him hot cocoa and put him to bed like a bairn, and sat there by him in Pa's seat and told him stories, once-upon-a-time stories, to make him forget the cold. And she stoked up the fire and put blankets on him, then the coats from the lobby, then the shawl off her shoulders, and still he said he was cold, so cold. And then he fell asleep, and she thought it was good, him sleeping like that, and she sat beside him, and sometime in the night she fell asleep in the chair, and when she woke she made him hot porridge for his breakfast, and came to wake him, but she couldn't wake him, for he was dead.

And Pa sat and stared, glaikit, as she spoke.

Then she got the doctor, she said. *Then* Joe from upstairs went running to fetch him, and the doctor came with his black bag and told her—and told her, yes, and she made the doctor a cup of tea, and the doctor said there would be no charge for his time that morning, which was decent of him. Then the doctor went away and Joe went looking for an undertaker, but the undertakers were all busy and not one would come till Monday: and so he lay there, her laddie, her youngest, and his soul had been called to the Lord, across the burning clouds it had gone into the land of morning.

And Pa stared, glaikit, as she spoke.

'And do you know what the last words were he spoke?' said Pa. '*Golden beaches.* Golden bloody beaches! And ships and all that. And he might have been, oh Christ knows what! Something big, something really fine. Because he had a first-class mind, your uncle Willie, he could have had an office to himself, and a car, and a house of his own on the southside maybe with a grand view of the hills. And instead of that, dead of pneumonia, and him no twenty years old, him a prince and deserving of life if ever any one was. I couldny understand it then,' said Pa, 'and I canny understand it even now. How such damn injustice can exist in the world. I could never understand it,' said Pa.

Pa grew sour and silent and bitter that winter after his return from Germany. He worked in the shipping office. He spoke to no one. He went to only one or two Party meetings and sat silent at them. He was asked to regale the comrades with horror stories about the Nazi state, about his sufferings at the hands of the fascist régime. He had nothing to say. When his subscription to the *Daily Worker* ran out, he didn't bother to renew it. He destroyed his diary and his poetry. He didn't walk in the Pentland

Hills any more. He took no interest in anything at all. He did his work very efficiently in the shipping office.

My godfather Joe—did I tell you about my godfather Joe, Pa's best and only real friend, the laddie upstairs?—well, Joe was the only one he talked to, and even Joe couldn't fathom him, couldn't understand why he didn't want to 'dedicate himself with renewed zeal to the work of the Party'—as Party piffle, not Joe, put it. Joe had a job as a boilermaker. He had saved up all his pennies. He ate a diet of white bread and margarine. One day he was going to go to the Soviet Union, he said. He was going to go proudly with his chin up to the homeland of the progressive proletariat undeterred by all the lies of the capitalist press, carrying his Party card like a torch, like a holy icon, and kiss the ground in Red Square.

Joe thought that a bit of healthy progressive proletarianism would do Pa good. Pa wished him luck, 'the best of British.'

That was in 1937.

The proud and desperate years. Joe's job took him to Liverpool. He went from there to Spain, but he didn't see much fighting. Eventually he got his dream—he went to Moscow with a delegation of British comrades to attend some International Brigade congress or other. Pa didn't hear from him again until the end of '38. Things had happened by then, things that made the headlines: the war in Spain was ending in a nationalist victory; the war in the rest of Europe was soon to begin. Suddenly everyone, even the folk in Marchmont Road, in Corstorphine among the gardens, in Leith among the cranes, knew the names of far-away places—Sudetenland, Munich, Czechoslovakia, Danzig. And there were things that hadn't made the headlines —things that were worse . . .

Standing here on the Granton shore looking at the waves running away from me in the first hint of day, there is a strange déjà vu, a 'been here before' about those evil years. They seem strangely nocturnal for one thing, as though from the trenches of the First World War to the landing beaches of the Second humanity had gone underground in a maze of tunnels. Just about everything man-made seems to have been ugly and oppressive —ugly buildings, ugly furniture, ugly music, ugly art, literature full of weariness and cynicism, politics either drivelling self-abnegation or braying supremacy and hate. And people, poor people, wandering through these mine shafts in their ugly flapper dresses, their ridiculous gangster suits, far away from the sun in a dwarves' kingdom lit by rainbow-coloured fantasies. And I ask myself, standing here in the shadow of Ivan's missiles, and Leroy's missiles—which years? What decades am I talking about in my cavern measureless to man?

Ugly years—even the dances were ugly. No, not the daft dances of the Bright Young Things kicking their legs and flapping their wrists on the Charleston floor. Not those, but the war dances of the lettered people, the celebrities and stars, the take-your-partners dance to the tom-tom drums. Pa had grown up with 'Onward Christian Soldiers' and 'Land of Hope and Glory'. The music-hall was full of patriotism; even while the Germans were still our friends Union Jacks decorated the stage, ladies with heaving bosoms trilled out 'Rule Britannia', and men with walrus moustaches joined the Volunteer Movement. In those days, the Tories were the bastards, the Hun-eaters, they were the warlovers with chestloads of medals, the red and hearty Majors (retired), the Colonel Blimps, the whole hang-the-Kaiser-and-shoot-the-conchies brigade. The Socialists then were the children of light, the strong and gentle martyrs, the simple working-folk whose honesty would prevail, the masses (led by This party, That party) moving slowly yet irresistably forward towards that red utopian dawn when war would be abolished, country unknown, and the man in the street would be happily reading his Shakespeare, playing the cello, and discussing art with George Bernard Shaw.

What happened? In 1933 the German Revolution happened, and—hey presto!—it was as though a wand had been waved, as though the band leader had shouted 'Take your partners, ladies and gentlemen, for—', as though the gym teacher had blown his whistle and the whole class stood on its head.

Yin

All of a sudden the Tories put their medals away, hung *Hang the Kaiser* in the wardrobe, discovered that Germany was a poor misunderstood and much put-upon land, discovered that the new German socialism was a practical, efficient, business-like thing quite compatible with traditional values and private enterprise, discovered that peace was good, and reconciliation a very fine thing. If the world was troubled, the Mothers For Peace, the Conservative Women Against War, the Peace Pledge Union, the Keep Britain Out Campaign, the non-interveners in Spain all knew that Hitler wanted peace too, that only the communists were mad, that only the Jewish bankers wanted strife. And they handed in their petitions, they signed their pledges in tears, they read poems for peace and gave concerts for peace, they damned the Czech refugees as criminals and the Spanish republic as a bandits' den. In Abyssinia they weren't interested, Poland they hadn't heard of, tales of the concentration camps were all lies.

—Haven't I heard it all since?

What happened?

Yang

All of a sudden the Socialists discovered the glory of arms and the bearing of arms, discovered the true communism of being a soldier marching in step with slung rifle and hearty song, discovered that Germany was a dark inferno, a jungle of raging slavering fascist beasts, discovered that Hitler's huns and the traitors who were in the pay of Hitler's huns intended to leave not a virgin unravished nor a trade unionist unhung in all these islands, discovered the excitement of flying with a planeload of bombs. If the world was troubled, the Workers' Olympic Committee, the Defence of Spain Committee, the Red Friends Of Russia, the join-the-international-brigades-and-knock-off-a-fascist-for-progress campaign all knew that, unlike the Nazi jackal, Stalin only wanted peace, and socialism in one country, and that the Hitler gang was part of a plot by international arms manufacturers who were preparing for war, so war had to be fought against them—war to the death, to the last man, to the end! War! In the Ukraine they weren't interested, the concentration camps they hadn't heard of, tales of the purges and show trials were all lies.

—And haven't I heard all that too?

—I who remember another invaded Czechoslovakia, the Cambodian massacres, the fall of Saigon, the boat people, Polish Solidarity.

—Haven't I heard it all too?

Yin yang, waves of the sea. *Yin yang*.

Listen, says the sea. Listen for one more time and I will tell you how Truth became.

Know that in the beginning of Creation was Night. The Night that preceded Creation created everything, a fire burning in the darkness.

And everything was whole that was created then. Out of that fire came both good and bad, came the country, came the city, came nature, came destruction, came both man and woman; and Night, to fill them all, created his favourite child whom he called Truth, and she was beautiful.

Then Night also created the Lie, and he was ugly, a weak crippled pitiful thing. And Night took pity on the Lie, for he was like a scarecrow hobbling over the earth, and gave him a sword with which to defend himself. But to the Truth who was strong and glowing with health he gave nothing.

Then one day Truth met the Lie in battle, and Truth the great gladiator laughed and hit Lie and knocked him to the ground. But the Lie had his sword, and scrambling to his feet he caught Truth off guard, aimed one savage blow, and sent her head flying.

Truth staggered, unable to comprehend what had happened to her, suddenly eyeless, mouthless, suddenly blind, deaf, speechless all at once. She groped for her head with fumbling fingers, searching the ground for it where it had fallen, and finding Lie collapsed there exhausted with the blow, she, thinking it was her own, seized on Lie's head and tore it off his shoulders.

So now Truth, Truth walks the world deceiving people with Lie's head, while Lie hobbles after her wearing the beautiful face of Truth, and Truth pulls her words out of Lie's heart, while Lie twists Truth's breath round his crooked tongue.

But Pa couldn't understand the spirit of those ugly years at all. He grew bitter, inward-looking, a world-weary man. Part of him was always to stay that way.

The part of him that was jealous. Looking back on it, I realize that now. He complained whenever I went out to play or just scive about with my mates Andy and Dougie and Eck. He complained in a loud petulant voice that I was 'wasting time', should be 'improving your mind'. He stood me in front of him and asked me very seriously what was the use, what was the purpose, of kicking a ball around a backstreet?—Didn't I know, he said, how ridiculous I looked, how unsuited I was to it, how unfit? Had I no conception of the contempt in which the others held me?—And what were the others, he continued; Andy whose Pa was a mechanic, Dougie whose folk owned a sweetie shop, Eck—did I know what Eck's father was? 'A bookie's clerk!' A bookmaker's clerk, a betting shop spiv—and did I think that was suitable company for HIS SON?—Did I now? Well, did I? *Did I?*

I didn't know what I thought, except that I resented his interference. Resented not being able to bring my mates home. Resented his sending Carol running away in tears when he caught me walking with her. Resented not having a gang, a clan I could be part of. Resented the books he kept thrusting at me, telling me to improve my mind with them.

Ma lost her friends too. Gradually they fell away under the barrage of Pa's martyred sighs, his furtive keeks at the clock, his overwhelmingly obvious patience with their intruding company, his sarcastic asides about the Women's Guild, bowls, tea parties, clothes, or whatever else it was they were talking about, his carefully managed stage-whispers—'Are these buggers going to be here all night?' And when he had finally driven them out, the beatific beam that would light up his face as he contentedly filled his pipe and settled himself into an armchair with a book.

'We've no need of anyone,' he said. 'We're sufficient to ourselves.'

And Ma looked bitter, and I looked angry, but I don't suppose he noticed that.

Of course I thought he did it out of pure malice. I didn't realize the fear and mistrust that people from the beyond, from the place where murders occur, had inspired in him. Had I known it, I still wouldn't have known why.

For it was all before my time, you see: part of that world I didn't know (pray God I never will) of militiamen with armbands, and blood running on the streets.

Joe came back from Moscow, and he came back a broken man. His visit had coincided with the climax of the Stalinist purges. That was in the end of 1937, the beginning of '38. Of course, he saw very little of it: he saw only frightened people. Stalin, who had been murdering for years, had finally begun to murder the murderers. In '37/38 he purged the Communist Party and the army officer corps. Police chief Yezhov sent his packs through the night. All the old guard bolsheviks went, all Lenin's comrades, all the heroes of the barricades, the flag-wavers, the visionaries of the great red dawn. Yezhov's men killed them all—a few of the most important with 'trials'; the thousands of the unimportant without even that. In Russian the year is called *Yezhovshchina*, the Yezhov terror. Then when Yezhov had served his purpose, Stalin had him killed as well, and some other gunman took his place.

There were arrests every night, said Joe. There were arrests every day. In broad daylight uniformed men would suddenly appear and cordon off a street and arrest everyone on it. The security police were fighting a war against the people, he said —*in the name of socialism!* But there was no resistance, everyone was cowed, in classrooms children were pumped full of lies and obedience—*in the name of socialism!* Joe had been a true believer, so had Pa. Both men had seen their beliefs raped before their very eyes. The other British members of the delegation Joe was with had seen it too—seen it, yet not seen it. They hadn't seen innocents arrested in broad daylight: they had seen 'the strong shield of the people's justice'. They hadn't heard of innocents being murdered by firing-squads: they had only heard of 'the liquidation of class enemies'. And they actually talked like that, said Joe, in phrases; those were the filthy phrases they used; and they were furtive and self-righteous at the same time; ashamed and guilty, and yet talking loudly and aggressively with snarling mouths and flashing eyes. Like rapists, said Joe, just like a lot of dirty wee rapists, his comrades. I never thought I would have lived to see the day, said Joe.

'I wish I hadny lived to see the day,' said Pa.

The two men were sitting in that dark room in Marchmont Road where, after the Second World War and the Atomic Bombs and the Korean War, about the time of the Suez Crisis and the

187

Hungarian Revolution and the beginning of the Algerian War and the Cuban Revolution, the Old Lady would say to me—

'Shush, my wee mannie, shush and I will tell you a story of the Land Beneath the Sea.'

The two men were sitting there, and the betrayal of Munich was already being planned. They were sitting there in quiet Marchmont, and Stalin's prison camps held twice as many people as the whole of Scotland. They were both socialists because Scotland's cities swarmed with the descendants of refugees from burnt Highland glens and the starved fields of Ireland; and they thought such things should not be in this world, so they became socialists—then went to countries where socialism was a tyranny that murdered.

Joe still believed—to the end of his life he still believed—in the Leninist path to socialism. His dear socialism had been defiled by lunatics, but still he loved her.

'It makes me feel less alone,' he said. 'Maybe that isny a very good reason, but, well, there you are.'

'I hate Hitler and I hate Stalin and I hate God,' said Pa. 'They're just all a bunch of fucking killers.'

When Stalin and Hitler signed their famous friendship pact and carved up Poland between them, Pa and his friend Joe took their red party cards to a red Party meeting in the Freemasons' Hall, tore them up dramatically and flung them on the floor. They were denounced as fascists, anarchists and Trotskyites. They stamped out and banged the door behind them.

Joe had a nervous breakdown a few weeks later.

Pa had always been a bookworm. He had read Marx and Lenin, Keir Hardie, Ramsay Macdonald and John Maclean. He didn't tear their books up. He read them again and wondered how it had all gone wrong. He had a couple of hundred volumes then—by the end of his life he had several thousand, and I still have them all, I've not parted with a single one—but he never did find out how it had all gone wrong. He poured over them like a monk over holy scripture knowing that the Truth must be in them *somewhere*.

'Books will never betray you,' he said, I don't know how often.

His meaning, of course, was that everything else will. Politics, men—women—everything. When he walked the streets of Edinburgh, he saw men with the eyes of murderers and wondered what they would look like in brown shirts and boots. Outside football grounds he heard the mindless chants he had heard on the Rhine. He went to the pictures for escape. He enjoyed Westerns with their uncomplicated Right and Wrong. He liked to see the countryside of Wyoming. He thought it was like Sutherland, though he had never seen Sutherland. Then he was called up. He didn't care. All his hopes and dreams had sailed away like black ships: they had faded into the night.

He was a cold, bitter man, my Pa, when the Second World War began—the war in which ss men would whistle 'The Ode To Joy' as they worked the machine guns at Babi Yar. There was no gentleness in him then.

Yet there was when I knew him: he had many faults, but much gentleness was there too, outweighing them all in the end. After the war—though his hair, once yellow, had turned so white that folk easily mistook him for my grandfather—he decided to become an English teacher, instil the beauties of the language Shakespeare spoke into children's minds, and point them towards a socialism which was all to do with life and loving, and as far removed from dictators and their stamping boots as anything could possibly be. And when he and Ma met in each other's loneliness after that war, they played snowballs in Marchmont Meadows, and walked along the shore to Cramond on fine days, and Pa pointed out the carving on Eagle Rock where the Roman soldiers had camped and raised their altar—*Matribus alatervis et matribus campestribus cohors II Tungrorum posuit*. They went walking together at the weekends in the Pentland Hills. He told her how, at the war's near end, he had been on sentry-go in Antwerp when the German flying bombs came over, and Flemish bairns had hidden from them under the skirts of his long army coat. And she loved him for that.

'To the Alatervian mothers and the mothers of the plains.'

And Golden Beaches

(When Willie died of pneumonia caught tramping the soaking docks he babbled not of green fields but of the sea's golden beaches—but perhaps they are much the same thing in the end. 'And you are that like him, sunshine,' Pa used to say. 'That like him.'

And he looked sadly at me, because his own father was dead in the sea, and he thought the sea was a curse and a place of death.

Dead as Ma was when they took her away to burn her. And Pa was crying, and the big polisman was sitting there uncomfortably, dangling his cap in his hands, rubbing the band of it. And on the wind, it being high above Leith and the sea not far off, and because the windows were open in the mild evening, there came the faint sound of waves on the concrete shore.

'I've got bad news for you, laddie. Your Ma's deid.'

Deid, he said. Your Ma's deid.

So I was never able to tell her . . .

The sound of the sea.

Deid.

And in that dark room when I was a wean and newly arrived in the world, where the great black range was a thing of wonder with its black kettle and saucepans and steaming bowls, and I was sitting in a high hard chair in a sombre corner listening uncomprehendingly to their talk about Willie who had coughed to death in the bad old days, and I was feared, being but three, of the black cat stalking me—then in yon dark room the Old Lady came and told me the tale of Conla and the bonny girl of the sea. Once upon a time, she said—

Conla—he heard her voice calling him—Conla . . . And he

looked out across the dark lapping waters and the white capped waves, and said—

'My Lady—you have come back.'

Then she smiled at him, the elfin girl, and her lips were red, and her teeth were white, her hair was gold as the sunlight, her skin soft and cool as the very water over which she walked to this world, the place of misery, from Land-Under-The-Sea where there is neither death nor sickness, and all the folk are kind. And she held out her arms to him over the crest of the waves. Then the boy's father, Conn of the Hundred Battles and his wizard Kernann, appeared on the cliff top. They couldn't see *her*, but they could see their Conla walking over the beach to the sea. They shouted to him, they begged him, they implored him, they told him that she was not what he thought, but a banshee, an evil thing. All to no avail. Then Kernann the wizard raised his staff and cast a reel of red fire around Conla that chained him to the land, reminding him of his duty as a son and as a soldier; and Conla hesitated and looked back over his shoulder at his father standing there . . . But then the elfin girl laughed and her laughter was like silver bells ringing out over the deep: she laughed, and her laughter shattered the chains of fire at a stroke. And Conla forgot duty and obedience and discipline and the burden of the past, and took her soft cool hands in his own.

'Come, Conla,' she said, 'come, and we shall love together in Tir-nan-Og for all eternity.'

And Conla turned his face to the door of the sea's house and followed her under the waves. On the cliff above, old Conn of the Hundred Battles stood and wept.)

They weren't silent, for that was impossible, but they showed no lights as the landing-craft made for the shore. The men didn't know exactly how many of them there were, except that there were thousands, and no one had ever seen so many ships. Yesterday they had stood about the decks and tried to count the grey ships on the blue Mediterranean, but they had lost count because the ships stretched to each horizon in their hundreds; so they had wandered about the cramped metal decks, the men in their khaki battledress, they had played cards, written letters home, someone had played a mouth organ, others had just leaned their elbows on the ship's sides and stared, wondering why on earth anyone could want to become a sailor and live on this boring unchanging same blueness that was the sea.

September evening before the Operation code-named *Avalanche*. Lights extinguished in the ships, four hundred and fifty ships all told steaming from the ports of North Africa, battleships, aircraft carriers, cruisers, destroyers, and troop transports sufficient to carry 100,000 British and 69,000 American soldiers and all their weapons. Above their heads the patrolling fighters, the ungainly barrage balloons: high above them the bombers, wave upon wave of them flying from Africa and Sicily, painted with the roundels of the Royal Air Force and the five-pointed white star of the United States, navigators crouched over charts, pilots staring into the darkness waiting to see the glimmering mouth of the volcano Vesuvius.

Listen! The loudspeakers on the ships crackle into life. It is 19.20 hours—7.20 in the evening—September 8th, 1943. A BBC newsreader announces the armistice with Italy. He repeats the words of General Eisenhower speaking on Radio Algiers: 'The Italian Government has surrendered its armed forces unconditionally and I, as Commander-in-Chief, have granted them military armistice terms which have been approved by the Governments of Britain, the United States, and the Soviet Union; thus I am acting in the interests of the United Nations. The Italian Government has bound itself to abide by these terms . . .'

The message ends. For several seconds men stand staring at the silent speakers, hardly believing their ears. Then the cheering starts on all the bigger ships. From ship to ship it goes, through the night, above the grumble of the engines. 'The Eyeties have jacked it in!' they yell. 'It's all over bar the shouting!' Ration bottles of beer and North African wine are passed around. Many of the men even think the war is over. This landing is going to be a cushy number. They are going to sail right into Naples harbour and land like Cook's tourists. Officers go to the microphones and tell them that the Germans are still in the war, and the Germans will fight, but the men want to be happy so they hardly listen. Instead they have a party—they cheer between the bunks and tell jokes, tip the bottles to the ceiling and organize sing-songs—

Roll out the barrel!
Let's have a barrel of fun.
Roll out the barrel!
We've got the Blues on the run . . .

Even the officers grab the last of their bottles of gin and whisky and go to celebrate with the ships' officers. Crikey, Italy's surrendered! Flash flash go the signal lights from blacked-out ships. Italy's surrendered! Flash flash.—And a company piper is instructed to hurry up and compose 'The Scots Guards' Entry Into Naples', and everyone is saying what a piece of cake it is going to be, this landing at Salerno.

Everyone?

—Hey, Donald, says a voice.

—What?

—Do you think the Jerries will pack it in?

No, he doesn't think so, the man with the lance-corporal's stripe, not by a long chalk.

23.20 hours. Twelve miles off shore the ships pause and the first landing-craft are dropped down the davits. Sergeants hiss at the men to shut up. The men are tense once more. Maybe it's not going to be such a walkover after all. I want to see Naples and live, says one of them. They sit in the craft holding their rifles between their legs. They stare at each other's faces, vaguely pale in the darkness. The sky is as black as the walls of the landing-craft: you can't tell where one ends and the other begins. Upstairs the stars are very bright. Men who haven't had a romantic thought in the whole of their lives look up at the stars. Somebody kicks someone else's shins. *'Kinell!* Shut it you noisy bastard! Silence from the men. The engine roars and gurgling foam swirls up behind them.

There are thirty-five men in each of the craft. They have stood on each other's helmets and fingers clambering down the netting. Compared to the big troop ships the little landing-craft are shaped like metal shoe-boxes, and they bob around on top of the water like corks. All the soldiers are more or less sea-sick. Twelve miles. The landing-craft take their stations in the forming-up area. None of the soldiers knows what way they are pointing any more. Somebody stands up and tries a keek over the side. Jock. Jock has a Bren-gun. Nobody likes him; he's a scrounger. He sits down again. It's that way, he says.

'How the fuck would you know?'

''Cos the place's fucking blazing, innit?' he says.

The men haven't heard the bombers above their own engines.

'The ships areny firing, but,' says someone.

''Cos it's the fucking airforce, innit?'

'I thought it was over,' says a quiet voice. Johnny. Johnny isn't much more than a boy. He's a nice boy from a Catholic home. On his last home leave he kissed a girl on the cheek. He's sitting holding a great big rifle between his knees. The lance-corporal is sitting beside him looking at the deck, stoically sucking a pipe. He grunts.

'It'll never be fucking over,' says someone.

'Shut up—shutfuckinup!'

CRASH

'Jesus!'

The columns of landing-craft are on the move now. It is still dark. The helmsmen keep station by the red lights in the stern of each vessel. Somebody makes a joke about this being a red light district. No one laughs.

CRASH

'They're fucking getting it over there,' says the helmsman.

The Bay of Salerno. The shore is a gentle crescent of sand overhung by bitter mountains. In the north the little towns of Amalfi, Maiori, Vietri, and Salerno herself sit right on the shore with mountain slopes rising out of the backyards. South of Salerno the beaches broaden. Inland, behind the golden dunes, lies Montecorvino airport and the railway station at Battipaglia, the little towns of Eboli and Persano, and, as the mountains encroach again, Paestum—once cried Poseidonia, the city of Neptune, god of the sea—and finally Agropoli. Between Salerno and Agropoli lies the Italian shore as the tourists would have it: gently shelving beaches, soft warm golden sand, and the sun shining over the blue waters. Now the bombers are pounding the roads and the railway line, they are bombing all along the beaches in case the Germans are there. They have been bombing intermittently these three months past. The towns are ruins now. The folk are refugees; they have abandoned their homes to live in the

194

hills. When the all-clear sounds they return to see if their homes are still standing, to salvage something from the rubble if they are not. Women, caught by surprise raids, run through the burning streets—they raise their hands to the sky crying *Basta! Basta!* ('Enough! Enough!'). Still the bombers come—in case the Germans are there.

But the Germans aren't there. The Germans are in the hills, crouching in trenches, manning their guns, waiting. They have, of course, been alerted: code-name *Orkan* (Hurricane)—'prepare to counter a major landing'. The men of the 16th Panzer Division are veterans of the Stalingrad front. They wait.

CRASH go the bombs, CRASH.

03.15 hours—3.15 in the morning, September 9th. The navy guns open up as well. The landing-craft come nearer and nearer. The orange glow from the burning shore can be seen quite clearly now. All those who can are looking towards it. A few mutter things to each other, squinting even to the point where they seem to be grinning in the glare of the fires. An Italian Glaswegian begins praying the Ave Maria. Now and at the hour of our death. Some poor bastard is having the jitters: he is asking for his mother. 'Where's mammy—I want ma mammy', he greets like a ten-year-old with scraped knees. Nobody swears at him. The men are packed together. The light from the fiery beach shines on all their faces. The lance-corporal finally looks up. Pa. His eyes are watery. He looks much older than he did just a few years ago. He holds his ungainly rifle as a tired man might hold his walking stick.

· Very lights, beautiful many-coloured lights, arch up, flares and star shells dance across the sky as finally the German guns open on the first wave: and somebody says, 'It's they fucking Eyeties canny be bothered unloading their fucking guns.'

All the men are standing, lining the walls of the craft. The lieutenant tells them to get down. A few minutes later they are back again. The lieutenant stands amongst them. 'I kent it was too good to be fucking true,' says Jock.

Hell must look something like the beach at Salerno.

'Whit daft sod said they wis Eyeties?'

'They're fucking Jerries all right.'

'Jerries.'—One word said in a quiet bitter sigh. For a moment everyone is silent. Jerries. That says it all. No one wants to meet the Jerries again, not after they'd all been thinking it was going to be a walkover, sunny Italy, *O Sole Mio* and all that, Italian men grinning amiably, Italian women . . . There had been Italian women in Tripoli and Tunis, and more in Bizerta. In Bizerta they had leaned out of windows holding their bare breasts in their hands and called to the boys, 'Hey, Tommy, come fuck; come fuck, Tommy.' In Bizerta, night before embarkation, Italian women had been mingling with the Arabs hanging round the camps, ready to fuck for a can of bully beef, ready to fuck for American cigarettes. Big discussion that night—are Italian birds better than Arab birds? Lewd laughter. Arab birds are funny, Arab birds like it up the bum, Arab birds would steal your eyeballs and come back for the lashes, fucking Arabs. Italian birds, but . . . Lewd laughter. Birds. And Jock the Bren-gunner clenches his fist. He pumps his hairy arm up and down from the elbow. See they womenfolk, eh? It's a right terror with the women he is! He's shagged more birds than he's had dinners, he says: from fucking Cairo to Tunis, Africa's just littered with the women he's shoved it up—Jock the hard wee man who is sweating like a pig now he stares at that God awful beach.

Jerries.

There's no walk-over with the Jerries. The Jerries'll fight. The Jerries are damn brave. Pa has been in the desert since the end of '41. Pa has heard the guns at Alamein. Fighting Jerries all that time. Oddly, he has never seen an armed Jerry face-to-face —only prisoners, and dead, and our dead, and Italian dead, and the bloody flies crawling all over them. And young Johnny, who has just joined, who has never heard a gun go pop since training camp, asks in a panicky sort of voice—

'Do you think they're going to fight?'

And Pa takes the cold pipe from his mouth and begins filling it.

'The Jerries? Naw, dinny worry about the Jerries, son. See Africa?—we made the Jerries run there all right! They chased us all o'er the fucking place.'

And Johnny manages to smile weakly.

'Mac,' says the sergeant, 'pit oot that fucking light!'—Then realizes the absurdity of what he has said, and somebody laughs, and the sergeant laughs, and everybody laughs. And the lieutenant says, 'Christ, Mackay, I didn't know you were Hitler's secret weapon, what?'—the lieutenant with his jolly voice, because Pa's pipe is a formidable thing, belching out smoke and sparks. And other voices say the same as the lieutenant, in other accents, with fouler words—the pitiful *fucking* this, *fucking* that flying like bullets in a battle—and there is much laughter, but Pa puffs away with dignity and wags two fingers at the lieutenant, who knows and grins, and Pa knows he knows, and he knows Pa knows, and the men are laughing, and they all know it's because they're damn near screaming, so shit-arsed scared are they.

The beach roars. There is grey on the mountains above it, but no one's looking at the sky, just at the burning burning burning beach, the hysterical flames there so red in the darkness. And someone produces a mouth organ and men begin to sing along with it, softly between their teeth—

I didny want to join the fucking army,
I didny want to fight the fucking war,
I want to go home, around the streets I'll roam,
And live upon the earnings of a highly connected lady.

I dinny want a bayonet in ma belly,
I dinny want ma bollocks shot away,
Post me back to Scotland, to bonny bonny Scotland,
And I'll fornicate ma fucking life away . . .

CRASH go the guns, CRASH.

03.45 hours. They're near enough the beach now to distinguish gun types by the sound of them: howitzers, mortars, naval guns—machine-guns, God save us.

'That's an 88,' says someone who has met the famous German gun at Alamein. The word goes round. 'The Jerries have got their 88s.'

'Oh fucking Jesus!'

From the other side of the craft a voice says, 'The Yanks are getting it down there.'

'Some sweet fucking consolation that is!'

In the southern part of the Bay of Salerno the Americans have held their fire—so also have the Germans. Their craft go in in silence. Silence until the ramps begin to drop. Then as the ramps hit the water the German guns open—and they rake the craft, they rake them. Many Americans die without even getting out of the landing-craft, without even setting foot on the oppressed continent they have come so many thousands of miles to liberate.

Grey light on the eastern mountaintops. Beneath them the Germans are firing all along the crescent of the Bay, from Amalfi in the north, south to Agropoli, from well-concealed positions in the dunes and the hills. They have strongpoints with masses of barbed-wire and mines, their guns have carefully prepared fields of fire, they have tanks driven into the backs of houses, hidden in haystacks and behind stone walls, completely camouflaged. Their strongpoints have names like battleships—Moltke, Scharnhorst, Schlieffen, Lilienthal. In them are men much like the men they are shooting at, who are shooting at them—men who have also got stories about Italian women, who have sung to themselves under the RAF's bombardment *Bitte, Tommy, fliege weiter* ('Please, Tommy, fly away'), and want to stay alive so they can meet Lili Marlene underneath the lamp-post by that barrack gate.

Death comes for them all.

04.17 hours. A burning landing-craft drifts past them. The men in it who haven't been killed by the guns are being killed by the fire. Overhead a burning bomber, its crew screaming silently. A parachutist comes down with his chute in flames. Salerno that was once a town beneath a blue headland, Salerno of the golden beaches, what love-lorn minstrel prepared you for what was to happen?

Crash go all the guns. Rat-a-tat, tat-tat-tat-tat-tat go the machine-guns.

And dawn is on the mountains above Salerno.

ZERAAACK

—Christ, what the fuck's that?

Sounds like somebody's fucking the bloody clouds.

ZERAAACK

—Nebel-thingumyjigs.

Nebelwerfers. Rocket throwers.

—They were using them on the Mareth Line.

'Oh fuck!'

Well, there's nothing else left to say.

Oh fuck.

Oh fuckfuckfuckfuckfuck.

Dawn brings a sea mist, and that makes things a little bit better. On the landing-craft the lieutenant calls them 'chaps' and tells them it is nearly their time. In light that is at last something other than star shells and flames the men can see the other landing-craft surging forward to the beach, and it makes them feel better, seeing that there are so many of them. It'll soon be time. The men swallow hard and grip their rifles, put detonators on their grenades. The lieutenant puts a whistle in his mouth and draws his revolver. He's standing up, right up at the front. They all look at the lieutenant. A German shell explodes on the water. Splinters hammer the walls of the craft. Another lands close by without exploding. It sends bucket-loads of water over the waiting men. Curses. Another—and another. Soon the tideless Mediterranean has breakers of tossing foam where the shells are landing. The lieutenant is still standing there, even with shrapnel explosions overhead. He says something about 'paying them back for Dunkirk'.

Zeraaack, crash, rat-a-tat-tat

Here it comes! The beach looms up. Yes! A heavy crunch and the landing-craft jerks to a stop. As fast as they can the sailors let the ramp down. The lieutenant blows his whistle and waves forward with his revolver. Everyone's on his feet. They run forward *splash* into waist-deep water, *splash* where the shells are landing, where the machine-gun bullets are splattering like rain, and the sea is churned up muddy and slicked with petrol and blood, and the air stinks of cordite and smoke. A lorry packed with ammo blows to bits. Zeraaack!—come the rockets. Crash! —the plunging shells. The men wade, rifles held above their heads. Bullets spurt around them. One screams—then another —another—another . . . More bullets. Beside Pa a man staggers back, still holding his rifle above his head, looking so surprised, so very surprised, then trips and falls backward into the water and appears never again.

Salerno, what minstrel prepared you for it? In the sea men are floating like rubbish, backs above the water, helmets hanging down, boots dragging the sand. The living lie flat on the water-line, half in and half out of the water where many of the dead are also lying. First wave troops are on the line of dunes across the beach, firing. One of them falls back and rolls down into the sand. White-taped markers on the beach. What's that there for? Nothing to fire at. The men lie still, holding their rifles out of the water.

Orders. The lieutenant blows his whistle again. Forward! They run forward, yelling. Machine-guns zig-zag the beach. Fortunately firing high. Most of the men double under the bullets, most of them. They shelter behind the first line of dunes. A ruined farmhouse in front of them. Dead British, dead Germans. Four frightened Germans run out of the farmhouse with their hands up. A navy shell—*crash*—two of them fall. One turns and runs back into the ruins. Nobody fires at him. The other one runs in circles, round and round in circles. Then he collapses. The men are firing over the dunes. Pa fires. The butt of his Lee-Enfield rifle against his shoulder. He pulls and releases the trigger, pulls and releases it mechanically. Fire to the front —Catterick training camp—always fire to the front. He fires to the front. There's nothing particular in front of him. He fires at it. *Crack crack crack crack crack*, reload five round clip, *crack crack crack crack crack*, reload again. Forward!—And they rush forward again with a few enemy snipers dodging about in front of them firing as they retreat, and here and there a man falls, but they cross a hard surfaced road, and on the other side are little orchards and flat muddy country with occasional fields of corn and grass—

Where they halt. Other officers have appeared—a captain, a major. The battalion padre bends over a wounded man. There are wee houses—crofts they would be called in Sutherland—and they are ruins, their yellow walls, their red roofs lie broken into rubble. Dead cows, dead goats lie in the warm sun. The men have time to notice that it is warm now the sun is up. The dead animals are filling with gas. Above each the flies hover like a cloud of smoke. In the desert Pa has seen dead men filling with gas as well. He chews a bit of melon pulled from a vine. Apart from the noise all about them, it is quiet now. The lads are picking fruit, filling their helmets with apples and olives. The

lads are saying, Och it wasny that bad. One of the lads is saying,
It's like drinking whisky, ken?—the first's the worst; once you
get that down you, the rest's no bother. They are trying to
swagger it off. They were all scared—now they're laughing
again. Pa looks around to see who is missing. He can't see
Johnny. What's happened to Johnny? He can't remember
seeing—

'Tanks! Tanks coming!'

They grab their rifles. Several grey tanks lumbering straight at
them. Panzer Mark IVs with infantry riding on the top. They all
fire their rifles, Tommy-guns, Bren-guns, Vickers machine-
guns at the damn things. The infantry disappear. The tanks
come on. The officers shout—

'Back! Back!'

Pa for a daft moment thinks they're shouting at the tanks. No,
they're shouting at the men. The men retreat as fast as they had
advanced. They scramble out of the orchard and over the field.
The tank machine-guns open on them. The lieutenant, but a
different lieutenant this time, shouting, pointing. Pointing at
what? Get onto the soft ground! The men scramble out of the
field and into a flooded area. They run. Down, down! voices
shout. They drop. Why don't those bastard tanks fire? Pa
panting, his chin in the mud. Why don't they? Some men are in a
ditch, waist-deep in muck. They are under the level of the tank
guns. They think they are safe. The first tank swings round. The
tanks are armed with flamethrowers. WHOOSH. It sends a forty
foot tongue of blazing petrol right into the ditch. Let's not talk
about what happens to the men in the ditch. WHOOSH it tries
for the men lying in the mud, who press their faces into
squelching mother earth to avoid the searing flames.
WHOOSH—but the fire can't quite reach them. Battalion anti-
tank guns open up from the crest of the dunes, but fall short. The
tanks don't want to go onto the soft flooded areas. They don't
want to sit and be shot at either. They back away.

Up, up, forward! The men get to their knees, get to their feet.
They look like slime monsters, dripping mud and ooze. Rifles
out, bayonets dull with muck they go forward again. American
planes fly overhead rat-tat-tatting. British planes circle, bombing. Splatters of anti-aircraft shells bursting across the sky. The

men regain the hard field. Regain the orchard wall and oh shit there are Germans in the orchard. Down they go. Down go the Germans. Everybody fires. *Crack crack crack crack crack*, reload. Their bullets go high, our bullets hit the wall. The Germans retreat, we advance. Back in the orchard. A dead German, the top of his head blown away. Across the orchard, a tomato field. Germans in the tomato field. *Crack crack crack*. Their bullets hit the wall, our bullets go high.

Barrage.

CRASH BANG WALLOP

—Christ, they're theirs!

—Christ, they're ours!

—Christ, everybody's getting it!

From the beach, British 25 pounders are blistering the area. From the hills, German howitzers are blistering the same area.

The barrage lifts. Navy guns begin firing at the German guns in the hills.

The British soldiers in the orchard and the German soldiers in the field raise their heads and begin shooting at each other again.

Another barrage. When it lifts, the Germans have gone.

'Forward! Forward!'

Cresting a small grassy hill, Pa looks back. Behind him the whole Bay of Salerno is packed with ships. Some are on fire. Grey-painted cruisers and destroyers are firing at the hills and mountains. Down in the south ugly smoke clouds hang over Paestum. And he thinks: Wonder how the Yanks have managed? Always in too much of a hurry, the Yanks. Wonder if they've lost many down there? . . . And then notices the sun in the west, the sun on the sea that stretches to Sardinia, and the sea now looking so blue and beautiful where the dead men were floating, and the ships there firing their guns. Where has this day gone? he wonders. I thought it was still morning.

Above the smoke and the shots, above the angry aeroplanes, a distant flight of seabirds passes westwards like specks of black dust.

Night. The men dig in. The Germans dig in. There is no lull in the shelling, it keeps on all the time.

Whispers—

'Joe.'

'Whit?'

'Are you alive?'

'No, I'm fucking deid.'

'I thought you was killed.'

'I thought I was killed too.'

'I fucking nearly *was* killed.'

'Shut up you noisy bastards.'

(Pause)

'Hey, Tam?'

'Aye?'

'What time is it?'

'How the fucking hell should I ken what time it is?'

'It's half eleven.'

'Is it? Ta. (Pause) It doesny look like half eleven, but.'

'Whit?'

(Pause)

'They flies is killing me.'

'Will yous lot fucking shut up!'

Flies. And mosquitoes, giant mosquitoes, hordes of the bastard things humming all round in the dark. The troops curse them more than the shells. There is nothing that can keep the insects off, neither repellent cream nor face nets. And in their millions they settle on dead bodies, humming contentedly. Some men are ill with the unaccustomed fruit they have eaten. Now they have violent diarrhoea. Because of the shells they daren't move. They lie in their foxholes feeling scared and sick and miserable. The voice of Jock the Bren-gunner complaining in the night—I could cope with everything if I hadny just shat my breeks as well. A voice actually praying—Please God, no more, no the shits too. I'm sorry about the smell, says the man in the next foxhole to Pa, but I canny help it. If only my mother could see me now, he says. Mosquitoes come to the excrement like bees to a honey-pot.

And somehow there in the midst of the stink and the squalor of it all, Pa manages to fall asleep . . .

Kicked awake. Dawn stand-to. Quick breakfast. Shells still falling. Pa lights his pipe. Orders. They begin to move forward, patrols out to the front and flanks. Pass a knocked-out tank, dead men lying beside it. Pass a ruined village, or maybe just a big farm with outhouses—ruined anyway. Dead pigs lying in puddles of blood. A few dead civilians. Sniper fire—machine-gun fire. The men stop, fire back, advance firing, cease fire. A wall with *Viva gli Inglesi* (Long live the English) painted on it.—Memory: a *Punch* cartoon, circa 1916. A wall somewhere in First World War Flanders, *Gott Straff England* painted on it. A kilted Highland soldier dourly scores out 'England' and chalks 'Great Britain' underneath. Cartoon caption: 'Scotland For Ever'.—The advance continues, Pa smiling at the memory of a *Punch* cartoon. Heavy shellfire—down! They wait and expect to be blown to hell. It doesn't happen. The shells are landing behind them. Up! They pass a road. An overturned civilian car. A dead cow. Another ruined house, this one with *Viva i Tedeschi* (Long live the Germans) painted on it. Men swearing at the Italian villagers—Fucking bastards, fucking two-faced peasants, dinny ken what fucking side they're on. Pa swearing like the rest of them—'Fucking wops!' More sniper fire. A man spins round and falls, face grey and pinched. Fire—cease fire—advance. A dead German sniper lying sprawled.

Advance. Shells falling, but not too bad, says somebody. Villagers in a hamlet, dusty pock-marked walls. They wave —the boys wave back. Ach well, you canny blame the poor bastards.

Ping, crack, rat-a-tat-tat.
—Where are we?
—How the fuck should I know? Italy somewhere.
—Where's Salerno then?
—It's yon big city up north.
—Naw. That's Rome.
—Naw it isny, that's Naples.
—Well, where's fucking Salerno then?
—I dinny ken, and I dinny damn well care!
—'Kinell!
Rat-a-tat, tat-tat-tat.
What's that over there? Tobacco plants. Nobody's ever seen tobacco plants before.
Crack crack crack—
Twelve foot high, damn nearly. Three officers squat over a

map. They don't bloody know where we are either. An armoured car burning, its ammunition exploding inside the turret. Wonder what the poor bugger looks like who was in there—wonder what he looks like now? A jeep drives past. German prisoners walk behind it with their hands on their heads. The men look at the Germans without hostility. Bren-gun carriers come up behind them and pass to the front. *Ping* of a sniper's bullet overhead. *Rat-a-tat* of a machine-gun.

The barrage when it comes is shattering. The earth leaps around. The men lie down under it; they clamp their hands over their ears and press themselves as close as they can to the earth. Pa will tell me later on that he can feel the earth trembling as though an earthquake is occurring, and he doesn't think about anything —his life doesn't suddenly flash before his eyes, or anything quite like that—he just has this feeling that even scared and hot and shitty-arsed as he is, it is still lovely to be alive, and he wants another gulp of life, a day or an hour or even a minute more of it, because oh it is so good. And they all feel like that, even the men who are being killed; they feel just like that, Pa says, the moment before the shells tear them apart and throw away the pieces.

Then the barrage lifts all of a sudden, but the men lie trembling for maybe another five seconds not believing it. One moves—a second—a third. Amazingly, most of them are still alive. One man whips up a Tommy-gun and begins firing it into the tobacco plantation.

'Tanks! Tanks!'

And here they come again, the metal monsters, crashing through the tall plants. The barrage has drowned the noise of their engines. Mark IVs and Tigers now, machine-gunning as they come, Panzer Grenadiers riding on their backs, Tommy-guns in their hands, throwing stick-grenades, Panzer Grenadiers in camouflage, their faces painted with streaks of green.

Pa trips over a man who is lying shaking. There is blood running out of the man's ears. Pa kicks him (*crack crack crack crack crack*, reload), but the man just rolls over. 'I canny hear!' he is shouting. 'I canny hear!' A tank goes over him. The battalion anti-tank guns fire, load, fire again, but the little 6-pound shells bounce off the massive steel hides of the Tigers. The British soldiers fall back, firing rifles and Tommy-guns at the slits in the tanks' visors. The tanks come on slowly, remorselessly, crushing anyone in their way, living or dead. One devoted soul jumps onto a tank, lifts the hatch cover, tosses in a grenade and slams it shut. He is shot before he can jump off. The tank blows up with a great roar, men burn in the flames, its signal flares hiss and splutter in all directions. Panzer Grenadiers firing as they come, shouting *'Hoch! Hoch!'*, German officers blowing whistles and shouting, waving their men forward. British officers waving theirs back. More men falling—Christ, how can we stop them? The men jump a wall, fire, Germans die under their fire. The tanks smash the wall down. Retreat over a field. Machine-guns sweep the field like hoses. Men go down screaming. Christ, can there be any of us left? Enough to line the ditch on the other side. *Fire!* They fire, they don't cease firing. On come the tanks. 'Fire! fire!' a sergeant yells. He stands and fires magazine after magazine—the bullets tinkle over the tanks like hailstones on an iron roof.

Tanks. No man who has survived Salerno can forget those tanks, the Mark IVs—the Tigers especially, with tracks as broad as conveyor belts. Pa sees one of them smash into the gable end of a house, hears it grind its way through the interior, and runs as it punches the wall out the other side, damn near on top of him, covered in bricks and dust, its great gun sniffing round for prey. He runs. He is running the wrong way. He runs right into a German. Pa fires and misses. The German fires and misses. Both men turn and run in opposite directions. Pa jooks behind a pile of rubble. The German is still going like the clappers. An 88mm gun pointing at the rubble. Pa sees it, runs, jumps into a crater as his place of refuge blows into the air. Pa gets plastered with dust. A stone hits his steel helmet. A signaller is already in the crater shouting into his wireless set—'For fuck's sake, we need ammunition! They Jerries has got a million bloody tanks up here!'—*Crackle crackle*, comes the answer: *let them get close and piss on them—maybe they'll rust: crackle crackle*. And Pa fires over the lip of the crater—fires off a clip thinking, I'm firing too high, must adjust my aim, fire lower: fires off a second clip thinking, I'm still firing too high, must adjust my aim, fire lower: fires off a third clip thinking the same thing: starts to fire a fourth clip still without adjusting his aim, knows what he has to do, still can't understand why he isn't doing it. Somebody grabs his shoulder. Pa looks glassy-eyed at a strange corporal bawling at him—'Get back, ye stupid bastard!' The signaller has been killed. Pa and the corporal scramble out together. Germans everywhere. Tanks everywhere. Pa and the corporal both run. The corporal disappears. Pa runs. He sees the camouflage backs of a group of Panzer Grenadiers also running. Pa runs through the midst of them. The Germans look at Pa: Pa looks at the Germans. A German jerks his rifle at him but doesn't fire. A tank burning. The Germans fling themselves flat on the ground. Pa runs on. British soldiers running, turning, firing, running again. And there, for Christ's sake, is the sea.

The sea.

The golden Mediterranean beach.

Yesterday's dead still lying on it.

Today's dead falling on it.

And piles of stores.

Boxes, crates, drums, jeeps, a huge Matador lorry burning right in the middle of it all, more boxes, crates, files of infantry-men diving behind the boxes, hope there's no ammo in those damn boxes, Bren-gun carriers, a grand piano, a dressing station—

A grand piano?

—a battery of howitzers banging away, and the gunners are cursing as the wheels slip in the shifting sand.

—And Jock the Bren-gunner running crazy along the beach shouting, 'We canny stick it! retreat! retreat!'

—And the sergeant-major after him with a revolver; 'I'll shoot you, ye bugger!'

—A loudspeaker voice shouts, 'Get onto the sand! Lie flat! Down!'

—And the men jump-roll over the last line of dunes, and roll down into the churned-up bloody sand that's covered with junk and corpses. And Pa lies with his rifle in front of his face, coughing sand, and in front of him a glimpse of thrawn sea as the destroyers come skimming in, white water foaming under their prows, and their guns swivel round

—As the first tanks crest the dunes

—And CRASH go the guns, CRASH

207

—And the tanks burn

—They burn

—And one big Tiger lumbers down in a mess of flames, down and over the beach it goes, ploughing over bodies, ploughing through a pile of crates, right into the sea, and the waves lap over it, and the fires sizzle and are extinguished, and the steam rises from the ruined monster as it slowly sinks out of sight.

—While from another a group of British soldiers fight to pull a Panzerman, and roll him in the sand to smother the flames that are spouting all over him, and he is screaming

—And somebody raises the cry, 'Here comes the cavalry!'

—And indeed it is the cavalry, the Sherman tanks of the Royal Scots Greys, counter-attacking inland.

—And the officers blow their whistles and shout.

And there on the beach the soldiers sort themselves out somehow or other, back into their original companies, original platoons, seeing faces they thought were goners, laughing, joking again, saying, 'Thank God we've got the fucking navy!', dusting off their clarty uniforms. They rest. All around them, the roaring of guns, the smell of burning tanks and burning bodies, of dead bodies mangled again and again and already rotting in the Italian sun. They rest. Cooks with petrol cookers prepare a hot meal. Mess tins of water are boiled for a brew-up. Then they parade in rough lines. Fresh ammunition is handed out. Then, with officers out in front, the lines advance. And as the shells start dropping again, an officer shouts—'Get off the beaches!'

Get off the bloody beaches!

And over the dunes and through the burning tanks and the dead and dying bodies they go.

Back into it.

Back where they came from.

Salerno. What minstrel prepared you for what was to happen, Salerno? . . .

On the ninth, or the tenth, or the eleventh day of the battle of Salerno, on a mountainside somewhere beyond Battipaglia, Pa sits and stares at the sky. Since landing on the golden beach he and his unit have faced days of non-stop fighting, nights of raid and counter-raid and sleep in snatches when the shelling isn't too rough. The whole countryside they have come to liberate now smells of death and smoke and fire. Every road, every path is pitted with craters, every village and farm a burnt-out, shelled and looted ruin. And the dead, the dead everywhere. Dead cattle, dead soldiers, British, German and American lying together now after so much discord, dead families from the ruined homes, men, women and children too all lying together—and the smell of these hundreds of unburied bodies rotting in the sun. The smell of putrefied corpses clings to Pa's skin and permeates his coarse khaki uniform. He stares at the sky. He no longer wonders if he will ever be free from the stink of death. He knows he will stink of death for as long as he lives.

Salerno—breakfasts of grapes and oranges by the wayside. Salerno—fresh graves among the olive groves. Salerno—dead bodies floating in the sea.

For the rest of his life these things will remain in his mind:

Screams coming from a blazing German tank, a dead officer jammed half in and half out of its turret hatch.

Americans, big amiable men who didn't advance properly, didn't dig in properly, and got shot down in swathes because they hadn't expected any serious fighting.

The way the navy's guns pounded the hills. The destroyers off the beach, and the battleship *Warspite* firing enormous shells fifteen miles inland.

The lads helping each other out—crawling under fire to bring in the wounded, or even just to give each other food and cigarettes.

Starving Italian children pointing to their mouths and crying *Niente, niente.*

A dying man with both legs blown off sitting propped against a tree and looking at his own blood seeping into the ground.

The German stretcher-bearers and orderlies who came over during a brief truce, who all turned out to be Russians captured from the Soviet army, and who were perfectly happy in their new role.

Some British and German wounded singing *Lili Marlene* together.

The man who couldn't take it any more and shot himself in the foot so he would get evacuated. The way they all pretended not to know what he had done.

How he missed a strong cup of tea and some hot food. How he would have sold his soul for a decent fill of tobacco.

The hospital ships in the bay with their big red crosses gleaming like a vision of the promised land.

Tracer bullets arcing across a valley. The way they seemed to come towards you so slowly, then speed up all of a sudden and pass you with a crack.

That awful smell of death!

'Get off the bloody beaches!'

And the warm wind blowing in off the sea . . .

A final memory:

Pa is sitting on a mountainside somewhere beyond Battipaglia with a rifle across his knees, and he is feeling utterly dazed and weary and sick of it all. Behind him the remains of the company have established a firing line and are shooting at Germans on the neighbouring slope who are shooting back at them. A few wounded men are lying beside Pa. Pa has a lump of shrapnel in his thigh. He is in pain, but somehow he isn't really aware that the pain is his.

He is just sitting there staring into space. Officially, as one of the 'walking wounded', he is guarding the company's rear. The hills are terraced with walls and dotted with thick woods of fir and olives. A few yards away on the slope below him is one such wall, looking rather like one of the dry stone dykes in the Pentlands, only bigger. It is topped with grass, and the stones are mossy and green. Beyond it, in a cleft of a mountain. Beyond that, Pa can see a burn running down the mountainside. In one place it spills over several black rocks in a little fall, and at that point the sun is catching it so that it shines like pure gold.

Then, as Pa sits admiring the golden river, he hears a noise, a very slight noise, in the vineyard on the other side of the wall. Behind him is the rifle and machine-gun fire of the company, and the echoes of it and the Germans' return fire rolling down the valley. He is so used to that perpetual rattling and cracking that he no longer notices it. This noise is slight, cautious. He thinks it might be a goat or a pig loose in the vineyard, but some extra sense tells him it isn't. Quickly he looks around. The company all have their backs to him, banging away at the Germans. None of the other wounded men are up to anything. Pa has his rifle and bayonet and one grenade. Using his rifle as a stick to support his wounded leg, he makes his way stealthily into the shadow of the wall. His feet are on soft grass that muffles his sounds. He listens. On the other side of the wall men are moving. He can hear the rustle of cloth scraping against the stone. Nearby is a place where soldiers have broken the wall down so stretchers can pass easily. Pa on his side of the wall, the others on theirs, are all moving to that same place.

Listen!

Voices—whispering . . .

He listens, tense. Could he be mistaken?

There is no mistake.

. . . *wir* . . . *Gluck* . . . (he hears).

. . . We're in luck (?).

The voices are German.

Pa glances once more at the company. About fifty yards away at least a couple of dozen men have their backs to that hole in the wall. He hears the whispering again—judges the position—draws his grenade, pulls the pin, tosses it over the wall, and lets himself fall to the ground.

The shrapnel wound comes alive and stabs him. He lies choking, blinking the tears. God! that a lump of metal can hurt so much!—And while he is thinking that, the grenade explodes with a dull roar.

Pa lies, feeling the pain and the rumble in his ears. Then cautiously he gets to his feet. He presses his ear against the wall. There is nothing, nothing on the other side. Just a sighing breeze in the vines. He moves to the hole in the wall. Quickly he keeks round the corner, and pulls his head back again. No bullets come at him. He takes another, longer, look. He climbs gingerly over the fallen stones.

His torn leg is running hot fire all through his body, but he isn't thinking of that. He has his rifle out and the bayonet pointed down. He limps forward a step—and a step—and a step.

Two Germans are lying there. One is on his back with his arms flung out. The grenade has torn his throat open—it's a great red gash. The other is lying on his stomach across his friend's legs. The palms of his hands are upwards, his head is twisted sideways. The back of his uniform has been torn right open and his shirt and the seat of his underpants are covered in blood. And their eyes are open. Neither can be any more than seventeen—perhaps not even that. And he has killed them both.

Their eyes are open. Dust settles on their paper eyes. A fly comes and crawls across one of them.

And there and then on that Italian mountainside among the broken and bleeding grapes, Pa goes onto his knees, lays his rifle aside, and clasping his hands in an attitude of prayer swears that if he survives this lousy war he will never fight again, he will live each day to the full for the sheer joy of living, and spend whatever years are left to him trying to teach the children of tomorrow the meaning of humanity and love.

Spring Tide

Look. Do you see it?

The eastern sky is grey as doves, its clouds are the colour of rose petals. That daily miracle is occurring, and no matter how often I see it I'll never get tired of seeing it again. At work, at night, in the Centre, I like to walk along the eastward-pointing corridor between the upper reaches of the sports halls when the ceiling lights are still on low night switch, just to stand and look out of the big windows at the end, over the outside track where the first birds are hunting, over Jock's Lodge and Restalrig, Craigentinny and Seafield, just to see the sun come up from out there over the Forth beyond the Isle of May.

Look—see it now? Between the arms of the Lothian and Fife coasts the sun is rising from Noroway o'er the faem, from Lapland, from the far mountains where heroes have their homes —and she is walking on the sea out there beyond Leith break-water, between Fife Ness and the headland of Fast Castle, between the Bass Rock and Pittenweem where the witches were burnt, where half-owre half-owre lie so many graves in the fathoms, out there the sun comes walking over the water, and her feet silver the waves as she passes.

Dawn, my new world. One by one the streetlights are going out over yonder in Aberdour, Kinghorn, Dysart, and all up the Fife shore to sweet Largo Bay: going out behind me on Starbank, going out on Lower Granton Road. And nobody notices, those urgent wires shivering their orders along, those automatic switches clicking, nobody notices because now the whole sky is glowing—and all of a sudden I don't care about missiles and bombs and war or anything else. If I am deluded, then it is dear life itself that is deluding me because somehow, despite the possibilities, probabilities and mathematical certainties, I just can't believe anywhere in my tingling body that such a thing will happen. Life this morning is too beautiful.

Do you hear me, Pa?

Beautiful.

On a winter's night twenty years ago some travellers came to our schoolhouse at Redheugh, down there on the Berwickshire coast. They knocked the snow from their shoes and coughed in the doorway. They were polismen. I liked them. They were big men, polite and apologetic. I made them mugs of tea. They held the mugs to warm their hands, and we talked about the weather. The inspector, in plain clothes and an overcoat, said he 'understood', told Pa he hoped he would be 'reasonable'. Pa was reasonable. He had lately become very tired. All the anger had gone out of him. He managed a joke with the polismen. The polismen all laughed heartily. Pa smiled a weary smile. 'Ach well, sunshine,' he said to me. We climbed into the waiting car . . .

Everybody was very reasonable. The education authority allowed him to return to his job. They put his aberration down to nervous stress and overwork following the death of his wife; and since it is a difficult legal point whether a widower father can abduct the child of whom he is sole guardian, no legal action was taken. Pa was summoned to the City Chambers, where he had been beaten on the head a quarter of a century before, and there no doubt he was read a long and reasonable lecture by some worthy soul or other who was not in the least afraid of the Bomb, and who truly believed that wonderful science and technology were leading us into a radiant future.

Back in the sixties folk believed things like that.

1963. I passed into the secondary school where Pa taught. Kennedy was assassinated, but there was no atomic bang. We had the satire boom instead, we had mini-skirts and the Beatles, and social problems on television. I grew up, exchanged the *Beano* and war comics for English literature, and fell in love with Audrey Hepburn. I was massaged by television, by all the American imports—*Perry Mason, The Virginian, The Man from*

U.N.C.L.E. When the Argyll and Sutherland Highlanders marched into the Crater District in Aden with their pipes playing, I felt proud and happy.

I lived with Pa, the two of us alone in that house back there with all its books. No one else ever entered it now unless it was to read the meter. We took turn about making the dinner (I'm still a passable cook). In my third year at school, when folk were all talking about flower power and wearing hair down their backs, I entered Pa's English class. He wasn't a particularly interesting teacher, but his pupils listened to him. He had that sort of wry wasted expression which commands respect. We got Chaucer and Shakespeare. We read *Julius Caesar*, and Pa got a class discussion going about the way politicians can manipulate a crowd by playing on its collective emotions. He took us to see James Mason and Marlon Brando in the film version showing at the Ritz in Rodney Street, where Ma and her Stanislaus had once sat. You never knew about that, Pa. I was thinking about them throughout the film. The class enjoyed it; it was like going to a Western, but I felt sorry for Pa because none of them could see what it was he was trying to tell them. Politics wasn't dark and threatening, not then, not in the swinging sixties. We passed on to *Hamlet*. Hamlet was boring. About war, for instance—

Hamlet: *Goes it against the main of Poland, sir,*
         Or for some frontier?
Captain: *Truly to speak, and with no addition,*
         We go to gain a little patch of ground
         That hath in it no profit but the name.

No, this meant nothing to us in the middle of the swinging sixties.

Pa died saving a wee boy's life. On the other side of the road, the Water of Leith was cluttered full of rubbish and long weeds, and a Primary School laddie who was capering on the footbridge lost his balance and fell in. His mates screamed, and Pa ran from the football match he was supervising in the park hardby and plunged in, Pa who was one year short of his retirement age. The boy was saved. Some of us reached the bank in time and dragged Pa out. He was flushed and coughing. He was having trouble

215

with his chest and his breath came in gulps. I phoned for the ambulance he didn't want, and climbed in the back with him. The heart-attack killed him before we reached the Infirmary. That's how Pa died.

Pa.

There was a light. It shone out over stormy waters. Mariners beheld it above the crashing waves. And to that light Pa and his whole generation went, as a moth to the flame. There was a light which shone in the darkness, but the darkness comprehended it only too well. There was a light that failed—and I grew cat's eyes and learned to walk without it, Pa, I have learned to walk without it.

Was that the lesson you wanted to teach?

So in the daylight I turn and walk back across the crunch of the shingle and the rope coils of blackened seaweed lying on the grey sand.

'Aye!—morning!'

'Morning!'

In the morning, at first light, beachcombers come down here to see what the night waves have left them. One old man walks along the sand with a metal detector, and a boy walks aimlessly by his side. Look, there he goes. A couple from the nearby flats exercise their dogs before going to work. A middle-aged unemployed man who has no hope of ever being employed again sits with a bottle and stares at the sea.

Edinburgh is a city like the sea.—There are whale jawbones standing in the Meadows.—Folk find fossil creatures in suburban gardens.

And on the horizon always sea and hills. To the north is the Forth, the big puddle, and the Fifeshire hills beyond it; to the south are the Pentlands and their blue reservoirs and clear cold burns; westwards is the Forth snaking inland to Stirling; eastwards is the sea the sea and beyond it Norway and mountains and dark forests, reindeer and snow—Ivan, his missiles, and the Soviet fleet.

And always the sea, the hills, merging together like a vision of blue peace and green leaves seen from the bottom of a damp and dirty well.

And at night the city is small and glowing and precious, buried like treasure in the heart of a black mountain, and all around the endless dark sea stretches; and beyond the tiny brittle shield of the atmosphere that protects us all, the great oceans of the universe stretch on and on, and the stars shine light years away to us like beacons on a stormy headland where a seal lies and beats the waves with her tail.

And in the morning the sun comes walking through the portals of the Firth, from the Isle of May to Inchkeith to the bridge where the trains are leaping; and we wait for her, we watchmen, we sentries, polismen, porters, guards, we gentlemen of the shade, travellers of the silver time, minions of the moon. We stretch and look around. This is life's good garden we have inherited and it owns neither Marx nor Jesus.

'Morning!' says one beachcomber to me.

'Aye!—morning!' says another.

On the Forth, a ship—black and orange and white and splotched with rust. British? American? Soviet? the *Ivan Susanin*? —A ship. And I think: Stanislaus, it was too soon to bring us and the Soviet Union together, but thanks for trying. It was too soon, Ivan: but don't kill anyone with your big missile yet —somehow we'll get together and try it again.

I walk back through the dark dripping tunnel. A bus goes rumbling past on Lower Granton Road, and I see sleepy faces through the glass. Lorries—and a gull crying overhead. Perhaps one day I will go to Sutherland of the mountains, make my home by Scourie shore, and sing peaceful songs to the waves. On the other side of the road a newsagent is open. I'll buy a paper over there and find out what the world is doing.

And behind me as I stand waiting for the lights to change, I can hear the sound of the sea.